THE HIGH
BY GEMMA

W9-ATP-923

NATIONAL READERS' CHOICE AWARD WINNER

DOUBLE RITA AWARD FINALIST
BOOKSELLERS BEST FINALIST
DAPHNE DUMAURIER AWARD FINALIST

"The High Heels Series is amongst one of the best mystery series currently in publication. If you have not read these books, then you are really missing out on a fantastic experience, chock full of nail-biting adventure, plenty of high jinks, and hot, sizzling romance." —*Romance Reviews Today*

"A highly entertaining and enjoyable series."
—*Affaire de Coeur*

SPYING IN HIGH HEELS

"Halliday's debut is a winner, with its breezy, fast-paced style, interesting characters and story meant for the keeper shelf."
—*Romantic Times BOOKreviews*

"Debut author Gemma Halliday has done a fantastic job of character development, dialogue, sizzling sexual chemistry, and story line, and delivers all this with empathy and humor."
—*Affaire de Coeur*

"Gemma Halliday's sparkling debut will give fans of Janet Evanovich and Linda Howard a wonderful new reason to celebrate!"
—Kyra Davis, author of *Sex, Murder and a Double Latte*

"This is a hilariously intelligent story that will keep you laughing out loud and thumbing through the pages. Gemma Halliday has a wonderful way with words and descriptions. She also knows how to weave a great murder mystery that will keep you guessing who the culprit is. This is a must read for all you chick lit fans. Mark my words readers, Gemma's one to watch."
—*Romance Divas*

"This charming debut novel by Gemma Halliday delightfully combines the best parts of chick lit with light mystery in the same vein as Janet Evanovich, *Size 12 Is not Fat* by Meg Cabot and *Sex, Murder and a Double Latte* by Kyra Davis. Smart, funny and snappy!"   —Fresh Fiction

"This book is a giggle-a-minute romp...A fresh and witty little number that will appeal if you like sparkling, good stories with a splash of mystery. Full marks go to Ms. Halliday on what promises to be a very successful debut to a fabulous career."
—Romance Junkies

"*Spying in High Heels* doesn't read like a debut novel. Gemma Halliday writes like a very seasoned author leaving the reader hanging on to every word, every clue, every delicious scene of the book. It's a fun and intriguing mystery full of laughs and suspense."   —Once Upon a Romance

"Maddie pops off the page. She is funny, funnier, funniest. She's creative, offbeat, and surprisingly realistic."
—The Romance Reader Reviews

"Fast-paced and intriguing."
—Lori Avocato, *USA Today* bestselling author

"Smart and stylish."
—Marianne Mancusi, author of *News Blues*

KILLER IN HIGH HEELS

"Drag queens meet the high-fashion mob in this fun, fast-paced follow-up to Halliday's delectable *Spying in High Heels*. This amusing whodunit scores big with inimitable characters like psychic Mrs. Rosenblatt, Maddie's tell-all mom and bad-boy Ramirez. Maddie's winning return, with her bold comical voice and knack for thinking fast on her strappy slingbacks, will elicit cheers from fans of the growing chick mystery field."   —*Publishers Weekly*

"For those of us who like Stephanie Plum by Janet Evanovich, this is the same type of tale that is a fun, witty mystery that will have you laughing out loud."   —*Midwest Book Review*

Other books by Gemma Halliday:

UNDERCOVER IN HIGH HEELS
KILLER IN HIGH HEELS
SPYING IN HIGH HEELS

Gemma Halliday

ALIBI
in
HIGH
HEELS

NEW YORK CITY

MAKING IT®

March 2008

Published by

Dorchester Publishing Co., Inc.
200 Madison Avenue
New York, NY 10016

ISBN 10: 0-8439-5835-9
ISBN 13: 978-0-8439-5835-5

The name "Making It" and its logo are trademarks of Dorchester Publishing Co., Inc.

Printed in the United States of America.

10 9 8 7 6 5 4 3 2 1

Visit us on the web at www.dorchesterpub.com.

Dedicated to the memory of our little angel,
SUZANNA CAITLIN SEEDS
November 5, 2006 – December 4, 2006.
May heaven be filled with soft blankies, warm teddy bears,
and an endless supply of pink binkies.

ALIBI
in
HIGH
HEELS

Chapter One

I love shoes.

I mean I really, really love them. If my tiny studio apartment in Santa Monica were—heaven forbid—to go up in a blazing inferno, the one thing I would rush back inside to save would be my favorite pair of strappy silver sling-backs. Granted, I'm single, live alone, and have never been able to keep a houseplant alive, let alone a pet. But still—it's bordering on obsession.

So it came as no surprise that when an incident of minor Internet fame resulted in a trendy Beverly Hills boutique asking me to design a line of shoes for them, I squealed, squeaked, and generally jumped around like a six-year-old minus her Ritalin. Thus far in my illustrious design career, the biggest break I'd had was working for Tot Trots children's shoes, where my SpongeBob slippers had been the top sellers at Payless last season. (Something to brag about or bury in a deep, dark corner of my résumé? I still wasn't sure.)

But then things got even better when the first pair of Maddie Springer originals was sold to an up-and-coming young actress who just happened to be wearing them when she got arrested outside the Twilight Club on Sunset Boulevard for drug possession. Suddenly my shoes were all over *Entertainment Tonight*, *Access Hollywood*, and even CNN. I got calls from the hippest boutiques in L.A. and Orange County, all clamoring to stock my line—aptly named High Heels Seduction.

And then the impossible happened. (Oh yeah, it gets better.) The most utterly amazing, best thing to enter my life since DSW started carrying Prada. Jean Luc Le Croix, the hottest new European fashion designer, asked me, little ol' me, to come show my shoes in his fall runway collection at Paris Fashion Week.

Paris!

I had died and gone to heaven.

Not surprisingly, I first had a mild heart attack, then did a repeat of the six-year-old-Ritalin-addict thing.

What was surprising, however, was my boyfriend's reaction to my news of the century.

"You're going where?" Ramirez asked.

"Paris." I sighed the word, visions of the Eiffel Tower dancing in my head.

Ramirez rolled over in bed to face me, his dark eyebrows drawn together. "What do you want to go to Paris for?"

"Are you kidding?" I sat up, covering myself with a sheet. Even though we'd been dating off and on for over a year now, I still had my modest moments around Ramirez. Probably due to the fact that I never quite knew what was going on behind those hooded eyes of his.

Jack Ramirez was a homicide detective with a very big gun, a very big attitude, and a very big . . . Well, let's just say that certain parts of his anatomy weren't entirely lacking in the size department either. He was tall, with a compact build that was all tight muscles and hard angles. Dark hair, dark brown eyes, and a dark, intense look about him that made men wary and women drool. One white scar cut through his left eyebrow, and he had a black panther tattooed on his bicep, the sleek, powerful lines of its back rippling along Ramirez's arm as he propped his head up on one hand, waiting for my answer.

"Why *wouldn't* I want to go to Paris? It's the fashion capital of the world! The home of haute couture, Chanel, Dior. The Eiffel Tower!"

"Where will you be staying?"

"Jean Luc has set up rooms for all of us involved with the show. We'll be at the Plaza Athéneé. It's all taken care of."

"Do you even speak French?"

I waved him off. "I know how to ask where the bathroom is and, 'How much do those shoes cost?' I'll be fine."

"I've heard the French can be pretty rude to American tourists."

I pinned him with a look. "Trust me—for Paris Fashion Week, I can handle a little rude."

"Hmph," Ramirez grunted, then shifted his weight, his half of the bedsheet slipping down his bare torso, exposing a six-pack to make Budweiser jealous.

For a moment I completely forgot what we were talking about.

"How long?"

"What?" I snapped my eyes back up to meet his.

"How long will you be gone?"

"Oh. Uh, a couple of weeks. Three at the most. Jean

Luc wants me there to help set up, and then of course I'll be there for the full Fashion Week. Maybe a few days after to help him pack up."

Ramirez shook his head. "I'm not thrilled about this."

"Come on, Jack. Why not?" Had he not heard the *Paris* part?

"Maddie, I don't like the idea of a woman being in a foreign country all by herself."

If the statement hadn't been so blatantly chauvinistic, I might have been touched by his concern.

"I won't be all by myself. There are tons of people involved with the show: models, producers, designers. Besides, most of the time I'll be with Jean Luc."

"Jean Luc." Ramirez mulled over the name. "I'm not sure that makes me feel any better."

"Don't tell me you're jealous?" I asked coyly, reaching one finger out and tracing a line down Ramirez's granite chest.

He grinned. "Of a guy named Jean Luc? You're kidding, right?"

I gave him a playful swat. "Well, don't be. You have no idea what kind of work goes into Fashion Week. I'll be lucky if I have time to sleep, let alone ogle the male models."

Ramirez narrowed his eyes at me. "*Male* models? Now you are trying to make me jealous."

I swatted him again. "Don't worry, I'll be fine."

"And what about me?" He gave my sheet a teasing tug. "What about you?"

"I'm not sure *I'll* be fine. Two weeks is a long time for a guy like me to be alone."

"I'm sure you'll manage."

"I don't know." He traced a finger down my bare arm, leaving a trail of goose bumps. "I'm getting kind of lonely just thinking about it."

"You're a big baby, you know that?"

His grin widened.

"Besides, may I remind you that this is the first time I've even seen you in two weeks anyway?"

His smile faltered a little. "Can't be."

"Oh, yes." I nodded my head for emphasis, my blonde hair bobbing up and down. "Last weekend you had to cancel because of a shooting in South Central. Then Wednesday it was the three-car pileup on the PCH, and Friday they found that stripper's body in the Hills."

Ramirez's one flaw in the boyfriend department was his devotion to his job. Not that I blamed him; he was damned good at it. In fact, it had been the way we'd originally met, when I'd stumbled onto a case of his involving my ex-boyfriend, $20 million in embezzled funds, and a string of dead bodies. But since then it had served only as a wedge between us, keeping Ramirez wrapped up at crime scenes and me at home watching *Sex and the City* reruns and waiting for the phone to ring.

Not, mind you, that I was complaining. Much.

"Huh. I guess it has been a while," he conceded.

"Thank you."

He blew out a long puff of air. "All right, then. I give in. I'll survive while you go make your shoes and visit the Eiffel Tower."

"Really?" I squeaked. Okay, fine, so I was *totally* going to go anyway. I mean, come on, it's Paris! But it was nice to know he wasn't going to fight me on it.

"Really." He paused. "Under one condition."

I arched an eyebrow at him. "One condition?"

Ramirez let his gaze stray down to the thin white sheet covering my barely Bs. He gave me one of those long, X-ray-vision stares. "Uh-huh." He nodded. Then he broke into his patented Big Bad Wolf smile—all big teeth and wicked eyes. "Tonight you're all mine."

A shiver hopped down my spine, ending somewhere south of my belly button. I did a dry gulp. Then nodded.

And dropped the sheet.

Currently I had two vices: Mexican food and (as you may have noticed) Mexican men. Thanks to an early morning shooting on Olympic that had Ramirez crawling out of bed at the crack of dawn (see, what did I tell you?), I couldn't indulge in the latter. Which left me with the former, in the form of a grande nachos supremo at the Whole Enchilada in Beverly Hills. And I had to admit the gooey cheddar-and-salsa-induced semiorgasm I was experiencing was almost as good as what I'd had planned for Ramirez that morning.

Almost.

"So did Ramirez spend the night again last night?" my best friend, Dana, asked, leaning both of her elbows on the table across from me.

I nodded. And grinned. I couldn't help it. After spending a night with Ramirez, there was nothing I could do to wipe that sucker off. "It was hot."

Dana licked her lips. "How hot?"

I picked up a stray jalapeño from my plate and held it up. "Ten of these and you still wouldn't even be close."

Dana sighed, then started fanning herself with a napkin imprinted with a dancing cactus. "You know, it's been so long I can hardly even remember what a one-jalapeño night would be like."

Dana was a blonde, blue-eyed aerobics instructor–slash–wannabe actress with the kind of body that had *Playboy Bunny* written all over it. Which generally meant she saw more action than a NASCAR fan. However, her boyfriend du jour was Ricky Montgomery, who played the hunky gardener on the hit TV show *Magnolia Lane*. Amazingly, my fated-to-short-term-romance friend had actually taken a vow of monogamy with Ricky, which, thus far, had lasted a record three months. I was pretty proud of Dana. Especially considering that as soon as shooting ended for the *Magnolia Lane* season, Ricky had flown off to Croatia to shoot a crime-drama movie with Natalie Portman. Ricky said the script was amazing and had Oscar written all over it. Dana said she was investing in a battery-powered Rabbit and praying they wrapped quickly.

"So, when is Ricky coming back?" I asked around a bite of cool sour cream and hot salsa. I'm telling you, pure heaven.

"Three more weeks. I'm just not sure I can make it, Maddie. This is the longest I've ever gone without sex."

I raised an eyebrow. "Ever?"

Dana nodded vigorously. "Since ninth grade."

Wow. I think in ninth grade I was still negotiating with Bobby Preston over second base.

"So, why don't you just go visit him?"

She shook her head. "Can't. The set's in a military zone. They needed all sorts of permits and things just to be there. 'Booty call' isn't exactly on the list of approved reasons."

"Sorry."

"Thanks." Dana sipped at her iced tea: decaf, sugar-free, packed with antioxidants. Dana was of the my-body-is-a-temple school of dieting. Me, I'm pretty sure my million-calorie nacho platter spoke for itself.

"If it makes you feel any better, last night was the only action I've gotten in weeks, too." Not to mention that I was currently substituting a morning of naked sheet wrestling with chips and refried beans.

Dana sighed again, giving my jalapeño a longing look. "Not really, but thanks for trying."

"How about some shopping? Retail therapy always makes me feel better.

Dana nodded, her ponytail bobbing up and down. "Sure. But just for a little while. I've got an audition at one. I'm reading for the part of a streetwalker on that new David E. Kelley show. I can so nail this one."

I looked her up and down, taking in her denim micro-mini, three-inch heels, and pink crop top. I hated to admit it, but she so could.

After I'd fully consumed my nacho supremo, stopping just short of actually licking the plate, Dana and I walked down Santa Monica, making a right on Beverly.

Now, normally actually *walking* two blocks in L.A. was an unheard-of phenomenon, but this was prime window-shopping territory. While the busy street was filled with sleek sports cars and imported sedans, the boutiques lining the street held windows full of designer purses, thousand-dollar tank tops, and Italian leather shoes with stitching so small you'd swear it was the work of leprechauns.

After drooling over a pair of crocodile boots, a fabulous deconstructed jacket, and two to-die-for evening gowns, Dana paused in front of the Bellissimo Boutique. "Ohmigod, Mads! Are those yours?" She pointed to a pair of red patent-leather Mary Janes with a black kitten heel.

I grinned so wide I felt my cheeks crack. "Yep," I said, beaming with a pride usually reserved for mothers sporting student-of-the-month bumper stickers. "Those are my latest. You like?"

"I love! Oh, I so want a pair. Hey, you think you could do something for me to wear to the premiere of Ricky's movie?"

"I don't know if you can afford me. I'm a pretty hot designer now," I joked.

"Well, with the way shooting's dragging on, it's not likely to be anytime soon." Dana pouted, staring longingly at the red heels as if they might magically turn into her leading man.

"So what kind of shoes do you want?" I asked, trying to cheer her up. "Any idea what color you'll be wearing?"

"Oh, I totally know what I want!" Dana said, instantly perking up. "I saw the cutest pair of wedge-heeled sandals on J. Lo at the MTV Awards. They were, like, black with this little line of sequins going down the . . ." But Dana trailed off. Her eyes fixated on a point just over my shoulder, then suddenly went big and round.

"What?"

I spun around and stood rooted to the spot. A little yellow sports car was careening down Beverly at Daytona 500 speeds. It sideswiped a Hummer, narrowly missing a woman carrying a Dolce shopping bag, then bounced back into traffic, tires squealing.

"Ohmigod, Maddie," Dana said, her voice going high and wild. "Look out!"

I watched in horror as the little car cut across two lanes, jumping the curb and accelerating.

Straight toward me.

Chapter Two

Ever had one of those moments where you're suddenly outside your body watching your own actions play out like some TV movie starring Heather Locklear and thinking, *Wow, her life really sucks?*

After a split second of deer-in-the-headlights, I jumped to the right, arms splayed out in front of me like Superman as I dove for the pavement. I'd like to think that had my belly not been weighed down by half a pound of Mexican bliss, I might have been quick enough to get out of the way. As it was, I felt the sharp bite of a fender colliding with my left leg as my head snapped back and met the sidewalk.

"Uhn." I closed my eyes, little bright pinpoints of light dancing in front of my vision. Adrenaline pumped through my every limb, my heart thudding like a jackhammer. I tried to move my mouth and tasted blood. I think I'd bit my tongue.

"Ohmigod, ohmigod! Maddie, are you okay?"

I blinked. Slowly. And saw Dana's face hovering over mine, along with a homeless guy wearing a faded

Abercrombie T-shirt, and two women in red hats with Chanel bags dangling from their wrists.

"I . . . I think so." I tried wiggling my fingers, arms, legs. I stopped at my legs. Pain shot up the left one, making me yelp like a puppy. I slowly propped myself up on my elbows and looked down. The yellow sports car was hovering just over my lower half. It was so shiny-new that it was still minus license plates and had a bright chrome mustang attached to the hood. The only thing marring its new-car perfection was the big ugly dent in the front fender.

I didn't even want to see what my leg looked like.

The Mustang's door flew open, and the driver stepped out. Or, I should say, wedged herself out. I was fully ready to unleash the wrath of a sexually frustrated blonde who's had her nacho buzz ruined until I got a good look at her. She was at least three hundred pounds and wearing a bright green-and-pink muumuu, Birkenstocks, and a shade of eye shadow that would make Marilyn Manson cringe.

I did a mental forehead smack.

Mrs. Rosenblatt.

Mrs. Rosenblatt was my mother's best friend, a five-time divorcée (always on the lookout for Mr. Six) who talked to the dead through her spirit guide, Albert. I know—only in L.A. Then again, I wasn't sure I should pass judgment so quickly. By the looks of the new car, the psychic business must not be doing all that poorly these days.

"Oh my word, Maddie, I didn't see you there, honey. It's this new stick-shift thingie. I got no idea how to work it. You'd think a body pays enough for a car like that, the thing would drive itself. Oh, lordy, your Mom's gonna kill me. I was on my way to meet her at Fernando's. Honey, can you move? Can you speak? Do you need a doctor? How many fingers am I holding up?"

I blinked. "Fifteen."

"She needs a doctor. Someone call a doctor!"

I let my head fall back on the pavement again while Dana dug a cell out of her purse and Mrs. R made me take deep breaths and count backward from ten. I'm pretty sure that was the standard routine for someone who'd ingested too many margaritas, not a woman who'd been hit by a car, but that moment I wasn't in a position to argue. At least the counting kept my mind off the pain, now slowly spreading up my thigh and settling into a throbbing rhythm as the shock wore off.

Ten minutes later our little crowd had grown to include half the people in Beverly Hills, or so it seemed as the paramedics fought their way through the looky-loos and eyed my legs. I was infinitely glad that I'd shaved them that morning.

The taller paramedic, a dark-haired guy with freckles, crouched down beside me and gingerly wiggled my left leg.

I saw stars and thought I might faint.

"This doesn't look good," Freckles said. "Could be broken."

Great. Some women cruise Beverly and go home with a pair of Jimmy Choos. I go home with a broken leg.

"Are you sure?" I whimpered.

"Not until we can get X-rays. Can you wiggle your toes?"

I concentrated on wiggling.

"The left toes."

"I *am* wiggling the left toes."

Freckles and the other paramedic shared a look; then he frowned down at my leg again. "Nope. Not good. We're going to have to cut this boot off."

"No!" I sat straight up. "I'm fine. It's getting better. Really. I'm okay. No need to touch the boots. Look, I can just unzip it here." I reached down and started to unzip. Bad idea. Pain shot up my leg, and the crowd began to swim before my eyes. I dropped the zipper and took a deep breath, trying not to vomit my nachos all over the sidewalk.

"Ma'am, your leg is swollen. It could be broken. We're going to have to cut the boot off."

"Do you have any idea what you're saying? These are Gucci! I had to design three pairs of Disney princess water shoes to pay for these."

Freckles exchanged another look with his partner. "Ma'am, you're in shock. Please lie still."

"No, wait. I think I feel the swelling going down already. Just give me a minute. I'm sure I can get the zipper."

"Ma'am, don't make us strap you down."

"Wait! Please, I . . . I . . . Dana?" I appealed to my friend, giving her my best helpless face. (Which, since I was currently pinned beneath a muscle car, wasn't all too difficult.)

Dana bit her lip. "Geez, Maddie, it looks really bad. Maybe you better just let them cut it."

I thunked my head back down on the pavement. What else could I do? I shut my eyes, trying not to cry as

I felt Freckles pull out a pair of scissors and desecrate my Guccis.

"Three months?" I blinked at the on-call doctor in her white coat and thick glasses, praying I had heard her wrong. Unfortunately, since I haven't been to Mass since last Easter, it was no surprise that God completely ignored me.

"Three months." The tight-lipped doctor nodded her head, consulting the manila folder in her hands. She was sans makeup, and her thick brown hair was pulled back from her face in a ponytail so tight it made her eyes crease. "You've got a tibial shaft fracture. You're going to need to wear the cast for at least three months to give the bones time to set. After that we can discuss a regimen of physical therapy. Keep your weight off it, and keep it elevated whenever possible to reduce swelling, especially in the first forty-eight hours."

I looked down at the big blue foam boot covering my left leg from my very unmanicured toes all the way to my hemline. From the knee down I looked like a bloated Smurf.

After slitting my Gucci right up the middle, the paramedics had whisked me away in their ambulance to the nearest hospital of my insurance company's choosing. Mrs. R had insisted on riding along, seeing as how she felt responsible and all. (I didn't point out that was because she actually *was* responsible.)

After I'd waited a mere thirty-five minutes in a tiny white room at the back of the ER, a nurse had wheeled me to X-ray, where they'd twisted my leg into all sorts of uncomfortable positions to take black-and-whites. Then I'd been wheeled back to the sterile room to wait while the on-call doctor reviewed my films, which had taken another forty minutes, all of them spent listening to the teenagers in the room next door puke their guts out after having eaten bad sushi at the Westwood Mall.

That was about the point when I told Dana I was fine and she should just go to her audition. She argued a little at first (because I was clearly not fine), but I knew how much she wanted that streetwalker part. Besides, there wasn't anything she could really do to help.

Now, though, surrounded by Mrs. R's Birkenstocks and Dr. Ponytail's loafers, I was kind of wishing I had an ally who understood just how badly this boot was going to clash with my entire wardrobe for, apparently, the next three months.

"What about showers? Can she take the thing off to shower?" Mrs. Rosenblatt asked. "My fourth husband, Lenny, broke his arm once, and he couldn't shower for two whole months. I tell ya, that sucker started smelling pretty ripe by the time they cut it off him. I think Lenny was starting to mildew a little."

I heard myself whimper.

"Baths would be preferable, and, no, no taking the boot off to bathe. You'll have to wrap it in plastic and stick it outside the tub."

I did another whimper.

"I'm going to prescribe you some pills for the pain," she continued, scribbling in my chart. Then she turned to a cabinet behind her and pulled out a pair of tall metal crutches. "You'll need to use these to get around. They're a little awkward at first, but trust me, you'll get used to them," she said, adjusting the height.

I took them, sticking one under each arm. *Great*. Not only was I a Smurf, now I was also Tiny Tim.

The doctor looked down at my one good Gucci, and a frown settled between her unplucked eyebrows. "And I'd suggest saying away from high heels until the fracture stabilizes."

"Hold on!" I put one hand up. "What do you mean, stay away from heels?"

"Besides the difficulty balancing, the elevated position of the other foot puts too much stress on the injured leg. Flats only for the next three months." And with that Ponytail left the room, still scribbling.

I stared after her, my mouth hanging open, tears starting to form behind my eyes. No heels for *three months*? Could this day get any worse?

As if to answer my question, the door flew open again.

"Oh, my poor baby!"

I looked up to see my mother burst into the room, head down, arms out, tackling me for a rib-crushing hug.

"Oh my baby, are you all right?"

"I'm fine." *Sort of*.

"I came as soon as Mrs. Rosenblatt called. Oh my poor baby, you could have been killed!"

"It's the damned clutch," Mrs. R said. "Too many pedals down there. I couldn't figure which one to press when. They need less pedals in them sports cars."

"Mom, I can't breathe."

"Oh, sorry." Mom stepped back, and for the first time I got a good look at her outfit.

I love my mother dearly, but let's just say I'm glad I didn't inherit her fashion sense. Today she was dressed in a pair of skinny jeans (clearly made for someone three sizes skinnier than she was), a blouse covered in tiny white ruffles, and a pair of black LA Gear high-tops formerly seen on MC Hammer circa 1989. She topped it all off with a shade of lipstick I could only describe as neon magenta, and blue eye shadow that reached all the way to her plucked eyebrows. When I was fifteen I sent applications to Oprah, Ricki Lake, and Jenny Jones hoping one of them would take Mom on their "Please give my mother a makeover" shows. No such luck. These days I usually just cringed in silence.

Mom looked down at my blue boot. "How bad is it, honey?"

"Not that bad," I said bravely. Okay, fine: It wasn't courage; it was denial.

"You know, they make some very stylish sneakers these days," my mom said. I looked down at her high-tops and felt tears well behind my eyes again.

"Ballet flats!" Mrs. R piped up. "They're all the rage. Last weekend I was doing aura readings down at Venice Beach, and all the young kids were wearing them."

I sniffled back the tears. "You think so?"

"Sure. You'll be just as pretty as a peach in them."

I sighed. "Paris just won't be the same without heels."

"Oh, well, there's no way you can go to Paris now," Mom said, still inspecting my boot.

"Whoa!" I held both hands up in front of me. Which, of course, made my crutches immediately slip out from my armpits and clatter to the floor. "I am *totally* still going to Paris."

"Maddie, you can't even walk!"

"I have crutches."

Mom looked down at the floor, then back up at me, raising one eyebrow.

"What? The doctor said I'd get used to them."

"Maddie, you can't possibly go to a foreign country like this. Honey, what about your luggage? And traveling through the airports? And customs? How will you even get around?"

I bit my lip. "I'll manage." *Somehow.*

I'll admit, though, she had a point. The more I thought about trying to navigate my way through LAX, let alone the French airports, while wearing Wonder Boot, the more my leg throbbed, my head started to hurt, and I really started jonesing for another comforting nacho platter.

But I was damned if one little NERF boot was keeping me from Fashion Week.

"Look, I've already committed to do this. Jean Luc is counting on me. I'm supposed to fly out this weekend. There's no way I can back out now."

Mom pursed her lips, her arms crossing over her chest as she gave me a good long stare. "All right, fine."

I gave an internal sigh of relief. "Thank you."

"Then I'm going with you."

"What?"

"Maddie, there's no way I'm letting my baby fly all the way to Paris all by herself with a broken leg. If you're so intent on going, then I'm going, too."

"But, Mom—"

"Well, then, I'm coming too," Mrs. Rosenblatt piped up.

I tuned to her, my mouth falling open. *"What?"* This could not be happening. Again I got that out-of-body feeling, as if my life were spiraling out of control into some late-night TV farce.

"I feel responsible. After all, it *was* my car," Mrs. R said.

"Besides," Mom chimed in, "I've always wanted to visit Paris. The museums, the shops . . ."

"The Eiffel Tower," Mrs. R added.

"Oh, the Eiffel Tower! Think how much fun this will be, Maddie," Mom said, grabbing my hand. "It'll be like a girls' night out. Only in Paris!"

The last time Mom and I had had a girls' night out she'd dragged me to a karaoke club, where we'd spent the evening sipping watery tap beer and listening to overweight businessmen butcher Diana Ross songs.

"No. No, no, no, no." I shook my head, a sudden headache matching the throbbing in my leg. "Look, I'm a grown woman. I can take care of myself. I'll get a skycap to help with the bags. They have bellboys in Paris. I'll be fine. I'm an adult, and I can take care of myself."

"Oh, honey," Mom said, tilting her head to the side and giving me the same look she gave me when I was five and told her I was running away from home to join the circus. "Don't be ridiculous."

Mental forehead smack.

There are few truly unstoppable forces in nature: tornadoes, hurricanes, an unexpected shift of the San Andreas Fault line. And—you guessed it—my mother.

Which was why, a few days later, as I hobbled through the front doors of the Plaza Athénée in Paris, France, I had a pair of awkward metal crutches shoved under my armpits and a pair of middle-aged women flanking my sides.

"Oh my God, Maddie, would you take a look at this place?" Mom's mouth gaped open.

"It's like where them rock stars stay," Mrs. Rosenblatt said. "I bet Gwen Stefani stays here."

"I bet the queen stays here."

"I bet this is gonna max out my Visa."

They were right: The place was amazing. The floors were a pale taupe marble beneath a sparkling crystal chandelier that was larger than my bathroom. Bright red fresh-cut flowers decorated the lobby, and the walls were done in delicately painted frescoes of wildflowers and serene lakes. The entire place felt opulent, glamorous, and oh, so very French.

Okay, so I was here with two postmenopausal chaperones. But I was here. In Paris. Despite the eleven-hour flight, I couldn't help the goofy grin that cracked my face.

"*Puis-je vous aider?*" asked a man behind the counter as we approached. He was in his fifties, tall and slim, with a large nose and a receding hairline exposing a shiny dome of a forehead.

"I don't know what he said," Mrs. Rosenbaltt commented, "but he sure looked good saying it." She gave me a suggestive elbow in the ribs.

The dome went red and his eyes hit the floor. "Ah, Americans," he said quickly, switching to English. "And how may I help you lovely young ladies?"

Mrs. Rosenblatt snorted. "We're *young* ladies," she said to Mom. Mom giggled.

I handed over my credit card. "Maddie Springer. And entourage," I added, glancing over my shoulder.

"Don't mind us. We're just here to sightsee," Mom said, waving me off.

"You, ah, got any recommendations where two *young* ladies could have a good time, Pierre?" Mrs. R licked her lips and leaned suggestively on the counter, her bright orange muumuu dipping down to expose a pair of breasts that gravity hadn't been kind to.

The clerk cleared his throat, going a deeper shade of crimson. "*Pardonnez-moi*, mademoiselle, but the name is actually Andre."

"Really? 'Cause you look like a Pierre to me. Must be that sexy French accent of yours."

Andre suddenly became engrossed in his computer screen. "Ah, yes, we have two rooms on the seventh floor. Adjoining."

"Oh, this is going to be so much fun, Maddie," Mom squeaked, giving my arm a squeeze. "It'll be like one big slumber party."

"Uh, do you have anything maybe not so adjoining?" I asked.

But unfortunately Andre was currently hypnotized by Mrs. R running her tongue suggestively over her lipstick-stained teeth. I admit it was kind of like a car wreck—hideously unreal, yet impossible to turn away from.

"So, what time do you get off work, Pierre?" Mrs. R asked.

The clerk gulped. "Uh, rooms 702 and 704. Enjoy your stay." He quickly slid the card keys across the marble counter, then scurried off to help the next customer.

"I think he kinda liked me," Mrs. R said.

"I think you kinda scared him."

"Oh, Maddie, we're in Paris! This is going to be so

fun!" Mom squeezed my arm again and steered me toward the elevators.

Visions of karaoke in French flashed before my eyes.

I was thankful Mom and Mrs. R decided to take a nap in their suite before going out for an afternoon of sight-seeing. I left them at their door, promising to call once I got safely to the site of Jean Luc's tent.

I slipped my card key in the door, stepped into my room, and suddenly felt like I'd entered a dollhouse. A white four-poster bed sat in the middle, draped in bright yellow floral patterns and piled high with about a million pillows. Beneath the window sat a long chaise, and on the far side of the room was a lovely antique bureau next to a small writing desk. The room was feminine, bursting with ruffles, and had *Paris* written all over it. I loved it.

I immediately went to the window overlooking the city and craned for a glimpse of the Eiffel Tower. I could see straight to the mountains, but sadly there was no tower in sight. Clearly not an Eiffel-view room.

I didn't stop to unpack, instead quickly changing into a breezy red spaghetti-strap sundress I'd bought at French Boutique on Melrose, a white shrug sweater, and red-and-white polka-dotted ballet flats (okay, *one* ballet flat and one ugly blue boot) before grabbing my purse and heading out to find a cab to Le Carrousel du Louvre—site of Jean Luc's show.

Fashion Week, here I come!

If you've never been backstage at a fashion show, there are few things in life that can compare to it: the excitement, the energy, the sheer chaos. And while Jean Luc's show wasn't scheduled for another week, as I neared the white tent with the words LE CROIX painted in bold black letters, the air was already electric with anticipation, and the chaos was in full swing. Men in white coveralls converged on piles of lumber, which in just a few short days would be transformed into runways the world would be watching to learn what they'd be wearing this season. Reporters with cameras slung around their necks stood in the corners, interviewing anyone who'd stand still. And models—tall, thin, almost inhumanly beautiful creatures—were everywhere, sipping from water bottles, smoking slim brown cigarettes, and strutting their impossibly long legs in impossibly beautiful couture.

This was as close to heaven as I thought I'd ever been.

In the center of it all, like a clever ringmaster, stood the man himself, Jean Luc Le Croix. He was tall and thick, in his forties. Jet-black hair, dark sunglasses, a look on his face like he were perpetually constipated. He wore black jeans, black snakeskin boots, and a black cashmere sweater with a big gold medallion hanging around his neck. He reminded me of an auctioneer, constantly barking out orders at whoever happened to be within earshot.

"Maddie!" he cried as I approached.

"Hello, Jean Luc." I leaned in and did a very French pair of air kisses at him.

"We've been expecting you. It is madness, yes?" he asked, gesturing around himself. "Come, come, we've got the models being fitted inside." Jean Luc led the way through the construction toward a large building beside the famous Louvre Museum. I hobbled awkwardly behind, trying to keep up with his long-legged gait.

The room he led me into was full of worktables, dress

forms, and tall, rail-thin models in various states of undress. Among them flitted assistants and seamstresses, long yellow measuring tapes draped around their necks. A chorus of different languages were being spoken: Italian, French, Spanish, and even a few words of English here and there.

Jean Luc barked to the models as we threaded our way through the room. "Tanya, darling, that's a top, not a skirt. Angelica, you need a necklace with that shirt. No, no, no, Bella, that color is all wrong on you. Take it off quickly, darling!" He turned to me. "You'll have to excuse me, the majority of the models came in only yesterday, and I'm still in the middle of a full-blown aneurysm."

I grinned. Despite his brusque manner, it was impossible not to like him.

"Becca! You're killing me," he shouted to a pouty redhead. "That's a front closure; you must wear undergarments with it!"

"Jean Luc," called a voice from the back of the room. "Jean Luuuuuuuuc." A short, slim brunette wearing all black, thick glasses, and a headset hailed him from across the room, making purposeful strides toward him.

Jean Luc closed his eyes in a minimeditation. "Not again," he mumbled under his breath. Then he turned around, all smiles.

"Maddie, meet Ann, my assistant."

"Charmed," Ann shot back, giving only a cursory glance in my direction. "Listen, Jean Luc, it's Gisella. She's lost her necklace for the finale."

"Christ, not again."

Ann gestured toward a tall, long-legged brunette with

stick-straight bangs and thighs so slim I could wrap my hands around them. She looked bored, jutting out one bony hip and contemplating her fingernails.

"She says she doesn't know where it is, and we can't find it anywhere."

"Fine, I'll be right there." Ann walked away, and Jean Luc turned to me. "I'm sorry, apparently my two-second break from crisis has ended. But come, I'll introduce you to Gisella."

I hobbled after Jean Luc again as he stalked toward the bored brunette.

"Maddie," Jean Luc said as I caught up, huffing just a little, "I'd like you to meet my lead model, Gisella Rossi."

"Nice to meet you," I said, sticking out my hand while simultaneously trying not to lose my grip on my crutches.

Gisella gave me a limp-wristed squeeze and a wan smile. "Ciao."

"Gisella will be wearing the black baby doll in the finale, so we'll need a tall heel for her. But nothing chunky."

"Got it. No problem." I had just the right shoe in mind for her already: a black, three-inch, pointy stiletto with a rhinestone-studded ankle strap I'd put the finishing touches on last week. I looked down at her feet, trying to gauge her size.

"Now, Gisella, darling, what's this I hear about the necklace gone missing?"

Gisella rolled her eyes. "I dunno where it is," she answered in heavily accented English.

"Honey. Sweetie," Jean Luc said, though the look on his face said he was mentally calling Gisella a whole host of less endearing names. "That necklace is irreplaceable. It's priceless. We have to find it."

Gisella shrugged again. "It could be anywhere."

"Where was the last place you saw it? Retrace your steps."

She blew a puff of air toward the ceiling, ruffling her bangs. "Last night I went to the party at Hôtel de Crillon. Then, after, I go back to my own room. I put the necklace in my room. Then I go to bed. I wake up, the necklace is missing."

Jean Luc started breathing hard, like he needed a paper bag. "You wore the necklace to the party? And took it back to your own room!"

Gisella contemplated her nails. "Yes. It is a fancy party."

Jean Luc looked ready to spout steam from his ears.

"You took a priceless piece of jewelry from *my* show to a private party?"

Gisella didn't answer, thoroughly engrossed in her cuticles.

Jean Luc pinched the bridge of his nose, struggling to compose himself. "At least tell me you put it in your room safe?" he finally mumbled.

Gisella bit the inside of her cheek. "I dunno."

"What do you mean, you 'dunno'?"

"It was a late party. I had a lot to drink. I can't remember."

Jean Luc took a deep breath through his nose.

"Maybe it is stolen," Gisella said.

Jean Luc visibly paled. "No. No, no, no, no. It cannot be stolen. It's on loan from Lord Ackerman's private collection. It is not stolen. You just misplaced it, Gisella."

Gisella shrugged. "We'll just have to get another one." And she stalked off, her long legs gliding with a grace that was at complete odds with her grating disposition.

Jean Luc pinched the bridge of his nose again. "Get another one? Christ, it's worth over 300,000 euros. Get another one! Good God, Lord Ackerman would kill me," he mumbled to himself as he walked away.

I did some quick mental math, converting euros to dollars, and couldn't help a low whistle as I realized the kind of money he was talking about: roughly $500,000. *Wow*.

Well, I guess life could be worse. I could be Jean Luc.

After settling in at a table in the back, I spent the rest of the day seeing one model after another, trying to match shoes to outfits. In most cases the shoes I'd brought with me were a little on the large size, something I'd been prepared for, bringing a whole bag of tricks to make large shoes fit a medium foot. One thing they'd taught us in design school was that it was always easier to fit a larger shoe on a small model than have her try to squeeze into a too-tight one. The only one that fit perfectly was, ironically, Gisella's. It was almost as if the black stiletto had been made for her foot. A good thing, too, as she wasn't the most patient of subjects, fidgeting and twisting in her seat the entire fitting.

By the end of the day I was beat. The pain pills were wearing off, my leg was throbbing, and I was seriously wondering what the French equivalent to Starbucks was. I was relieved when Ann walked through the workroom, announcing they were packing it in for the night.

One cab ride later (during which I had my nose pressed to the glass the entire time, trying to catch a glimpse of the Eiffel Tower), I was dragging my tired self through the lobby of the Plaza Athénéé. It took all the energy I had left to concentrate on keeping my crutches from slipping on the marble floor—not an easy thing to do. And one that inevitably led to my running smack into some poor soul getting off the elevators.

"Oh, I'm terribly sorry," I mumbled to the ground. "*Je suis* . . . uh . . . *muy, muy* sorry." No wait, that was Spanish. "Uh, *je suis* . . ."

"No problem, Maddie."

I froze—and looked up into the man's face for the first time, sucking in a breath of surprise. There, standing in front of me, was the last person I expected to see in Paris.

Felix.

Chapter Three

Two years ago I had investigated the disappearance of my former boyfriend, who, as it turned out, had been involved in an embezzlement scheme that ended in murder. I'd confronted the killer head-on, and during the resulting struggle I'd inadvertently popped one of her saline breast implants with a nail file. And then stabbed her in the side of the neck with a stiletto heel. I know—very girlie of me. But what can I say? Shit happens.

Unfortunately it was just the kind of story that the *L.A. Informer*, Southern California's sleaziest tabloid, lived for. That was my first encounter with Felix Dunn, the only reporter in all of L.A. County who had published no fewer than five articles revolving around Bigfoot's secret love child with the Crocodile Woman. Felix had taken the popped-implant story and run with it, even going so far as pasting a picture of my head on Pamela Anderson's body under the caption: *Big Boobs Beware!* I'd briefly contemplated hiring a hit man.

Since then Felix and I had, on occasion, worked together for the greater good. Okay, I'd worked for the greater good. Felix had worked for a juicy story to land him on the front page. He had the moral fiber of pond scum, which came in handy when dealing with the criminal element, but I wasn't entirely sure he wouldn't eat his young to sell a few more papers.

During brief moments Felix did, I admit, appear to have a human side. Born in England, he wore his cropped blond hair a little on the messy side, had twin dimples that appeared in his tanned cheeks quite frequently, and had the Hugh Grant–charm thing down pat. And, at least once he'd expressed genuine concern over my well-being. It was during one of those rare moments that I'd last seen Felix. I'd been spending the night at his house and, in a completely accidental move, kissed him. On the lips. With tongue.

The kiss had been meant for his cheek, but I swear he'd turned his head at the last minute. Like I said, complete accident. But considering we hadn't seen each other since then, I still felt heat creeping into my cheeks, and the taste of his lips slipped to the forefront of my memory as I stood in the lobby of the Plaza Athénee staring up into his blue eyes.

"Maddie. How are you, love?" he asked, his voice holding the slightest hint of a British accent.

"Fine." I cleared my throat. "Uh, great. Wonderful."

His gaze strayed down to Wonder Boot. "You don't look all that great-wonderful."

"Gee, thanks. Just what every girl wants to hear."

His eyes crinkled at the corners, those dimples making an appearance. "That's not what I meant." His eyes roved appreciatively over my red dress. "And you know it."

My cheeks went Lava Girl again. "Tibial fracture," I blurted out. "I collided with a Mustang. Mrs. Rosenblatt. I'm fine."

Felix clucked his tongue. "You've got to be more careful, love. Let me guess, stumbled over a heel? Not the most practical footwear, now, are they?"

I resisted the urge to stick my tongue out at him. "Fashion is not about practicality. And, no, I didn't stumble. I was the victim of a psychic who couldn't work a clutch."

Felix chuckled. "Only you, Maddie."

I ignored his amusement at my expense. "What are you doing here, anyway?"

Felix raised an eyebrow at me. "It's Fashion Week. What do you think I'm doing here?"

"Hoping one of Versace's models runs off with the Loch Ness Monster?"

Again those dimples flashed. "Actually I'm here with my auntie. She never misses Fashion Week, but she does hate coming alone."

I narrowed my eyes at him. Dutiful Nephew didn't fit Felix's usual MO any more than GI Jane fit mine. I could hardly see him accompanying a doddering blue-hair to runway after runway.

He paused, then added, "And, of course, if some top model should happen to trash her hotel room or collapse from an anorexic laxative overdose while I'm here, so much the better."

Ah. Now there was the Tabloid Boy I knew and loved. I mean, hated.

"And you? What brings our Maddie to Paris?"

I lifted my chin, making the most of my five-foot-one-and-a-half-inch frame. "I happen to be showing this week."

He raised a blond eyebrow, suitably impressed. "Really?"

"Yes, at the Le Croix show. All the models will be wearing Maddie Springer originals."

"I should say you've finally arrived then." He looked down at my one polka-dotted ballet flat. "This from your collection?"

"No. Thanks to the broken leg I'm on a no-heels diet."

"No heels?" He did a mock gasp. "Good God, how will our Maddie survive?"

"Ha, ha. Very funny, Tabloid Boy."

"Well, congratulations on the show. I'll look forward to seeing you there. Now, if you'll excuse me, I'm afraid I'm keeping Auntie waiting. Good to see you again, Maddie. Uh . . ." He gestured down to Wonder Boot. "Need a hand getting up to your room, love?"

I squared my shoulders (not easy while holding on to a pair of crutches, by the way). "No, thank you. I'm quite capable of taking care of myself."

Again with the grin. "Suit yourself." Felix did a little bow, then took off in the direction of the hotel's restaurant.

I watched his retreating back. He'd traded in his usual uniform of a white button-down shirt and rumpled khaki pants for a more sophisticated look of tailored slacks and a soft gray blazer. The color of the jacket brought out the highlights in his blond hair, the line of the slacks accentuating his long, lean form. I had to admit it looked good on him.

Not, mind you, that I was looking.

I turned and hit the elevator button, immensely relieved that for all his teasing, at least Felix hadn't mentioned the Kiss (accidental as it was). I'd expected some snide comment, but he hadn't even hinted. In fact, it was almost as if he'd completely forgotten all about it. Good. Perfect. Me too. What kiss? See? It never happened. Completely forgotten.

The carriage arrived, and I awkwardly hobbled into the elevator, glancing briefly toward the restaurant as Felix disappeared inside.

I had to remember to ask Ramirez whether he owned a blazer.

I opened the door to my room and immediately spied a note on hotel stationery slipped under the door. Ditching the crutches with a clattering thud on the carpet, I leaned down and picked it up. *Went to Moulin Rouge. Don't wait up. Mom.* Mom and cancan dancers. Now, there was a combination.

I hopped over to my ruffled four-poster bed on one ballet flat and flopped down on my back, spread-eagled. I closed my eyes and lay there, contemplating the back of my eyelids. One day down, six more to go until show day.

I was hovering in that place somewhere between semiconsciousness and dead-to-the-world sleep when "The William Tell Overture" started singing from the region of my purse. I groped, refusing to open my eyes as I blindly fished for my cell. "Hello?" I asked as I flipped it open.

"How's my favorite designer this morning?"

Ramirez. Despite the tired ache in my limbs, a smile lifted the corners of my mouth at his smooth voice, sounding deceptively close.

"Evening. It's eight o'clock. I'm beat."

"Aw, poor girl. Slide a little closer. I'll give you a massage."

I grinned in the dark. "Don't tempt me. It's only an eleven-hour flight."

"Paris is that bad, huh?"

I sighed. "No. Actually, it's wonderful. Absolutely amazingly, exhaustingly wonderful."

"Good. I'm glad to hear it." Though I'd swear a tiny corner of his voice almost sounded disappointed.

"I still haven't even gotten a glimpse of the Eiffel Tower yet, though."

"I'm sure Jean Luc wouldn't mind your taking a little time off to do some sightseeing."

"Ha! You don't know Jean Luc."

"What if you just go in a little early tomorrow and take a quick trip to the tower in the afternoon?"

I rubbed my temples. I had to admit it wasn't a bad idea. "Maybe."

"Hey, by the way, I dropped by your place last night and watered your plants."

Last spring Ramirez and I had finally taken the plunge and exchanged house keys—probably the biggest commitment I could ever expect out of a guy like Ramirez. When I'd shown Dana the pink copy of Ramirez's house key that he'd had made for me, she'd warned that once the keys came out, the ring wasn't far behind. I'd had a brief moment of panic until I realized a) this was Ramirez we were talking about, and b) Dana's longest relationship thus far had been with her treadmill. She wasn't exactly an expert.

I frowned into the phone. "Um, honey, I don't have any plants."

"Okay, I dropped by and watched the game on your TV. Cable was out at my place."

"You are such a guy."

"And that's a bad thing?"

I felt myself smiling in the dark again. "No. Definitely not."

"So, when are you coming home? Your place isn't the same without you."

"A week from Sunday."

Ramirez groaned into the phone. "That's a long time."

"Only ten days."

"Only?" He groaned again, though this one held a hint of his wicked Big Bad Wolf smile behind it. "You know, I think you're going to have to make this up to me when you come home."

I quirked an eyebrow in the darkness. "Oh, yeah? What did you have in mind, pal?"

"Oh, I've got a couple of ideas. How do you feel about whipped cream?"

I giggled into the phone, even as my body went warm in places completely inappropriate to talk about in mixed company. "Whipped cream, huh? What am I, an ice-cream sundae?"

There was that growl again. "Uh-huh. With maybe a cherry or two on top. Then I'd lick—"

But he didn't get to finish that thought as Ramirez's pager chirped to life in the background. I heard him shift, then curse under his breath. "Shit. Maddie, the captain's paging me. I gotta go. Call you back?"

I swallowed down a lump of disappointment. Just when we were getting to the good part. "Sure."

"Five minutes. Promise," he said. Then a click and silence sounded in my ear.

I looked at the phone in my hands. I swear, if Ramirez paid half as much attention to me as he did his captain, we'd be married and making babies by now. Not that I necessarily wanted to be a baby maker, but quite honestly I wouldn't thumb my nose at a night of being a human ice-cream sundae. I closed my eyes, wondering just how Ramirez had anticipated finishing that last thought.

There went that inappropriate heat again. I stared at my cell. Five minutes, huh?

I got up, rummaging in my suitcase for something suitable to wear while having intercontinental phone sex with my boyfriend. Unfortunately, the best I could come up with were the flannel pajamas with little ducks printed on them that I'd packed. Not necessarily Frederick's of Hollywood, but they'd have to do. I slipped the top on, giving up on the bottoms as they stretched and strained around Wonder Boot. I guess I could have taken the boot off. But I only had two more minutes. Besides, the shirt was long enough to cover all the important parts. I grabbed my cell, flipped the lights off, and crawled back into bed with one minute to spare.

I sat there staring at my phone. A minute went by. Then another. One more. *Okay, don't panic.* Five minutes, ten minutes . . . *What's the difference, right?* I decided that a watched cell never rang and grabbed the remote on the night table, switching on the TV to wait it out. Surely Ramirez would call any second.

I surfed through one channel after another of people speaking way too quickly me for me to catch even a word or two, until I found a station airing *Friends* reruns dubbed in French. I still couldn't understand what they were saying, but I remembered this one as the episode where Rachel got drunk and confessed her attraction for Ross, and could follow the plot well enough from memory.

Fifteen minutes later Rachel was blasted, leaving on Ross's answering machine her thoughts on closure, and I was staring at my own very silent phone.

"Ça, mon ami, est aboutissement," Rachel said with a smirk. Canned laughter erupted. The screen switched to a commercial for either tennis shoes or fitness water—I couldn't really tell.

I looked down at my cell readout. Completely dark. *Five minutes, huh?* I flipped open my phone. Yes, the battery was charged. No, I hadn't missed any calls. *Damn.*

I'd give him another ten minutes.

By the time *Friends* was over and I was watching a dubbed *I Love Lucy* rerun, in which Ricky told Lucy she had some *explicitation* to do, I realized a) my libido had completely faded into exhaustion, and b) I'd been stood up.

While I was disappointed, it was depressing to realize I wasn't entirely surprised. When the choice was between me or a case, I knew exactly where I stood with Ramirez. When a homicide came up, Maddie disappeared. I flipped off Lucy and closed my eyes, wondering if I'd ever have Ramirez's full attention.

Bright and early the next morning my alarm blared, a Black Eyed Peas song breaking through the predawn light. For half a second I seriously had second thoughts about my getting-up-early plan. But it was the Eiffel Tower we were talking about. Reluctantly I dragged myself out of bed and hopped (quite literally) into the shower, doing a one-leg-in, one-leg-out thing with Wonder Boot, which resulted in shampoo in the eyes, a funky shaving job on my one good leg, and an aerobic workout to rival Dana's step-and-sculpt class. Twenty minutes later I felt like I'd run a marathon, but I was clean and dressed in black jeans (one leg rolled up past my knee), an Ed Hardy shirt with a skull and daisies printed on it, and a silver ballet flat (just one). I had the doorman grab me a cab and made tracks through the crisp morning air toward the Louvre, this time with a large café au lait from the Plaza's café. Don't ever let it be said that I'm not a fast learner.

By the time I arrived the sun was just starting to peek out from behind the buildings, illuminating from behind the impressive glass pyramid structure in the Louvre courtyard. The light reflecting off the angles and slopes gave it an almost otherworldly look that reminded me of the huge, crystal-studded ball that dropped every New Year's in New York. I took a moment just to watch the spreading pink hues of the sunrise reflecting off its surface as I finished my café au lait.

I made a mental note to buy a disposable camera before coming in tomorrow morning as I chucked my paper cup into a nearby trash can and hobbled through the plastic flaps of the Le Croix tent.

But I didn't get far as I ran smack into Jean Luc.

"Oh, I'm so sorry, I'm still a little clumsy on these things. The doctor said I'd get used to them, but—"

Jean Luc cut me off, grabbing me by both shoulders. His face was white as a sheet, his eyes wide, the pupils dilated. "Maddie," he said in strangled voice. "It's Gisella."

He gestured toward the newly constructed runway. It was missing a few boards, and the sides were still unfinished. Flanking it on one side was a pile of lumber scraps and on the other a sawhorse, ready for the coverall fellows to resume their work.

And in the center of it was Gisella, Jean Luc's top model. Lying faceup. Her stick-straight hair fanned around her head, which was being consumed by a thick, dark pool of crimson. One of my pointy-toed, black ankle-strap stiletto heels was sticking out of her jugular.

Chapter Four

I staggered, my crutches slipping out from under me. I focused my eyes on the ground, the flapping plastic doorway, the image of the perfect Parisian sky beyond. Anywhere but at the ugly red pool of blood surrounding Gisella's head. I took in a deep breath. Bad idea. It held a cloyingly sweet scent that made my stomach roil in protest. Quickly I made for the door. If I was going to puke, I didn't want to contaminate the crime scene—because it was painfully obvious that was what this was.

The stiletto heel to the neck. Just like I'd done to Miss When Mistresses Attack right after popping her implant. It had been unnerving then, but seeing a repeat of the same scene was creepy enough to make my coffee feel like motor oil in my stomach.

And it didn't help that the shoe sticking out of her neck was *my* design.

The landscape wavering, I slipped to the ground outside the tent, my good leg giving out. I put my head between my knees, closed my eyes, and took deep breaths that smelled like coffee, wet grass, and leather ballet flats.

"We've got to call the police," Jean Luc said beside me, his voice sounding oddly far away.

With a shaky hand I reached for my cell phone. After staring at the buttons for what seemed like way too long, I realized I had no idea who to call and handed the phone over to Jean Luc.

Then I promptly stuck my head between my knees again.

Minutes later the tent was swarming with people.

Jean Luc had, luckily, known exactly who to call. And within minutes they had arrived in droves: policemen in blue uniforms that looked strikingly similar to American ones, crime-scene technicians in black windbreakers with cases full of evidence baggies, and two men in long coats who'd wheeled in a metal gurney and black tarp. Then the second wave had arrived, the paparazzi. Flashbulbs went off, notepads came out, and TV cameras from every country of the world fixed on the white flapping door of the tent, waiting for a glimpse of Gisella's mangled body. I periodically scanned the crowd for Felix. I knew he wouldn't be far from a story like this.

Ann, Jean Luc, and I waited off to one side, next to the growing group of models dabbing at their eyes with tissues and muttering subdued *ohmigod*s as they arrived and heard the news. Ann's headset was eerily silent as we watched the scene unfold. Jean Luc was a sickly shade of yellow, popping antacids into his mouth like Pez. Me, I was still crumpled on the ground, my crutches splayed out beside me. Though, I was happy to report, my stomach had stopped trying to relieve me of my morning caffeine fix.

"I . . . I can't believe this," Jean Luc said, his voice

shaking as he popped another chalky white tablet into his mouth. "This just can't be happening. Not a week before the show!"

"It is," Ann assured him, her dark eyes intently watching the growing number of reporters.

"First the necklace, now this." Jean Luc was wringing his hands. "I've got to call Lord Ackerman. He's going to be livid."

The tent flaps opened and we all held our breath, the paparazzi straining forward for one last shot of Gisella. Instead, a tall, stoop-shouldered man with a mustache that looked like a small furry animal had died on his upper lip emerged. He wore a cheap gray suit that was at least two sizes too big and had a cell phone glued to his ear. He spoke quickly into it in French, then snapped it shut, scanning the area until his eyes settled on our little group.

"Which one of you found the body?" he inquired in accented English as he approached.

I cleared my throat, grabbing my crutches and struggling to a vertical position.

"I did," Jean Luc piped up. "And, shortly after, Maddie arrived."

"Ah. Mademoiselle"—the man pulled a small notebook encased in leather out of his pocket and consulted it—"Springer?" he asked, nodding in my direction.

I nodded.

"Detective Moreau." The detective didn't offer his hand, instead flipping the notebook shut. "Yes, I'd like to ask you some questions."

I took a deep breath, trying to inhale some bravery I certainly didn't feel. "Go ahead."

"Actually, I would prefer to speak with you in private." He shot a look at Jean Luc, whose face was whiter than a Goth girl's. "Is there somewhere we can go?" he asked, gesturing around the courtyard.

"The workroom," Ann supplied. "This way."

She led the way through the growing crowd across the courtyard to the workrooms, unlocking the door and letting Moreau and myself in.

"*Merci*," Moreau said with a tiny bow. Then he gave Ann a pointed look that was clearly a dismissal.

Ann took the hint. "Let me know if you need anything else," she offered before leaving.

Moreau shut the door, then indicated a hard-backed chair behind a worktable holding a half-sewn pencil skirt. "Please take a seat."

I did, as Moreau pulled out his notebook again, along with a stubby yellow pencil that looked like the ones they issued you when miniature golfing.

"So, you were the one who found the deceased. Gisella"—he consulted his notes—"Rossi?" he asked as if he'd never heard the name. Clearly he didn't subscribe to French *Vogue*.

I nodded.

"When was this?"

"I don't know. Maybe an hour ago. As soon as we found her Jean Luc called you guys."

"Jean Luc. This would be Monsieur Le Croix, your employer, yes?"

I nodded again, starting to feel like a bobble-head doll. "Yes."

"And he called the police right away?"

"Yes."

"When was the last time you saw Gisella, Mademoiselle Springer?"

I thought back. The previous day had been a blur of activity. "I-I'm not sure. There was so much going on yesterday."

"You didn't see her this morning, then?"

"No, not until . . ." I trailed off, my eyes cutting to the door.

"Right. And where were you earlier this morning?"

My head snapped up. "What?"

"I asked where you were this morning," he said, leaning two hands on the table.

I gulped. "Why? Am I a suspect?"

Moreau stared at me. "This isn't the first time you have come across a dead body, is it?"

I bit my lip. I had to admit it wasn't. Call me unlucky, but I seemed to be jinxed that way. "No."

"Isn't it true, in fact, that you once before stabbed a woman with a shoe?"

I paused, then nodded slowly. "Yes, but—"

"And isn't it true," he continued, raising his voice to steamroll right over my objections, "that she was also stabbed in the neck?"

I said nothing. Damn, news traveled fast.

"An interesting coincidence, no?"

"Look, I didn't have anything to do with this. I barely even knew Gisella. I just met her yesterday. Yes, it's just a weird coincidence." But even as I said it my mind was rejecting that thought. What were the chances of a something like that happening twice? "Look, stilettos are sharp. They're pointy. They're a good weapon."

He looked unconvinced, his dead-squirrel mustache twitching with every breath.

"It could have been anyone! Gisella wasn't exactly popular, you know."

"You are the designer of the shoe in question, are you not?"

"Um . . . yes?" I said, only it sounded more like a question.

"Another coincidence that she was stabbed with your shoe?"

I jutted my chin out defiantly. "Yes. Another coincidence."

Moreau snorted. "That's quite a few, isn't it?"

I pursed my lips, refraining from comment—mostly because I didn't have one.

A knock sounded at the door, and an officer in blue appeared. He was carrying a black bag with him and said something in French to the detective. Moreau responded with a, "*Oui, oui,*" and waved him in.

The second guy laid his bag on the table and opened it, pulling out a long stick with a cotton swab on the end that looked like a supersize Q-tip.

"Since this is all one giant *coincidence,*" Moreau said, heavy on the sarcasm, "I don't suppose you would mind giving us a sample of your DNA? To rule you out, of course."

I looked at the Q-tip, then back to Moreau. I squared my shoulders. "No, of course not."

Moreau nodded to the uniform, who gestured for me to open my mouth. I did, and he stuck the Q-tip in, gently scraping it along the side of my cheek. Then he placed it in a plastic case and snapped the top shut, dropping it into his black bag. He mumbled something else in French to Moreau, then nodded and left the room.

I stared after him, suddenly wary, though I wasn't sure why. Surely whatever they did with my DNA would prove me innocent, right?

"You never answered my initial question, Mademoiselle Springer," Moreau said, scrutinizing me.

I snapped my eyes back to meet his.

"Gisella was killed between one and four A.M. Where were you this morning?"

"I woke up and came straight from the hotel to here. Where I found Gisella."

"Alone?"

"Yes. No. I mean, I was with Jean Luc."

"All morning?"

"No, just when we found her."

"What about last night?" he asked, his questions falling rapid-fire one on top of another.

"I was working."

"Alone?"

"No. I was with Jean Luc."

"All night?"

"Yes."

"So, you are lovers?"

"What? No. I mean, no, not all night, not like that."

"Like how then?"

"I . . . we . . . we were working. Until late. Or at least it felt late with the jet lag. Then I went to my own room."

"Alone?"

"Yes," I said vehemently.

"So, you were alone then. No alibi?"

"What? No, wait, I wasn't . . . I mean . . ."

Damn, he was good. He'd effectively gotten me to say exactly what he wanted to hear. "Look, I didn't do this."

"So you say."

"It's true!"

"Yet you were alone, you have no alibi, your shoe was used as the murder weapon. And the crime fits your . . . how do you say . . . MO to a *T*."

"What MO? No, I'm not a criminal; I don't have an MO! I . . . I . . ."

I was rapidly losing this battle. For all his ridiculous looks Moreau was good. Too good. So good I had a bad feeling that if he was convinced I'd done this, he'd find a way to prove it. Even if it wasn't true.

I was just about to pull out my one and only secret weapon—crying like a girl and hoping for mercy—when the door swung open and a vision in khaki Dockers and a rumpled white button-down filled the doorway.

Felix.

"What the hell is going on here?" he asked. "Why is that chap taking her DNA sample?"

Okay, so white knight he wasn't, but I'd never been so glad to see anyone in my life.

Moreau, on the other hand, didn't look at all pleased. "And you are . . . ?" he asked.

Felix squared his shoulders. "Lord Ackerman."

I blinked.

"Lord Ackerman?" I asked. *"Lord?"*

Felix shot me a look that clearly said, *Shut up*. Which I did, clamping my lips together to keep from laughing.

"I'm sorry, Lord Ackerman," Moreau said, his voice suddenly filled with a note of respect despite Felix's worn Skechers sneakers and I-just-rolled-out-of-bed hair. "But this is an official *murder* investigation." He emphasized the word, throwing a pointed look my way.

Damned if I didn't *feel* guilty under his gaze.

Felix narrowed his eyes at the detective and shot back, "*Qu'est-ce que tu fais?*"

Wow. Item number forty million I didn't know about Felix. He spoke French.

Moreau seemed a bit surprised, too, his mustache twitching ever so slightly. But he parried back quickly, responding in rapid French something that prompted Felix to throw up his hands in an exasperated gesture, then shout something in return. I watched the two of them go back and forth, wishing like anything I'd taken French in high school instead of ceramics. The ability to make a clay pencil holder that said, *Happy Mother's Day*, was completely useless right now.

Finally Felix thumped his hands on the desk, bringing home his point (whatever it was) and grabbed me by the arm, hauling me to my feet. "Let's go, Maddie. We're done here."

I expected the detective to protest, but instead Moreau just watched, intent on Felix, his eyes narrowing above his mustache (which was twitching double-time now).

I tried not to look too smug as we left the room.

"What did you say to him?" I asked as Felix navigated the hallways, one hand still firmly clasped around me.

"I said that if he came near you again without a warrant, I'd have his badge."

I stopped. "Warrant?"

We were just outside the tent, police vans and numerous cop cars circled around the courtyard, the long stretch of press and tourists being held back by wooden police barricades. The main point of interest at the Louvre was definitely not the Mona Lisa today.

"Do you seriously think he'd get a warrant?" I asked.

Felix turned to face me, his eyebrows hunkered down in concern. "Maddie, she was killed with one of your designs. And you have to admit the shoe to the neck . . . not a common way to kill someone."

I gulped. I knew. I also knew I didn't do it. Which meant someone not only wanted Gisella gone, but had tried to make it look like I'd been the one to do it—a disconcerting thought. Sadly, thanks to the *L.A. Informer*, my past exploits weren't exactly a secret. Anyone could have heard about the shoe to the jugular.

"That was genius, by the way," I said as Felix steered me through the crowd, signaling for a taxi. "The whole pretending to be Lord Ackerman. Really got Moreau's attention."

Felix gave me a funny look over his shoulder as a black-and-white cab pulled up to the curb. "I wasn't pretending."

"What do you mean, you weren't pretending?" I asked, slipping onto the vinyl seat.

Felix spoke to the driver in French, giving him the address of the hotel, before turning to me.

"I really am Lord Ackerman."

I snorted. "No, you're not. You're Felix."

He didn't say anything, but the telltale amused twinkle I'd come to associate with his teasing was noticeably absent from his eyes.

"Ohmigod, you're serious? *Lord* Ackerman?"

Felix nodded slowly.

I turned to Felix, pretty sure my mouth was unattractively gaping open. "You've got to be joking. What, did you buy the title online or something?"

Felix gave a wry grin. "Worse. I was born into it. On my father's side, a quite distant cousin of the queen's."

"The *queen*? Wait, are you trying to tell me that you're actual royalty?"

"Oh, don't worry, only about a hundred people would have to die before I'd come close to the throne."

"So, hold on here." I held up one hand. "You're telling me that Gisella's half-million-dollar diamond necklace was on loan from *you*?"

Felix nodded slowly, carefully watching my reaction, which I was pretty sure was a cross between pure shock and total disbelief.

I'll admit I'd never really known that much about Felix's background. I knew his mother was Scottish, which was where Felix claimed he inherited his "thriftiness," as he called it. Though I'd pointed out to him on more than one occasion that tipping a waiter in nickels wasn't thrifty; it was downright cheap. All I knew of his father was that he was English and Felix had inherited a good deal of family money from him at some point. And, apparently, a title. I'd always referred to Felix as a cheap rich guy. But I'd never imagined him as an actual member of the aristocracy.

A titled tabloid reporter. What was this world coming to?

I didn't have a chance to question the lord any further as my cell rang from the depths of my shoulder bag. I pulled it out and flipped it open, checking the caller ID. Ramirez.

I closed my eyes and did a little minimeditation before clicking the on button.

"Hello?" I asked tentatively.

"Hey, beautiful."

Despite the morning I'd had, I felt comfort wash through me at the sound of his voice. I suddenly really wished he weren't an ocean away.

"Look, I know what you're going to say, and it's not my fault," I quickly said into the phone. "I just found her. And I know it's a huge coincidence the way she was killed with the shoe in her neck and all—well, at least Moreau thought it was—but that's all it is! I swear! I had nothing to do with it. All I wanted to do was come to Paris for Fashion Week and maybe catch a glimpse of the Eiffel Tower, and then the accident and this stupid cast, and now they're taking my DNA, even though they don't have a warrant, and saying I don't have an alibi!"

There was a pause on the other end. Then Ramirez's voice came in a slow, deliberate cadence. "Maddie, what is going on over there?"

"Don't you know?"

"No," he said, concern lacing the word. "I just called to tell you I was sorry I didn't get a chance to call you back last night. What the hell is going on? What's this about DNA and warrants?"

Oh, hell. I swear, one of these days I'd learn to keep my mouth shut. Obviously today wasn't that day.

Quickly I filled him in on the morning's events, pussy-footing the best I could around my interrogation, lest I reveal just how blonde I'd sounded. I must not have done a very good job, however, because when I finished he was silent. I heard just the sound of his breath coming in tightly restrained pants.

"Hello? Are you still there?"

"I'm booking the next flight."

"No!" I shouted into the phone. Okay, I'd kind of freaked out facing Moreau. And having Felix show up had been a huge relief. And I'll admit the second I'd heard Ramirez's voice I'd instantly felt better. But having him fly halfway around the world just to hold my hand was tantamount to saying that he was right. That I couldn't take care of myself. That I did need a chaperone as badly as he and my mother thought. No way was I admitting that.

"No, really, I'm fine."

"You're not fine, Maddie. You're a homicide suspect."

"Well, sort of, but—"

"Look, I don't want you there alone."

"I'm not alone," I said, glancing over to Felix, who'd been pretending not to listen to the conversation up to this point. "Felix is here."

Silence. Then, "Felix? As in, the reporter Felix?"

"Uh, yeah."

"The same Felix who got you kidnapped in Vegas?"

"Uh . . ."

"And the same Felix who gave you a gun last spring?"

"Well, um . . ."

"And," he said, really gaining steam now, "the same Felix who looks at you like you're dessert and he hasn't eaten in weeks?"

"He does not!" I glanced over at him again. Did he? "But, uh, yeah. That Felix."

"I'll be there by morning." Then he hung up.

I stared at the silent phone in my hand, then up at Felix, still looking out the window, pretending not to eavesdrop.

Great. Just what I needed—a pissing contest.

Chapter Five

When we got back to the hotel I was beat, mentally and physically, the jet lag catching up to me big-time.

The front of the hotel was crammed with paparazzi. As if the Fashion Week photographers weren't enough, now every newshound in Europe was covering the sensational death of their favorite supermodel. I could see Felix mentally sizing them up, his hands fidgeting in his lap with nervous energy. If there was one thing Felix hated, it was to be scooped.

The cabdriver pulled as close to the front doors as he could manage, then dropped Felix and me off at the sidewalk. I awkwardly angled Wonder Boot out of the cab, sticking the crutches under my armpits, hobbling toward the hotel doors, and leaving Felix to pay the fare. Hell, he was related to the queen. He could handle it.

By the time I made it to the glass front doors Felix had easily caught up, and we pushed our way through the crowd. Unfortunately the lobby wasn't any less populated, the chatter of reporters echoing off the marble floors. I kept my head down and plowed straight for the elevators, letting out a sigh of relief as the doors closed behind us. Two minutes later I was at my door, fumbling in my shoulder bag for my card key.

As it turned out, I didn't need it. The door flew open.

"Oh lordy, Maddie, I'm so glad you're okay!" Mom grabbed me in a big bear hug, knocking both crutches to the ground.

"Mom, I can't breathe."

"Sorry." She stepped back. "I was just so worried. You're on every TV station. Not that I can understand most of what they're saying about you."

"Is it true? Did you stab that model with your shoe?" Mrs. Rosenblatt asked, waddling up behind.

"Of course it's not true!" Mom shouted, turning on her. Then she paused and leaned in close to me. "Is it?"

"No! It's just a coincidence."

"See," Mom said to Mrs. R. "I knew it wasn't true. I knew you couldn't do the horrible things the TV says you did."

"What are they saying?" Felix asked, walking into the room behind me.

"They're calling her the Couture Killer," Mrs. R piped up.

Felix winced. "Wish I'd thought of that," he muttered under his breath.

I resisted the urge to kick him. Mostly because I couldn't balance on one foot.

"Who's this?" Mrs. Rosenblatt asked, gesturing to Felix.

"This is Felix Dunn."

"The reporter?" Mom narrowed her eyes. She knew all too well how I'd felt about my head being pasted on Pamela Anderson's body.

"The one and only." Felix bowed. "I've heard so much about you, Mrs. Springer. It's lovely to finally meet you." He grasped one of Mom's hands in both of his.

Mom blushed. "Oh, well."

"And you," he said, advancing on Mrs. R, "you must be the charming Mrs. Rosenblatt. A true pleasure, ma'am." He leaned down and kissed her hand.

Mrs. Rosenblatt giggled. "I could get used to these European men."

Oh brother.

"Maddie, what exactly happened today?" Mom asked, gathering my fallen crutches for me.

I hopped over to the double bed and sat down, pillows floofing around me. Reluctantly I filled Mom and Mrs. R in on the events of the morning. I glossed over my run-in with Moreau as best I could (in case you hadn't noticed, Mom tends to be a little overprotective), but by the time I was done she still had her lips clenched together in a tight white line.

"How could they possibly think you had anything to do with this, Maddie?" she asked.

"Wow. Creepy finding her like that. You've definitely got some bad karma issues, *bubbee*," Mrs. Rosenblatt said, putting a sympathetic hand on my arm. "You want an aura cleansing?"

What I wanted was a long, hot bath, a handful of pain pills, and a nap. But I had to agree with her: My karma did suck.

"What she needs is a lawyer. The nerve of that policeman, questioning you," Mom said.

"It sounds like a setup to me," Mrs. Rosenblatt offered. "Someone's trying to make you look guilty."

Which, thus far, was working splendidly.

"Who would want to do that to my baby?" Mom asked, her eyes going big and round beneath her powder blue eye shadow.

"You pissed anybody off lately, doll?" Mrs. R asked.

I shrugged. "How could I? I don't even know anyone here. It's got to be a coincidence."

"The real question is, who would want Gisella dead?" Felix piped up from the corner.

He'd been so quiet I'd almost forgotten he was there, sitting at the minidesk, absently doodling on a pad of hotel stationery. His forehead creased as he went on. "Anyone could have read about your exploits, Maddie, and decided you'd make a convenient scapegoat. The real question we should be asking is, who had issues with Gisella? When was the last time you saw her?"

"Yesterday. Jean Luc introduced me to her right after she lost the necklace. Then I did a fitting for her shoes right before we left for the night."

"Hold on." Felix stopped me. "Go back. What necklace did she lose?"

"Lord Ackerm—" I started. Then I checked myself. "I mean, uh . . . yours."

Felix lifted an eyebrow. "Mine?"

Oops. "Uh, Jean Luc didn't tell you?"

He shook his head from side to side. "Care to fill me in?" he asked, leaning forward.

I quickly related the scene I'd witnessed the day before between Gisella and Jean Luc. When I finished Felix looked deep in thought.

"So, the necklace goes missing; and then Gisella ends up dead."

"I betcha it was stolen." Mrs. R nodded sagely, her chins (plural) bobbing up and down. "You know France is crawling with them cat burglars."

I rolled my eyes. "Only in Cary Grant movies."

"But then why kill her after they already stole it?" Mom asked, pursing her drawn-on eyebrows.

"Good point. Why kill her if they'd already gotten away with the necklace?" I asked.

"I say we start with the necklace anyway. It's our best lead," Felix decided.

"This wouldn't have anything to do with you wanting to recover it, would it?" I asked.

Felix shrugged. "It's insured. But, yes, I wouldn't mind if it showed up."

"I have an even better idea," I offered. "How about we just leave this to the police?"

Three pairs of eyes turned my way.

"So they can arrest you?" Mom asked, voicing everyone's thoughts.

"But I'm innocent."

Silence.

"I am!"

Mom reached over and patted my arm. "Of course you are, baby. *We* believe you."

I looked around the room. Clearly I was outnumbered.

"Okay, fine. Where do we start?"

Taking Felix's suggestions, Mom and Mrs. Rosenblatt decided to find out all they could about Gisella by doing some serious Googling downstairs in the hotel's business center. Felix said he had some things he wanted to check on (though I suspected he really wanted to call the story in to his editor at the *Informer*) and would meet up with me in the lobby later that afternoon. For lack of a better idea I decided to see if there were any new developments at the show site. In lieu of actually braving the paparazzi (not to mention risking a run-in with Moreau) I dialed Jean Luc on his cell.

He answered on the third ring.

"Yes?" he barked out, his voice tense.

"Hi, Jean Luc. It's Maddie."

"Oh," he answered on a sigh. "Maddie. Are you all right? What happened to you?"

"I'm fine. I'm back at the hotel."

"Thank God! I was afraid they'd taken you into custody."

I winced. *Not yet.* "Have there been any new developments since I left?"

Jean Luc sighed into the phone. "Not that I know of. They've been back and forth with their evidence bags all day. Maddie, I swear I'm on the verge of a breakdown. They've taken every last pair of your shoes into evidence."

I grabbed a bedpost for support. "They've taken my *shoes*?" I repeated, hoping I'd heard him wrong, visions of my Paris debut fading faster than a bad dye job.

"Can you believe it? What am I supposed to do, send all the models out barefoot? Good God, this isn't some mall; it's Fashion Week!"

I felt a mini–heart attack coming on. This could not be happening.

Jean Luc's voice got high and whiny as he continued, voicing my exact thoughts: "This cannot be happening to me! Not only do I have to find a replacement for Gisella when everyone who's anyone is already booked, but now I have no shoes, too." I heard Jean Luc unwrap another antacid and crunch down loudly on it.

I closed my eyes and took deep breaths. Okay, so they'd taken my shoes. It was fine. They'd dust them, process them, whatever it was they did with evidence, and see that I did not kill Gisella. So, really, this was a good thing, right? (Am I the denial queen, or what?)

"Do you have any idea who could have done this?" I asked.

Jean Luc paused, and I could hear the silent question.

"I didn't do it!" I yelled.

"No, of course you didn't, Maddie."

Why was it that no one sounded completely convinced when they said that?

"Look, I didn't even know Gisella."

Jean Luc sighed again. "Honestly, I'm not sure any of us knew her that well. She tended to keep to herself. That is, when she wasn't complaining. I hate to speak ill of the dead, but she wasn't exactly the easiest person to work with."

"How about the other models? Was she particularly close with any of them?"

Jean Luc paused, and I could picture his eyebrows furrowing together. "Close, yes. Friendly, no. She spent most of her time with Angelica, but they had a very love-hate relationship. Mostly hate. Angelica was jealous of Gisella's contracts, and rumor has it Gisella apparently fueled this by stealing Angelica's boyfriend."

I perked up. A stolen boyfriend was a strong motive for a stiletto to the jugular.

"Is Angelica there now?"

"No, she left about an hour ago. Said she was going back to the hotel."

I crossed my fingers. "Any idea what room she's staying in?"

"1245."

"Thanks. Let me know if you hear anything new."

Jean Luc promised he would and hung up as he crunched another tablet.

I hopped into the bathroom, splashed a little cold water on my face, and added a fresh swipe of Raspberry Perfection to my lips before grabbing my purse and crutches and making for Angelica's room.

Five minutes later I was knocking on the door to room 1245. I could hear a loud bass beat playing inside, but no one answered. I waited a couple of seconds, then banged my fist on the door again. This time it opened a crack, the security bar still in place.

A redhead with Casper-pale skin, thick curls, and huge brown eyes appeared. "Yeah? What do you want?" she asked, her accent an indistinguishable (at least to my ears) eastern European.

"Angelica?"

She narrowed her eyes. "Who are you?"

"I'm Maddie Springer. I'm doing the shoes for the Le Croix show."

Angelica's eyes went round as recognition dawned. "You! The murderer!"

I rolled my eyes. "I didn't do it!"

"They said on TV that you did."

"Don't believe everything you hear on TV. Listen, can I come in?"

"I don't think so."

"Please?"

"You might kill me."

If I hadn't been holding a pair of crutches I would have thrown my hands up in exasperation. As it was I just said a silent curse on the head of all misinformed reporters.

"Look, I didn't kill her. If I had, do you think the police would have let me go?" Never mind that it had been touch and go there for a few minutes.

Angelica chewed her plump bottom lip while she thought about this.

"Listen, I just wanted to ask you a few questions about Gisella. Jean Luc said you knew her."

Angelica sank her teeth into her lip for another beat before shutting the door and lifting the security latch. She pulled it back open wide, allowing me entry.

"Okay."

"Thank you."

"But keep your hands where I can see them."

I tried not to roll my eyes as I stepped into the room. It was a carbon copy of my dollhouse, only her ruffles were a pale sky blue, and the place looked like housekeeping hadn't been there in weeks. Clothes covered every available surface, empty minibar bottles spilling out of the trash can, and a hip-hop song punctuated with a lot of "yo, bitches" played from an iDock on the dresser. Out of habit I crossed to the windows, futilely looking for a glimpse of the Eiffel Tower as Angelica turned the music down.

"So," she asked, plopping down cross-legged on the bed, "what do you want to know?"

"Jean Luc told me that you and Gisella were close."

Angelica smirked. "Well, we weren't BFFs or anything," she responded, the Americanism seeming oddly comic coming through her thick accent.

"You'd had some issues with her lately?"

"Bitch stole my Sam away."

Unlike Jean Luc it was clear that Angelica had no problem speaking candidly about the dead woman.

"Sam?"

"Someone I was dating."

I perched on the edge of the desk. "What happened?"

Angelica shrugged. "It wasn't like I was even that into Sam. Totally cute, but short-term, you know? Anyway, the first time Gisella sees me at a club with Sam, she starts flirting all over the place. The next thing I know Sam's telling me we should see other people, and then *they* show up together at the Posen opening."

"When was this?" I asked, gauging her reaction. I had to admit she didn't exactly seem heartbroken over the guy, casually picking at her nail polish as she spoke.

"A couple months ago."

"And was she still seeing Sam?"

Angelica laughed. "Hardly. She dumped Sam after a few weeks. Like I said, it was all about stealing what I had. Gisella was like that. She didn't want anyone to have something that she couldn't have. She was always jealous of me."

I raised one eyebrow. "Really?" Jean Luc had indicated that their relationship was the other way around.

Angelica nodded, her red curls bobbing up and down. "Sure. When I landed the cover of *Elle* she was livid. She was on the phone to her agent fifteen times a day trying to get her own cover. And then when I was booked for Jean Luc's show, she had to be booked too."

"But I thought she was Jean Luc's lead model?"

Angelica's eyes narrowed. "*Was.* I'm the lead now." Her lips curved into a little smile that I wasn't sure reached her eyes. With friends like this, Gisella didn't need any enemies.

"So," I said slowly, watching her reaction, "she gets the lead in the show and she steals Sam? Some friend, huh?"

Angelica shrugged her bony shoulders, curling one leg under her frame. "Like I said, I'm the lead now, so it all worked out."

Yeah, except for poor Gisella.

"If Sam was history, do you know if Gisella was seeing anyone new?"

Again with the shrug. "I couldn't say. Though she was with a guy at the Hôtel de Crillon party a couple nights ago."

I perked up. The one where she'd worn the necklace. "You were at the party, too?"

Angelica nodded. "Everyone was there."

"Did you know the guy Gisella was with?"

"No. But he was cute. Average height, I guess. Sorta dirty-blond hair."

"Did you catch his name?"

She shook her head. "Sorry. Gisella didn't introduce me."

"Did you notice the necklace she was wearing?"

"Well, duh!" she said, shooting out another American-ism. "Everyone noticed the necklace. Gisella made sure of that. She told everyone that Jean Luc was letting her keep it in her room for the evening. The little liar. Jean Luc would never."

Great. So, a roomful of people who knew exactly where to find it. *Sorry, Felix.* I had a feeling the necklace was long gone.

"When was the last time you saw Gisella?" I asked, changing tactics.

Angelica cocked her head at me. "You know the police already asked me this stuff?"

Right. They would have. And as sure as I was that Moreau was on the wrong track, I had a feeling he was covering that track very carefully.

"Humor me."

Angelica grinned. "All right. Last night. After the fittings were over. I saw her in the bar, and then later I heard her in her room."

"You heard her?"

"Uh-huh. Her room is right next to mine."

I glanced at the shared wall. "What exactly did you hear?"

"She had a guy in there. At first I just heard her voice. A lot of giggling, you know. Then some moaning and tumbling around. It was quiet for a few minutes after that. Then the fighting started."

"Fighting?" Now we were getting somewhere.

"Uh-huh. He never raised his voice much, but I could tell it was a man. Now, Gisella, she was shouting, yelling, throwing a terrible fit."

"When was this?"

Angelica pursed her lips, letting a thoughtful frown settle between her brows. "I first heard her go in a little after midnight. But the fighting started closer to one."

"Could you hear what they were arguing about?"

"She was saying that she didn't deserve this. That she was a supermodel. That she wasn't going to take it lying down."

"And did he respond?"

"I'm not sure. Like I said, she was doing most of the yelling."

"What happened next?"

"That's it. I heard the door to her room open and slam shut, then nothing. She was silent."

"But you never saw the guy?"

She shook her head. "Like I cared who Gisella was screwing."

I thought about the implications of this new information. Maybe it had been quiet after Mystery Man left because Gisella was already dead. Was it possible that she'd been murdered in her room? I thought about the pool of blood on the runway. Not likely. But she could have been drugged, unconscious. Maybe he'd left, only to come back later, drag Gisella to the runway, then kill her. Either way Mystery Man bore some looking into.

I thanked Angelica and left her room. As soon as I stepped into the corridor again I heard the bass beat resume. At least Angelica wasn't taking the death of her friend too hard.

I glanced to my right. Gisella's room. No crime-scene tape, no policemen guarding the door. I looked down the hallway to my left. Empty.

Gingerly I hobbled over and tried the doorknob. As expected it didn't budge. On a whim I shoved my own card key into the slot. No green light. Obviously not going to work. Unless I had a lock pick in my purse, I wasn't getting into Gisella's room. Which, of course, I didn't.

Luckily, however, I did happen to know someone with a full set.

As soon as I stepped off the elevators into the lobby I spotted Felix. He was leaning against a marble pillar, his back to me, talking to a blonde woman I didn't recognize. She was tall, almost the same height as Felix in her heels, long blonde hair expertly colored, with trendy highlights shot throughout. She wore a black dress that looked painted on her slim form. Tanned skin, long legs—one of those women men instantly drool over and other women instantly hate.

As I watched Felix lean in closer and drape an arm around the woman's waist an odd sensation shot through me. I wasn't exactly sure what it was, but it came with a satisfying vision of clawing the woman's perfect blue eyes out.

I didn't get to examine it any further, though, as my cell started singing from the depths of my purse. I pulled it out, checking the caller ID. Dana.

"Hello?"

"Maddie, ohmigod, what's going on there?"

"You heard, huh?"

"Are you kidding? It's all over every station! I was on the stepper at the gym and almost fell over when they showed your face on CNN."

"CNN? Seriously?"

"Maddie, they're saying you're a suspect." She paused. "You're not really a suspect, are you? I mean . . . you didn't do it, right?"

"Why is everyone asking me that? I did not stab a woman with a shoe! I would never do that." I paused. "Again."

"Right. Of course not."

"Look, it's just a coincidence." Though the more times I said it, the harder it was becoming to believe. But being set up sounded so melodramatic. Outside of a Robert De Niro movie, was anyone ever really set up?

"So, what happened?"

I glanced across the lobby. Felix was whispering something in the woman's ear now. Something that made her laugh and toss her hair over one shoulder. My stomach did that funny clenching thing again.

I ignored it, instead filling Dana in on my day, ending with the conversation I'd just had with Angelica.

"So, Mystery Man did it," she said when I'd finished.

"Maybe. Or the jealous model. Angelica could have done it herself and made the whole Mystery Man thing up."

"What about Jean Luc?" she asked.

"What about him?"

"Well, maybe he killed Gisella. I mean, he admitted himself that she was a pill. Besides, look at all the free publicity he's getting. His name is, like, everywhere."

I shook my head. "No, Jean Luc is freaking out right now. Angelica's the show's new centerpiece, but he's still short one model. And everyone in Europe is already booked for Fashion Week."

"Ohmigod, me!" Dana squealed. "Me, me, me! I could totally fill the spot."

"You? Dana, you're an actress, not a model."

"Big diff. I played a model in that pilot last spring,

Runway Rascals. And I've done a few mall things and boat shows. I could so do this!"

"I don't know, Dana. . . ."

"Look, I have experience, I'm available, and I could totally help you clear your name. Please, please, please!"

I'd like to say it was the *please* that got me. But in actuality, the idea of having a friend on my side here was just too tempting. Between the foreign language, foreign press, and foreign police officers watching me like a hawk, I was feeling just a wee bit ganged up on. Call me selfish, but against my better judgment I felt myself saying, "All right. I'll suggest it to Jean Luc."

Dana gave a squeal so high I was pretty sure poodles from Santa Monica to Marseille yelped in protest.

"Oh, thank you, thank you, thank you, Maddie! I'm gonna go start packing right now."

"I said I'd *suggest* it," I reminded her.

But she didn't hear me. She'd already hung up.

I looked up to see Felix guide Miss Long Legs over toward the lounge, his hand flirting with the small of her back. I told my clenching stomach that I so did not care who Felix fraternized with as I keyed in Jean Luc's number and prepared to convince him that one beach-blonde aerobics instructor from L.A. was the perfect addition to his European collection.

Chapter Six

Jean Luc's phone went right to voice mail, so I left him a message touting Dana's abilities and the number of her booking agent. Then I snapped my phone shut and headed for the lounge where Felix and his filly were seated in club chairs, sipping cocktails. Felix was leaning back, one leg crossed over the other, a mellow look on his face, as if the cocktail were doing its job already. The woman sat forward in her seat, talking animatedly, her hand stopping to rest on Felix's arm every so often. It was such a perfect little scene of romance in Paris that I almost hated to interrupt.

Almost.

"Felix?" I called as I approached.

His eyes swept toward me. "Maddie, I was just waiting for you."

Yeah, I'll bet. I looked over at the blonde, her dress hugging a chest that made my barely Bs look like bug bites.

"Any luck, love?" he asked.

"I talked to one of the other models. Angelica."

"And? Any news?"

"Sort of. I have a favor to ask of you." I looked at the blonde again. "Maybe we should speak in private?"

Felix looked over at his companion. "No worries, love. I've already told her everything. Maddie, this is Charlene. Char, this is Maddie, the designer I was telling you about."

Charlene put out a slim manicured hand. "Lovely to meet you," she said, her British accent matching Felix's.

I shook it, surprised at the strength of her grip. "Pleasure," I muttered.

"Funny, you don't look like a killer," Charlene said, giving me an up-and-down, her eyes settling on Wonder Boot.

"I'm not!" I protested, maybe a little too loudly. Two guys in business suits at the next table stared at me over their glasses of chardonnay. "Look, it's just a coincidence. I swear."

"Maddie, she was just kidding," Felix said, his eyes crinkling at the corners.

Charlene gave me a wan smile.

I faked one back, though I'm not entirely sure I pulled it off.

"And how do you two know each other?" I couldn't help asking.

Charlene laughed. "Oh, I've known our little Felix all my life. I'm his auntie."

I think I swallowed my tongue.

"Maddie, I told you I was accompanying my aunt Charlene, didn't I?"

Accompanying his dear old auntie? Yes. The fact that said auntie could double for a Playboy Bunny? No.

Definitely not. Not, mind you, that I cared who Felix spent time with. I didn't. He could be dating the entire squad of Lakers girls, for all I cared.

So I wasn't entirely sure why my stomach did that clenching thing again as Auntie Charlene laid her hand casually on Felix's knee.

"Uh-huh, sure. Only I wasn't expecting someone so"—*stacked, flirtatious, slutty*—"young."

Charlene laughed again, a sound some men might call tinkling. Me, I found it fake as hell.

"Well, Felix's father was the oldest. Twenty-five years later my father remarried, and he and his new wife adopted yours truly. Turns out my nephew is actually two years older than I am. Isn't that a lark?"

Quite. And, I noticed that the "adopted" part meant they weren't really blood relatives at all. My eyes rested on Charlene's groping hands again as my stomach rolled, and I wondered if the milk in my morning coffee had been spoiled. Clearly I was coming down with something.

"So, what kind of favor?"

"Huh?" I snapped my eyes back up to meet Felix's.

"You said you needed a favor from me?"

"Oh. Right." Only in the face of Auntie Charlene, I wasn't quite sure that I wanted to blurt out the fact that I'd like to use his lock-picking expertise to break into a murder victim's hotel room. I wasn't entirely sure I trusted her.

And not just because she was fondling her nephew's thigh.

"Um, I was wondering if I could borrow you for a few minutes, Felix."

"Auntie made dinner reservations for us. We were just about to leave. Is it urgent?"

Considering that Gisella wasn't coming back to the room, and the police had likely already done their worst to it, I figured *urgent* didn't exactly describe the situation.

"No," I conceded. "Not exactly."

"Oh, why don't you come with us?" Charlene suggested. She turned a big beauty-pageant smile on me that was all teeth. "I'm sure it wouldn't be any bother to change the reservation to three."

"Thanks, but no, thank you. I, uh, I'm not feeling all that well. I've got a little stomach thing going on."

"Oh, too bad," Charlene said. Then she gave Felix's thigh a squeeze. "I was so looking forward to getting to know one of Felix's little friends."

My turn to flash the fake smile.

"Tomorrow, then?" Felix asked, rising from his chair. Auntie Charlene did the same, quickly linking one arm through Felix's.

"Sure. Tomorrow."

"Right. I'll call you in the morning then. Night, Maddie."

"Night," I said to his retreating back.

I wondered why the hell the sight of Charlene's minidress-encased hips wiggling back and forth beside Felix should make that bad latte rise like bile in my throat.

I got back to my room and, considering my ill state, promptly ordered a bowl of chicken soup from room service. *There. That oughtta shut my stomach up.*

I then chucked the crutches and settled down on the chaise by the window to check my messages.

The first one was from Mom, saying she and Mrs. R had printed out a ream of papers on Gisella, and to call her as soon as I got in.

The second message was from Ramirez. I felt that clenching sensation in my gut fade as his deep voice filled my ear.

"Hey, it's me," he said. "I'm at LAX. I booked a seat on the red-eye. I'll be there by morning."

Okay, so I knew I'd put up a fuss about him coming over, but in all honesty it made my little heart go pitter-patter that he was racing across an ocean to be by my side.

That is, until he added, "Don't do anything stupid until I get there."

I stuck my tongue out at the phone as it clicked over. "End of new messages." I deleted both of them, hung up, and tried Mom's cell. It went to voice mail, so I left a message of my own saying I was in the room.

Since room service still hadn't made it up with my soup, I grabbed the remote and flipped on the TV to wait.

Unfortunately the first thing that hit the screen was a picture of my own face staring back at me. I sat straight up, stabbing a finger at the volume control. The sound filled the room, but I couldn't understand a word they were saying. *Damn.* I strained, trying to pick out any phrases from the *French for the Traveler* book I'd picked up in the airport. Unfortunately they clearly weren't asking where the bathroom was or what time the train arrived, so I was out of luck.

The only thing I did understand was the headline that shot across the bottom of the screen as the picture switched back to the anchor at the news desk:

THE COUTURE KILLER STRIKES PARIS.

I was in the Le Croix tent, flashbulbs going off, music pumping through the speakers, models in various states of undress running back and forth behind the stage. The show was in full swing. Jean Luc barked orders from one end of the room, a long line of models standing at the head of the runway, waiting for their cues to strut its length for all the world to see.

Suddenly Ann grabbed me. She said something in French, which I didn't understand in the least. I shook my head, trying to tell her I couldn't understand. But she just kept talking, getting more and more upset. Finally some English came through.

"You're next!" she told me.

I looked down. I was wearing one of Jean Luc's creations—the black baby doll that I'd seen him fitting Gisella for the day I'd arrived.

Ann shoved me ahead of her toward the runway, to the front of the line of waiting models.

"Wait!" I cried. "I'm not a model. I don't know how to do this!"

But it was too late. She pushed me through the white flap and onto the runway.

The lights were blinding, I couldn't see a thing except the white flashes of cameras going off. I couldn't make out faces, but I knew the tent was packed. I heard a chorus of voices oohing and ahhing. I took a tentative step forward. Then another, feeling my way down the runway through the blinding spotlights. I finally felt as if I were getting the hang of it. People started clapping, and I started strutting in earnest.

Until my toe hit something.

I tripped, falling forward, my arms splayed out in front of me to break my fall, which seemed to go on forever. The ground was suddenly miles away from me. And as I looked down to see what I'd tripped over, I heard myself scream.

There, lying beneath me, was Auntie Charlene in a pool of blood. With a stiletto heel sticking out of her neck.

I sat straight up in bed, my heart pounding, my ducky jammies sticking to my sweaty body.

I was not on a runway. I was not falling. I was not looking down at a pool of blood. I was in my hotel room, surrounded by ruffles and very civilized French decor. I closed my eyes, letting my head fall back on the pillows, and I took great big gulps of air, trying to rein in my heart rate from autobahn to something slightly less hectic than an L.A. freeway.

First a stomach bug. Now nightmares. *Come on, girl, get a grip.*

Throwing off the covers I set my good leg down on the ground and hopped into the bathroom.

One steamy hot quasi-shower and three layers of mascara later I was feeling more like myself again. I slipped on a white empire-waisted sundress, a cropped red cardigan, and one red sandal with white beading along the strap and just the teeniest, tiniest half-inch heel. I know: If Dr. Ponytail saw it she'd probably have a cow. But considering that half the population of France thought I was a murderer, I needed a little something to lift my sprits. Even if it was only half an inch.

I was just making my way through a café au lait and a *pain au chocolat* (a croissant filled with gooey, delicious chocolate—do Parisians know how to do breakfast or what?) from room service when my cell rang and Felix's number popped up.

I flipped open my Motorola. "Yeah?"

"Do you always answer your phone that way?" Felix asked.

"No. I checked the caller ID. I knew it was you."

"Ah. So, you save your most charming self just for me then, that it?"

I ignored the sarcasm and shot back some of my own. "How was dinner with *Auntie*?"

"Lovely. How was your evening? Stab anyone else I should know about?"

"I hate you."

"Yet you continue to call."

"Hey, you called me, pal."

"Because *you* asked for a favor. Considering which, one would think you'd be nicer to me."

I shoved a large piece of croissant in my mouth to keep from shooting something nasty back at him. Mostly because he was right: I did need his help.

"So, what's the favor?" he asked as I chewed.

"I 'eed 'ur 'icks."

"What?"

I swallowed the bite. "I need your picks. Your lock-picking set. I want to take a look in Gisella's room, and it's locked."

He was silent for a moment. Then: "Here in the hotel?"

I nodded at the phone. "Yes."

"Maddie, these aren't the kind of locks you can just jimmy open. You need the card key."

"Okay, how do we make one of those?"

Felix sighed. "Well, first you'd have to know the code for that particular room. Then you'd have to program the card with the proper code."

"Like with a computer?"

"Trust me, these hotels are very secure. We cannot just make a card key."

Damn. I shoved another piece of croissant into my mouth, chewing thoughtfully. "Okay, how about I go to the front desk and tell the clerk I'm in room 1243 and that I've lost my card key?"

"Hmm . . ." Felix said on the other end. "That might work. I'm sure the clerk wouldn't check your name against the hotel register, and even if he did I'm sure he wouldn't put it together with the stream of reporters outside, all vying for statements about the dead woman whose last residence was room 1243."

"You know, you're a very sarcastic person."

"It's one of my better traits."

I gave my phone the finger. "Okay, Felix, you come up with a better plan."

He sighed. "All right, if you're determined to get into Gisella's room I'll meet you there in half an hour."

"And exactly how will *you* get us in?"

"Trust me." And he hung up.

Trust me—famous last words.

If I'd had any better ideas I might have exercised them. As it was, I finished my breakfast, grabbed my crutches, and made my way to the elevators and up to room 1243.

Felix was standing outside waiting, fresh pair of rumpled khakis on, his hair a little wet, as if he'd just showered.

"So?" I asked as I approached.

He flashed me a smile large enough to create dimples, then held up a card key.

"No way!"

He nodded. "Yes way."

He stuck the card in the slot above Gisella's door handle, and, amazingly, the little light turned green.

"Okay, spill it, Tabloid Boy. How did you get the card?"

"It pays to be Lord Ackerman," he said, opening the door.

"What about the dead woman, the press, all that? What, just because you're Lord Ackerman, Pierre gave you the card key?"

"No, he gave it to me because I'm Lord Ackerman, who told him that I was dating the deceased and had left a priceless family heirloom in the room the last time I'd been in here and didn't trust the police not to make off with it."

"And he bought that?"

Felix gave me a look. Then he held up the card again.

I shook my head. Like I said, Felix may be one step above pond scum, but he knew how to think like a criminal. Which, in certain situations, like this, came in very handy.

I shut the door behind myself, flipping on the light switch and flooding the hotel room with fluorescent light. While the room was situated to get morning sun, the frilly yellow curtains were drawn tight, creating a tomblike atmosphere that was downright creepy, considering the circumstances. The bed was unmade, dozens of tiny pillows having fallen to the floor. Clothes covered the chairs, while numerous tubes of lipstick, eye shadows, and concealer littered the top of the dresser.

Felix went immediately to said dresser, opening the top two drawers.

"What exactly are we looking for?" he asked.

"Evidence," I replied, crouching down to look under the bed.

"Of what?"

"Well, I'm not going to be terribly picky at the moment. Anything that will clearly state to the police, 'Maddie didn't do this.'"

He paused, and I could feel his eyes on me.

I straightened up. "What?"

He shrugged. "Nothing."

"Oh, no. Not you, too. You *know* I didn't stab her, Felix."

He held his hands up in a defensive gesture. "I never said you did."

"Yeah, but you gave me a look."

"What look?"

"It was a look."

He grinned. "Yes, I was looking at you. But I was merely thinking how cute you looked all crouched like a sand crab down there on the floor with your one giant foot."

I narrowed my eyes at him and thought a really dirty word.

"Maybe I'll just go check the bathroom," he said. Then he called over his shoulder, "You might want to try the desk."

"I'd already thought of that," I lied. I awkwardly hobbled across the floor, my crutch catching on a discarded Wonderbra as I tackled the small writing desk by the window, hoping that whoever Mystery Man was, he'd left some trace of himself behind.

Nothing but hotel stationery and a pen in the first drawer. The second held a mishmash of receipts, postcards, papers, and a slim silver camera. I picked up the camera and turned it over in my hands. It was one of those digitals that could take either stills or video. I hit the power button and watched as the little screen came to life. I'll admit I'm not the most technologically clever person in the world. I can work my iPod and check my e-mail, but beyond that I'm pretty much clueless. So, it took me a few minutes of aimlessly pressing menu buttons before I came to a list of what looked like video files. They were all labeled with names. Rocco. Marcel. Charlie. Roberto. Ryan. Next to each name was the date the file was created.

Curiosity got the better of me. I scrolled down to the one marked ROBERTO and hit the play button.

Instantly the sounds of moaning and panting filled the room as visions of naked body parts flashed across the small screen. I cringed, trying not to look as I searched for the stop button.

"What are you doing out there?" Felix called.

"Nothing!"

"It doesn't sound like nothing."

I pressed all the buttons, hoping one would work. Finally one did, not only making the video disappear, but all the files as well. I stared at the little screen, the words NO FILES FOUND where *Gisella Does Paris* had just been.

Felix poked his head through the door.

"What's that?"

"Just a camera."

Felix raised an eyebrow. "Any pictures on it?"

"No." At least, not anymore.

He shrugged, then popped back into the bathroom.

I turned the camera off but, on the off chance the files could be retrieved, slipped it into my purse. Quite honestly I wasn't sure I'd recognize a guy again from the videos Gisella had shot unless I went around asking men to drop their pants. But just for good measure I pulled out the hotel stationery and wrote down the names of all her files before I forgot them. While I couldn't remember the dates beside them, I did know they were all made in the last two months, with Ryan being the most recent, dated just two days before Gisella's murder. Which could mean nothing, but at least it was a place to start.

I moved on to the piles of papers in the desk drawer. Most were receipts from taxicab rides, boutiques, restaurants. Almost all were written in French, though I could clearly make out the boutiques she shopped at. Gisella had expensive taste. There were several shops in Paris whose names I recognized, as well as three top-tier Italian designers.

"Hey," I called to Felix.

He popped his head back out again.

"Check the closet, would you?"

"What am I looking for?" he asked, crossing the room and sliding back the mirrored doors.

"A de la Renta coat."

Felix paused, flipping through her wardrobe. "And a de le Renta would look like . . . ?"

"Fur."

He rummaged around. "She has three furs."

As much as I was against killing defenseless little animals for the sole purpose of looking cool, I felt my heart clench just a little. "Three?"

He nodded.

I couldn't help myself; I needed just one little look. I hobbled over to his side. Sure enough, one de la Renta, one Alta Moda, and one vintage Chanel. I ran my hand over the Chanel, making little moaning sounds that were strikingly like the ones I'd just heard on Gisella's camera. "You have any idea how much this is worth?"

Felix was checking the pockets of the Alta Moda. He shook his head. "No. Tell me."

I couldn't. It was priceless. Women had given their firstborn children for less.

"I can tell you, however," he said, his face breaking into a smirk, "how much this one is worth."

I raised an eyebrow at him. "Oh, really? All right, Mr. Fashion Knowledge. What's it worth?"

Felix pulled his hand out of the pocket, then held it open. In the middle of his palm glittered a necklace, three perfectly cut diamonds suspended from a thick gold chain. "Exactly five hundred and thirty-three thousand, three hundred and two dollars. Last time I had it appraised."

I sucked in a breath. "Your necklace?"

He nodded.

"Do you know what this means?"

"That I don't have to deal with the insurance company?"

"That Gisella had the necklace all along. She really did misplace it."

Felix stared down at the necklace, turning it over in his hands. "Or she'd planned on keeping it for herself."

"You mean Gisella stole it?" I raised one eyebrow in his direction. Now, there was something I hadn't thought of. I was just about to ask him what prompted that train of thought when a sound outside the door made us both freeze.

"What was that?" I whispered.

Felix shook his head, shoving the necklace in his pocket. "I think that's our cue to get out of h—"

But he didn't get to finish, the sound of the door flying open cutting him off. Three policemen in blue uniforms came bursting into the room, practically filling it, guns drawn, arms straight out in front of them.

The first one shouted something in French.

"What?" I asked.

He repeated his command.

"I'm sorry, I don't speak French."

He pointed his gun at me.

Yikes! Okay, that I did speak. I put my hands up in a surrendering motion.

"Look, I can explain. This is Lord Ackerman, and we were just here because he left a priceless family heirloom last time he slept with Gisella."

"I never said I slept with her," Felix protested, doing a mirror image of my hands-in-the-air thing.

"Play along," I whispered out the side of my mouth.

"Maddie, I don't think—"

But again Felix was cut off as the second officer traded in his gun for a pair of handcuffs, which he promptly placed on Felix's wrists, clasping them together behind his back.

"Wait, no, you're making a mistake," I protested. "Okay, fine, we're not really here looking for a family heirloom. That was just a cover. We were looking for evidence that would clear my name. See, I'm the Couture Killer."

Officer Number One raised an eyebrow at me.

"No, wait—I'm not really a killer. I mean, just in the press. But it's not true. None of it's true. I mean, yes, I am a designer, that part's true. And I do love couture. In fact, I'm actually even showing this year at the Le Croix—"

"*Voler!*" shouted Officer Number One.

"What?"

"He said we're thieves," Felix translated as Officer Number Two patted him down.

"No, please, you're getting this all wrong," I protested. But I realized it was futile as Officer Number One gestured toward me, prompting Officer Number Three to pull out a pair of handcuffs of his own. He grabbed my hands, snapping the cool metal around them (which, of course, made my crutches clatter to the ground at my feet). However bad having my picture plastered on the news was, this was worse—much worse.

And then things got even better.

"*Capitaine!*" Officer Number Two shouted to the first guy.

We all turned to face the second officer, who was holding Felix in one hand—and pulling the diamond necklace out of his pocket with the other.

Officer Number One looked from Felix to me, a smug smile on his face. *"Oui, voler."*

Felix and I looked at each other.

Oh. Shit.

Chapter Seven

No matter what country you travel to, what culture you come from, or what language you speak, there is one almost universal truth about human beings—we don't like to pee in front of one another. Which was why, as I sat on a wooden bench in the square ten-by-ten holding cell, I uncrossed, then recrossed my legs for the gazillionth time since officers One, Two, and Three had brought me here in handcuffs.

They'd split Felix and me into two separate cars, and I had no idea where they'd taken him, or even if he was in a cell of his own somewhere. Or, for that matter, where my cell was. Somewhere in Paris was about all I knew. I'd tried talking to Officer Number One on the car ride over, but either he didn't speak English or he just didn't want to talk to me.

Luckily the booking officer had spoken English and explained that I was being charged with trespassing, breaking and entering, and burglary. All of which I protested vehemently as I'd been fingerprinted, photographed, and shoved into a holding cell to wait. Oddly enough, if you traded in doughnuts for croissants, the entire process had been eerily similar to the American one. (Don't ask me how I know this. Let's just say my karma *really* sucks.)

And similar also was the lone toilet sitting in the middle of the room. I uncrossed my legs again and tried not to think of clear streams, faucets, or waterfalls as I checked out my cellmates. To my left was a short brunette woman in spandex tights and a stained T-shirt. She was mumbling to herself, and her hair looked like she'd attacked one side with a pair of safety scissors. Across the room sat two women in black jeans, flannel shirts, and bandannas, looking like they'd walked straight out of Compton. And next to them was a woman with stubble on her upper lip, in a tube top and hot pants, with a red feather boa draped around her neck.

I glanced at the toilet again, wondering how long I could wait.

I closed my eyes, wishing like anything that I hadn't had that second café au lait that morning, and wondered where Felix was. Surely he had explained to the officers that the necklace was his. I mean, you couldn't really be arrested for stealing something that already belonged to you, could you?

Which made me wonder, had Gisella stolen the necklace? She hadn't struck me as the sharpest crayon in the box when I'd met her, but I guess it didn't take a whole lot of brains to pocket a piece of jewelry. If she had stolen it, what did that have to do with her death? Had someone found out she was pocketing the jewelry? Maybe someone who'd seen her wear it at the party? Maybe Mystery Man. But that didn't explain why they'd want to kill her. I mean, why not just turn her over to the police? Or Jean Luc? It still didn't make sense. And I still wasn't 100 percent convinced that Gisella hadn't just shoved it into her pocket after one too many glasses of champagne and forgotten all about it.

"Bonjour."

I opened my eyes and yelped. Miss Tube Top was sitting so close to me she was practically in my lap.

"Uh, hi." I scooted to the left.

"Ça va?"

"Uh, sorry, I don't speak French."

She just looked at me.

"I. Don't. Speak. French," I said again, louder and more slowly.

The woman grinned, showing off a row of slightly yellow teeth, most of which were all still there. "I heard you the first time, my girl," she said in perfect English.

"Oh."

She leaned in, and I could smell her breakfast vodka on her breath. "Tell me, what's a darling little thing like you doing in here?"

I heard myself gulp loudly as Tube Top gave me an up-and-down, then licked her lips.

"Uh, a slight misunderstanding."

She gave a short bark of laughter. "Ha! Me, too, doll." She reached over and laid a hand on my knee. "Wanna tell me about it?"

Suddenly peeing in public had just gotten replaced as the worst thing about being in a holding cell by being groped by a prostitute of ambiguous gender.

"Springer?" A tall, thin officer with a crooked nose opened the cell door.

I popped up from the bench like a jack-in-the-box,

shoving my crutches under my armpits. "That's me!"

Tube Top looked disappointed, but gave me a little one-finger wave as the officer took me by the arm and escorted me down the hallway.

I breathed a sigh of relief. I had a feeling I'd been one knee grab away from being someone's be-atch.

My relief was short-lived, however, as the officer steered me around the corner and I spotted the man who had sprung me from the pokey. Arms crossed over his broad chest. Eyes dark and unreadable. Lips pursed into a fine white line. Jaw set into those granite-hard angles of Bad Cop.

Ramirez.

"Uh . . . hi." I gave him a little wave. No reaction. "I see you made your flight." Still nothing. "Nice to see you, honey?" I tried.

Ramirez ignored me, addressing the officer. "I'll take it from here." He put his signature down on the officer's clipboard, then grabbed my upper arm in a vise grip and steered me down the length of the hallway.

"See, the proper response here would be, 'Hi, nice to see you, too, Maddie,'" I said as I hopped to catch up to him. "Or maybe, 'Are you okay? Wow, how traumatic this must have been for you.'"

Ramirez paused just long enough to shoot me a death look, then propelled me past booking, the front desk, and the glass doors of the police station, outside onto a street that was busy with afternoon shoppers and sightseers. He walked me a full block in silence before backing me into an alleyway that smelled like urine and rotting fish and spinning me around to face him.

"What the hell were you thinking?" he growled, his

voice so tightly restrained I knew it could easily snap at any moment.

"Look, it was all a misunderstanding. We just wanted to look around. Angelica said they'd been fighting."

"Who?"

"Angelica. The friend who's not all that friendly."

Ramirez just stared at me.

"Look, we were just trying to find evidence that someone else did this. We were going to put everything back where we found it. Well, except maybe the necklace."

Ramirez's Bad Cop face didn't give away any emotion, though I could tell from the long blue vein in his neck that was starting to bulge just a little that I wasn't making any headway with him.

"Didn't I distinctly tell you," he ground out between clenched teeth, "not to do anything stupid until I got here? I think this qualifies."

I put a hand on my hip. "Yeah, about that—"

But he cut me off, shaking his head. "God, do you know how guilty this makes you look, Maddie? Being found pawing through the victim's belongings?"

"I didn't do anything wrong. You and I both know I'm innocent."

He stared at me. Silently.

For one horrible second doubt hit me as I looked into his unreadable eyes.

"You *do* know I'm innocent, right? Jack?"

He rubbed a hand over his face. "Jesus, Maddie, of course I know that."

I let out a breath I hadn't realized I'd been holding. "I'm sorry you got dragged down here. Thank you for getting me out."

His eyes softened, and he reached out a hand, running the tip of his fingers lightly along my cheeks. "What am I going to do with you?"

"Well," I said tentatively, "you could start by giving me a kiss hello."

His Bad Cop face cracked, the corner of his mouth lifting up into a deceptively boyish grin. He leaned in close and brushed his lips softly over mine. I tasted the mingled flavors of coffee and Dentyne, and I think I sighed out loud.

"What about Felix?" I mumbled against his lips.

He froze. "Felix?"

I nodded. "We were arrested together. Did he get bailed out, too?"

Ramirez pulled back, his eyes going dark and unreadable again. "I don't know."

"Well, you have to find out."

"Oh, I do, do I?"

"Yes! Felix doesn't belong in jail. He's not a criminal."

Ramirez planted his feet hip-width apart and crossed his arms over his chest. "He broke into her hotel room."

"To look for evidence."

"He was found with half a million in diamonds in his pocket, which he readily admits he took from the victim's room."

"But the diamonds are his! She stole them first."

"He carries a lock-picking kit."

Okay, he had me there. I never quite got a straight story out of Felix about his wild teenage days, but it wasn't every guy who carried a lock-picking kit around in his cargoes.

"But he didn't use it." *This time.* "I was with him the

whole time. He didn't do anything illegal." I paused. "Well, not very illegal, at least. Look, we just needed to search her place. You don't understand. I have no alibi. They think I'm the Couture Killer. Moreau wants to lock me up."

"He's not out to get you, Maddie. He's just doing his job."

I narrowed my eyes. "Don't tell me you're taking *his* side?"

"What are you talking about?"

"I should have known. It's a cop thing, right?"

"Jesus, Maddie, I'm not taking sides."

"So what happens if Moreau arrests me for murder, Jack? Is he still 'just doing his job'?" I asked, doing air quotes with my fingers.

Ramirez looked to the sky as if asking for help from somewhere above. "Look, Moreau is investigating a crime. Which you are not making any easier."

"Oh, so now I should be trying to make his job of building a case against me easier? Someone's trying to frame me, Jack!"

"Which doesn't give you license to break into the murdered woman's hotel room."

I crossed my arms over my chest, which was not easy to do with crutches stuck in my armpits, but was worth the effect. "So, what, you gonna lock me up?"

Ramirez breathed in deeply through his nose, nostrils flaring as that vein in his neck bulged in earnest now. "No. They're letting you go into my custody. I convinced them it was a language-barrier thing."

"And Felix? I'm not leaving without him."

Some indefinable emotion flitted across Ramirez's

face. "This guy really means that much to you, huh?"

"Of course not," I said, a little too loudly. "He doesn't mean anything to me. I just . . . It was my idea. He went along with it. I owe him."

Ramirez bit the inside of his cheek, doing the stare-down he usually reserved for criminals he was trying to intimidate a confession out of. I held my ground, still crossing my arms, jutting my chin defiantly, trying to squeeze one more half inch of height out of my already stretched spine.

"At the very least, they'll want him deported back to England."

"Hey, as long as he's not rotting in jail, I don't care where he goes."

Ramirez made a sound halfway between a snort and a growl. Then he turned around without a word and hailed a passing cab. He opened the back door.

"Get in," he commanded.

"Where am I going?"

"Back to the hotel."

"And you?"

His jaw went granite again. "To find out where they're holding Felix."

I dropped the defensive posture. "Thanks." I stood on tiptoe (just one foot) and planted a kiss on his cheek.

"Hmm," he grunted. Though I thought I saw that vein in his neck relax just a little.

I got in the cab and watched his retreating form as he walked back to the police station. Okay, so maybe he wasn't always the easiest guy to get along with. But he did bail me out of jail. You had to love the man for that.

The ride to the hotel seemed to take forever, and by the

time I'd fought my way through the paparazzi standing vigil outside, I was tired and hungry, and I really, really needed to go to the bathroom. I took care of the latter first before collapsing on the bed and dialing room service for the biggest order of crepes they had. I was just digging into them when the adjoining door to my room popped open.

"Maddie! There you are! Where have you been?" Mom asked, bustling into the room with a handful of shopping bags. Mrs. Rosenblatt waddled along behind her, her bright blue muumuu accessorized with three strands of yellow plastic pearls. I swear, I needed sunglasses around the woman's wardrobe. Mom was more subdued today—white stretch pants under a black skirt with a stretchy black-and-white polka-dotted top and her black high tops. Okay, so maybe *subdued* was a stretch. But this was Mom we were talking about.

"Where was *I*? Where have you two been? I tried to call you last night."

"Last night we dragged that Pierre fellow to the Eiffel Tower," Mrs. R said.

"The tower?" I asked, my voice going high. Great— they went to the Eiffel Tower and I went to prison.

Mom nodded. "Oh, Mads, you should see it at night, all lit up. It's the most magical thing I've ever seen in my whole life. I have to come back here with Ralphie. It's so romantic."

Mrs. R let a frown settle between her draw-on brows. "Pierre didn't think it was romantic. He didn't even try to kiss me."

Imagine that.

"So what have you been up to?" Mom asked.

"I had a little run-in with the police."

"Police?" Mom swayed in her high-tops, falling back on the bed beside me. "Oh, my baby," she said as she dove in for a patented rib-crushing hug. This time, though, I let her. After spending the morning in a holding cell, I'll admit I could use a hug.

"What happened?" Mrs. Rosenblatt asked.

I filled them in on my adventures in the French criminal-justice system while I devoured the plateful of crepes. By the time I was finished Mom was back to hugging me again.

"Mom, I'm fine. Really." I wriggled out of her death grip. "So, what's with all the shopping bags?"

"Well," Mom said, straightening up. "Like I promised, we spent yesterday gathering info on Gisella." She gestured to Mrs. R, who pulled a sheaf of papers out of one of the bags and handed it to me. "Did you know she was booked to do seven different shows this week?"

I shook my head. "No." I thumbed through the papers. They were printouts of various fashion Web sites, online gossip columns, and industry blogs.

Mrs. R nodded. "Yep. The Le Croix was her only lead, but she was doing runway for six other designers. So, your mom and I figured we'd check 'em out today."

"We went undercover as Fashion Week tourists," Mom said, her eyes shining.

I looked down at the bags. "Mom, you *are* tourists."

"Anyway, you'll never guess what we learned, Mads. That necklace you said went missing at the Le Croix show? Four of the other designers Gisella was working for said they've had pieces go missing as well. We asked, but only a couple of them had reported the thefts to the police. The others figured the pieces were just misplaced in the chaos of getting ready for the event and would turn up soon enough."

"Just like Jean Luc."

Mom nodded. "Interesting coincidence?"

As much as I was beginning to hate that word, I had to agree with her. I wished we'd had time to check the pockets of Gisella's Chanel. I'd bet my ballet flats there were more than hankies in them.

"All right, so let's assume that Gisella was taking the jewelry. Then what? What did she intend to do with it?" I asked.

Mom shrugged. "Sell it?"

"On the black market! She had to have someone fencing the jewels for her. A partner," Mrs. R said. "My third husband, Alf, had a pawnshop for a while. They're real particular about what they take. They don't wanna get busted. It ain't as easy as it looks to unload hot stuff."

"So, assuming it was Gisella, who was unloading it for her?" I wondered out loud.

"Another model?" Mom offered. "Mystery boyfriend?"

"Maybe her agent?" Mrs. R piped up.

I thought about that. Angelica had said that Gisella called her agent numerous times a day. Maybe the calls hadn't been about booking a cover after all, but about where to get rid of half a million dollars in stolen diamonds. "Did you find anything on who her agent is?" I asked, shuffling through the computer printouts.

"Here," Mrs. R said, pointing to a page that read, *Girardi Models*, across the header. "Donata Girardi. She's based in Milan, Gisella's hometown."

"Oh, I saw something about that," Mom said, grabbing the stack from me. More shuffling. "Ah!" She pulled a gossip column out. "Donata Girardi is staying at the Hôtel de Crillon. She's the one who threw the party where Gisella wore the necklace."

I stared at the party photos. I wasn't entirely convinced that Gisella was a master thief, but I figured it wouldn't hurt to have a conversation with her agent.

"Okay, first thing tomorrow we'll question her."

"Question who?"

Mom, Mrs. Rosenblatt, and I snapped our heads up in unison, all eyes pointing at the adjoining doorway, where Ramirez's frame had suddenly appeared.

"Who are you going to question?" he repeated, stepping into the room.

"No one," I said quickly. Then I gave Mom and Mrs. R serious psychic vibes to ix-nay on the estions-quay. "We're not questioning anyone."

"Okay." Ramirez narrowed his eyes. "Maybe I should rephrase. Who are we *not* questioning, then?"

I planted my hands on my hips. "How did you even get in here?" I asked.

"The door next door was open. This"—he held up a red shopping bag with the word *Dior* on the side— "was wedged in the doorjamb. And don't change the subject."

"Oops," Mrs. R said, taking the bag from his hand. She looked from Ramirez's narrowed eyes to my hands-on-hips. "Uh, maybe we ought to leave you two alone."

She gestured to Mom, who quickly dumped the printouts into an Hermès bag and followed Mrs. Rosenblatt to the door. She gave me a quick coconspiratorial wink and mouthed, *Call me*, behind Ramirez's back as they slipped out.

Ramirez latched the door shut behind them before turning his catlike eyes on me. "Okay, you want to tell me what that was about now?"

I bit my lip. And shook my head.

Ramirez sat on the double bed beside me. Close beside me.

Despite our little standoff, I was suddenly reminded of how much I'd missed him.

"Maddie, I'm serious," he said. "You've got to let the police handle this."

"But the police think I did it."

He let out a long breath and rubbed his temple. "I don't want you questioning anyone."

I opened my mouth to protest, but he quickly put a hand over my lips and talked right over me.

"I don't want you nosing through anyone's stuff for some sort of nonexistent evidence. I don't want you following anyone, spying on anyone, or impersonating anyone."

Wow. He knew me well.

"And most of all," he said, leaning in until the scent of his aftershave settled over my senses like a mellow fog. "Most of all I don't want you anywhere near Felix Dunn again." He pulled his hand away from my mouth. "That guy is bad news. Every time you're around him he gets you into trouble."

"Well, technically it was me who got him into trouble this time."

He gave me a look. "Promise me."

I took a deep breath of Ramirez-scented air. And nodded.

He looked so relieved I almost felt guilty that I'd had my fingers crossed behind my back.

"Good," he said. "Oh, and one more thing."

I raised an eyebrow at him. "What now?"

His eyes crinkled at the corners, going all dark and warm as his face broke into a Big Bad Wolf grin—all teeth, like he might eat me up at any second. "This."

He dipped his lips to meet mine, his stubble tickling my cheek as his tongue brushed against my lower lip.

Instantly my mind went mushy. The prison cell, Felix, Moreau, the whole mess the press was making of my life all disappeared as I leaned into his kiss, my lips melting under his. I closed my eyes as his arm wrapped around my middle and he laid me back on the bed. In an instant the hard planes of his body were covering mine. One hand dove into my hair, the other hiking up the hem of my skirt as his hips pressed into mine. I kissed him back—hard—as I fumbled with the top button of his jeans. When I popped it open he growled low in the back of his throat.

"It's been too long," he mumbled into my mouth.

"It's only been a couple of days."

He paused, then looked down at me, his eyes glazed over with a look that could only be described as pure lust. "Yeah, like I said, too long."

I laughed as he dove back in, his lips locking on to my throat, nibbling at my pulse in a way that made my body shiver from my head clear down to my toes. I wrapped one bare leg around his torso, navigating my gimpy leg out of the way.

Ramirez looked down. "Can you have sex in that thing?" he asked, gesturing to Wonder Boot.

I felt a devilish grin of my own sliding across my face.

"We're about to find out."

Chapter Eight

I awoke to the sounds of room-service carts being wheeled down the hallway outside my room. I gingerly opened one eye, then the other. It felt like I'd been asleep for days, my mouth full of that morning gym-socks flavor. I turned over and looked at the digital numbers of the alarm clock: seven fifteen.

"Mmmm," Ramirez moaned beside me. He rolled over, wrapping an arm round me and pulling me to him, spoon fashion. "Good morning, beautiful," he mumbled into my hair.

I grinned, wiping the sleep out of my eyes. "Yes. Yes, it is."

"I had a dream about you last night," he said. He rubbed his pelvis against my bare tush, leaving very little to the imagination as to just what kind of dream I'd awakened him from.

"Was I good?" I joked.

"Oh yeah," he growled, his breath tickling my ear. I ducked, giggling.

"And just where do you think you're going?" he asked. He pulled me onto my back and sat up, straddling me.

Then he slid one hand down my arm, twining his fingers with mine as he stared down at me.

"Police brutality," I teased, wiggling beneath him.

He just flashed me a wicked grin and raised his eyebrows suggestively. "You ain't seen nothing yet." He leaned in close, his eyes intent on my lips.

"Halt!" I quickly covered my mouth with my free hand. "I have morning breath."

He chuckled. "Me too. Who cares?" He zoned in again.

"Gross. You may be cute, but I am so *not* kissing you with morning breath," I mumbled behind my hand.

He paused. "Seriously?"

"Seriously."

He let out a deep sigh, then rolled back to his side of the bed. "I fly all the way to Paris just be denied by the morning breath."

I swatted at him, throwing my good leg over the side of the bed and hopping to the bathroom. "Give me five minutes."

"Four!" he called as I shut the door.

I loaded my toothbrush with Crest and, figuring I might as well go all the way, turned on the shower and quickly did a shampoo and rinse. I towel-dried my hair into a fairly passable sexy wet look and threw on a little makeup. Hey, just because we'd seen each other naked didn't mean Ramirez had to see me without my eyeliner. By the time I emerged from the bathroom, a white hotel-issue towel wrapped around my midsection, Ramirez was propped up in bed, one hand behind his head as he watched a soccer match on TV.

"That was one hell of a toothbrushing."

I shrugged. "What can I say? I'm a hygienic sort of gal."

He shook his head at me, the corner of his mouth twisting up until a dimple flashed in his left cheek. He curled an index finger at me. "Come 'ere."

I shook my head. "Uh-uh. Your turn."

His grin faltered for a half a second before he conceded, sliding out of bed. "All right. But that towel had better be history by the time I come out," he warned.

I shot him my best come-hither look as he brushed past me and into the bathroom.

And as soon as he shut the door I sprang into action. I dropped the towel and threw on a denim skirt, pink baby tee, and a deconstructed jacket to match my one black ballet flat. Fortunately I still heard the water running as I grabbed my purse and crutches and bolted out the door.

I know—totally dirty trick to play on Ramirez. Especially when he was being all cute. But there was no way I was going to question Gisella's agent with Ramirez playing bodyguard. And, as much as I loved him, there was *no way* I was leaving all this to the police.

The thing about Ramirez was that he wasn't a guy who did gray. Life was either black or white to him. Cops: good. Criminals: bad. Victims were victims, and if you found yourself behind bars there was probably a good reason for it. Which was why Ramirez and I spent 90 percent of our time together butting heads. Me, I was all about the gray stuff. Sometimes I wasn't entirely sure Ramirez could handle a girlfriend who, once in a while, found herself sitting in a holding cell. Or who, on the rare occasion, had been known to do a little B and E for a good cause. I wasn't sure Ramirez could handle gray. And on days like this, I wasn't sure how much longer he'd continue trying to for my sake.

Especially when he found the hotel room empty.

I tried to shrug that thought to the back of my mind as I grabbed a cab outside the hotel. As we pulled away from the curb I glanced over my shoulder, afraid that any second now Ramirez would come bolting out the front doors wearing nothing but his boxers. Luckily we were weaving our way into morning traffic before my cell rang, my own room number showing up on the caller ID.

I bit my lip, then hit the ignore button with a deep pang of Catholic guilt.

Even if Moreau never formally charged me with Gisella's killing, I could tell the press had already convicted me. Unless I found out who had really done this, my career as a designer was in the toilet.

So, really, I was sure Ramirez would understand. I was just doing *my* job.

Fifteen minutes (and two more phone calls) later we pulled up to the Hôtel de Crillon. Fortunately it was relatively paparazzi-free, every newshound in town still haunting the Le Croix tent and the Plaza Athénée. I stopped in the lobby only long enough to a) grab a cup of coffee and b) ask which room Donata Girardi was staying in. Of course, the kid on duty, a short, chubby guy with bad acne, said it was against hotel policy to give out that information. Instead he handed me a courtesy phone and dialed Donata's number for me. Luckily she was in. And, after I briefly explained who I was, she agreed to see me.

I downed my coffee and made for the elevators. With no small effort I ignored "The William Tell Overture" ringing from my purse yet again as I knocked on Donata's door. I heard movement on the other side; then it was opened by a slim woman in her fifties, with thick black hair, thick black lashes, and—I suspected without the help of Nair—a thick black mustache. She wore a pale blue tailored suit with a cream scarf knotted at her neck, and pointy-toed leather heels on her feet. Her eyes were slightly squinty, as if she'd had an aggressive face-lift in the recent past, and her lips puckered in an unnatural way beneath her coral-colored lipstick. Despite the obvious work, I could tell by her high cheekbones that she was once a very naturally beautiful woman. She was slim through the hips, with long legs, and had the faintest hint of a small, heart-shaped birthmark just above her left cheek at the hairline. I immediately got the sense that, like so many other agents, Donata was a former model herself. The idea was reinforced as she ushered me in and crossed the room with a grace I sorely coveted at the moment. I awkwardly hobbled through the door, setting my crutches down as I clumsily plopped into an armchair by the window.

"Your purse appears to be ringing," she said, a soft Italian lilt coloring her voice.

I waved the comment off. "Voice mail will get it."

"I see. So, you are one of Le Croix's designers, *sì?*"

I nodded. "Yes, Maddie Springer. I'm doing the shoes for his collection."

She nodded. "The black stiletto heel."

I cringed. "Yes. And I want to express my sincere condolences. I'm sorry for what happened to Gisella."

She raised an eyebrow. "You are sorry?"

"Yes. I mean, no, not that I'm sorry like I'm apologizing. I mean I'm sorry it happened, not that I'm sorry I did it. Because I didn't. I had nothing to do with it happening. This was just a coincidence."

"I see." Though I noticed she scooted her chair a fraction of an inch away from me. Clearly she wasn't entirely convinced.

Join the club.

"And what is it I can do for you, Signorina Springer?"

Tell me who was fencing stolen property for your client. But I figured the subtle approach was probably best. "I was wondering what you could tell me about Gisella's social life."

Donata looked out the window. "Gisella was a very social girl. She loved parties."

"Like the one you threw here in the hotel?"

Donata nodded. *"Sì."* She clasped her hands in her lap but didn't elaborate. I had the feeling she was a woman who had learned to play her hand close to her heart.

"Do know if Gisella was seeing anyone?"

"Gisella always had men around."

"Anyone special?"

She shrugged, a barely detectable movement of her shoulders.

"What about Ryan? Does that name ring a bell?" I asked, reciting the last file entry from Gisella's camera.

Donata paused. "She mentioned a Ryan. I think they may have dated."

"Did she happen to mention Ryan's last name?"

She sucked in her cheeks. "Jones? Jeffries? One of those, I believe. He was English."

My phone took that moment to chirp to life inside my purse again. I ignored it.

"Do you know if Ryan was here in Paris with Gisella?"

Donata looked down at my Kate Spade. "Are you not going to answer your phone?"

I shook my head. "Nope."

She raised an eyebrow at me, but said nothing.

"So, was Ryan in Paris?"

She shrugged. "I could not tell you. Gisella and I, we were not so close that she would inform me of her boyfriends' whereabouts."

"But you did talk often. Several times a day?"

She nodded. "*Sì*. For work."

Hmm . . . Modeling work or burglary? "When was the last time you saw Gisella?"

Donata's lips twitched. She looked down at her hands to hide some emotion flitting across her eyes, though whether it was guilt or genuine sorrow I'd be hard-pressed to answer.

"The night before she died. I went up to her room to fill her in on the next day's fitting schedule. But I was there only a brief time. She said she was expecting company."

I wondered if that company was Ryan Jones-slash-Jeffries.

"Did Gisella bring Ryan with her to your party?"

Again Donata shrugged her slim shoulders. "I did not notice. I was busy playing hostess. But I would not be surprised. Gisella was almost never unaccompanied by a man. Now, if you will excuse me, I have a client to meet with." She rose and walked to the door, effectively ending the interview. I grabbed my crutches and followed her, though she already had the door open and was waiting by the time I got there. I paused before stepping through the doorway.

"Do you have any idea who could have killed Gisella?" I asked, starting to sound desperate now.

She didn't answer, instead giving me a pointed look.

I rolled my eyes.

"Besides me."

Donata slowly shook her head. "Her death is a tragedy. She will be missed," she said, sounding as if she were reading off a teleprompter.

And with that she closed the door behind me. I stood in the hallway a moment, listening, hoping to catch some sort of sound on the other side. Nothing.

Great. I hadn't really learned anything more about Donata and still wasn't sure where the jewels fit into all this. If they fit into it at all.

But I did glean one little kernel of info from Donata. Ryan's last name.

I was heading through the Crillon's lobby when my cell rang again. I almost didn't even pull it out of my purse, but the odd stares I was getting as I hobbled across the marble tiles to the tune of "William Tell" finally made me slip it out. And I was glad I did. Dana's number lit up my LCD.

"Hello?"

"Mads! Guess where I am?"

I shifted the phone to the other ear, trying not to drop it as I leaned on my crutches. "I give up."

"Paris! I got the spot in the Le Croix show."

Perfect timing. "Dana, you are amazing. Where are you?"

"I'm still at the airport. My plane just landed. I'll meet you at the Plaza in about half an hour."

"Uh . . ." Visions of a pissed-off Ramirez flitted through my head. "That might not be a good idea. How about meeting me at the Hôtel de Crillon instead. I'll be . . ." I paused, looking around the lobby. I spied a café across the street through the glass front doors. ". . . across the street at the café."

"Cool. Just let me drop my bags and I'll be right there."

I shoved my cell back into my purse, feeling guilt gnaw at me again as I noticed the THREE NEW MESSAGES alert across the screen. Instead of dwelling on it, I hobbled across the street to the café, where I ordered a large café au lait (a girl could get addicted to these things) and a pastry made of flaky, buttery crust and a sweet, honey-like filling.

While I waited I tried Felix's cell. Hey, I promised Ramirez I would stay away from him, not lose his number. And I was away. Besides, I wanted to make sure he had gotten out of police custody okay.

Unfortunately, there was no answer. I left a voice mail, then dialed Jean Luc to thank him for hiring Dana and to see if there were any new developments at the tent. He informed me that the police still weren't giving back the shoes, and he was starting to seriously panic.

"I've tried begging, pleading, even threatening. Nothing. They won't give them up. Maddie, what are we going to do?" he asked, crunching down on an antacid.

I closed my eyes, letting a bite of buttery croissant melt on my tongue. "Listen, is there any way you could get some replacement shoes shipped to the tent? Just plain black pumps, maybe?"

"Plain black pumps?" he shouted, as if I'd suggested his models wear Birkenstocks.

"Don't worry—they won't go down the runway that way. I can do some quick alterations and embellish them."

"You think it will work?" he asked, still not entirely convinced.

"Trust me, if I can make SpongeBob flip-flops look good, I can make this work. Besides," I reasoned, "it's not like the police are giving us any other option."

Jean Luc let out a deep sigh. "All right, I'll order the pumps and let you know when they come in. God, this show has disaster written all over it," I heard him moan as he clicked off.

I shook my head. Didn't I know it.

As soon as I hung up my cell chirped to life again with Ramirez's number. I hit ignore. I know, he was so gonna be pissed later, but what could I do?

I finished my coffee while I waited for Dana.

Fifteen minutes later she came through the doors wearing a pair of black stretch leggings, a black long-sleeved tee with a picture of a tiny pink poodle on it, and a jaunty black beret.

I looked her up and down, and I'm pretty sure my expression betrayed my thoughts as she said, "What?"

"Poodles?"

"I'm in Paris! I'm doing French chic. You like?" She did a little spin, and I couldn't help but grin.

"It's very French."

"Thanks." She sat down, depositing her purse on the empty chair beside her. "So, what's the latest? Spill it."

I did, catching her up-to-date on the Googling twins and my chat with Donata. By the time I'd finished, my coffee was history and Dana was swirling the dregs of her herbal tea in her cup, her strawberry-blonde brows drawn together in thought.

"Okay, so putting aside the whole jewel-thief thing for a moment, this Ryan guy was likely the last person to see her alive?"

"Right. Well, before the killer. If he isn't the killer, that is."

"So, what do we know about him? Just that his name is Jones or Jeffries?"

"And that he's English."

"Do they have a yellow pages for England?"

I gave her my best get-real face. "Yellow pages?"

"What?"

"I say we go talk to Angelica again. Who knows? Maybe this was another stolen boyfriend."

"Perfect! I told Jean Luc I'd check in with him today anyway. How freaking perfect is this, Maddie? Not only do I get to strut a designer runway, but ohmigod, I get to do it in the most romantic city on earth!"

"Speaking of romance, how goes the long-distance thing with Ricky?" I asked as we gathered our things and hailed a cab.

"Ugh! Don't ask."

"That good, huh?"

"I take it you haven't seen the latest issue of the *Informer*?"

I shook my head. "I try to steer clear of Felix's smut. Why?"

"Well, according to their sources, Ricky was seen *kissing* Natalie Portman outside the set."

"According to their sources, the Loch Ness Monster is the product of toxic dumping in Canada. You can't believe a word they print."

"You think?"

"I know. What does Ricky say?" I asked as a taxi stopped at the curb and I tried to angle Wonder Boot in.

"He denies it, of course. I told that bastard I'd gone a whole month without sex for him. He'd damn well better not be kissing Natalie Portman."

I craned around in my seat as the cab took off in the direction of the Louvre.

"What are you looking for?" Dana asked.

"I'm trying to see the Eiffel Tower."

"It's that way." Dana pointed out the other window.

"How do you know?"

"I saw it on my way here from the airport."

"You saw it?" I asked, jealousy washing over me. "I've been here three days and still haven't seen it."

"You should. It's totally cool."

Ten minutes later we were back at the Le Croix tent. Any evidence that it had once been a crime scene was completely gone, the interior a hum of preshow activity. The only difference was the runway being reconstructed by the coverall crew, the stained boards having been confiscated into evidence by Moreau and company.

I introduced Dana to Jean Luc, who immediately whisked her away to the fitting rooms. I tagged along (Wonder Boot precluded any sort of whisking on my part) and spied Angelica being pinned into a pleated miniskirt at a back table. I hobbled my way over to her.

"Hi," I said as I approached. "Remember me?"

She nodded. "The Couture Killer."

The seamstress pinning Angelica snapped her head up.

"I didn't do it," I reassured her.

She looked from me to Angelica, then got up and mumbled something about a measuring tape before backing quickly away.

"Wow, you're popular," Angelica observed.

No kidding.

"Anyway," I continued, "I wanted to ask you if you knew a man named Ryan Jones, or possibly Jeffries."

Angelica scrunched up her face, squinting her brown eyes. "No, I'm sorry. Doesn't ring a bell. Why?"

I felt my hope deflating. "It's possible he was dating Gisella."

"I didn't really keep track of her current boy toys."

"Hmm, well, how about these? Any of these names stand out?" I handed Angelica the list of names I'd gotten off Gisella's camera.

She stabbed a finger at the first one. "Oh, sure, I know Rocco. He was this Italian guy we met while doing a shoot in Venice. Total meathead, but really cute. Gisella took him back to her place after we wrapped, but it was just a one-night kind of thing. This one," she said, pointing to Roberto, "I think I met at a club in Milan. He might be working in New York now. But the others, no idea."

"Thanks anyway." I slipped the list back into my pocket as the seamstress returned, deeming it safe to approach Angelica again.

For lack of anything else to do I hobbled to the back table to wait for Dana. I sat down beside my empty shoe rack and felt a lump forming in my throat.

Okay, being accused of murder was bad. It really, really sucked. But the thought of missing my one big chance to show at Fashion Week was enough to make my insides shrivel up and cry. I bit my lip to keep the tears at bay as I prayed Moreau was being nice to my babies.

"Maddie?"

I sniffed back an unshed tear and turned around to find Ann hovering over my table.

"Yes?"

"Angelica told me you were asking about Ryan Jeffries."

I sniffed again, a little bubble of hope welling in my chest. "Do you know him?"

She nodded, her headset bobbing up and down. "He used to model for Ralph Lauren. A couple years ago I did a show with him. Why are you looking for him?" she asked.

"I heard a rumor that he may have dated Gisella. Maybe even recently. Do you have any idea how I could get in touch with him?"

She pulled a BlackBerry from her pocket, punching in numbers. "Last I heard he was living in London," she said, scrolling through numbers.

I waited, trying not to get too excited. As I nervously tapped my ballet flat against the floor, craning to see the numbers on Ann's organizer, my purse started to ring again.

She looked down. "You're ringing."

"I know. I think it's broken."

Ann gave me a funny look but didn't comment. "Okay, here it is." She handed the device to me. I grabbed a scrap of tracing paper and quickly copied down the address and phone number.

"Thank you so much," I gushed.

"No problem. Trust me, anything to put this behind us

and get on with the show. I think Jean Luc's had four separate strokes today." She tucked her BlackBerry back into her pocket just as her headset crackled to life. "See what I mean?" she said, then started talking into the headset as she walked off to deal with another crisis.

I stared down at Ryan's number. I slipped my cell out and dialed. It rang four times, then clicked over to a machine.

"Hi, this is Ryan," came the voice of a very British-sounding man. "I'll be out of town until the fifteenth, but leave a message, and I'll get back to you as soon as I'm home." I didn't, instead hanging up.

I looked down at the address. It was indeed in London. And today was the fifteenth.

Maybe had I not been sitting next to a completely empty rack of what were formerly my shoes, I wouldn't have contemplated it. Maybe if I hadn't thought the police were set against me, that a killer was out to frame me, and, hell, that even my own boyfriend wasn't sure whose side he was on . . . maybe had I not had to deal with all this while dragging around a giant NERF toy on my foot, I might have been more patient. I might have tried Ryan's number again. I might have left a polite message and waited to hear back from him.

But I didn't.

Instead I picked up my cell and dialed my travel agent, booking two seats on the next available flight to London Heathrow.

Chapter Nine

I drummed my fingers on the wooden tabletop, waiting for Dana to finish her fitting. A skinny guy in tight jeans and a painted-on Polo shirt was pinning a dress around her frame, periodically pausing to tell her to keep still. Even as I waited I couldn't help the little puddle of drool forming at the side of my mouth as I took in the dress she'd be wearing down the runway. It was a pale green silk number, falling to midthigh, with a crosscut back and a keyhole front. It was the kind of dress that you bought whether you had an occasion or not.

And hoped some hot guy would end up tearing it off of you.

Finally the guy with the pins slipped it over Dana's head and let her free. She came skipping over to me.

"Ohmigod, Maddie, did you see the dress?"

I wiped at my mouth to make sure the drool wasn't showing. "The sad thing is, I had the perfect pair of white pumps that would have gone with it—if they weren't in an evidence locker."

Dana frowned. "I'm so sorry, Mads."

"Me too. But, listen, you think you could get Jean Luc to let you off the hook tonight?"

Dana raised an eyebrow. "Why?"

I quickly filled her in on Ryan's whereabouts and our reservations on the seven-thirty flight into London.

"We're going to play Angels again!" Dana cried, jumping up and down.

For a brief moment I had second thoughts. The first time Dana and I had played Charlie's Angels she'd dressed me up as a hooker and we'd ended up getting shot at. Then there was the time we'd tried to outwit the mob, which had ended with Dana blowing a hole in some guy's chest. And, last but not least, the time we'd gone undercover on a TV set and nearly ended up becoming the next victims of a Hollywood strangler. Suffice to say, the term *playing Angels* didn't totally thrill me.

On the other hand, that dress had screamed for my white pumps, and if there was any chance of my getting them out of Moreau's evidence locker before the show day, someone had to be the crime-fighting hotties. It might as well be us.

"Okay, but I get to be Farrah this time," I told her.

Dana did a shoulder-shrug, nose-scrunching shriek thing, then promptly skipped (yes, I swear she actually skipped. Wonder Boot and I were supremely jealous) off to inform Jean Luc she would be back in the morning.

We stopped off only long enough to grab a couple of *tartines*—open-faced sandwiches—at a sidewalk café along the way (Dana's a low-fat grilled veggie, mine a ham-and-cheese loaded with mayo. Hey, hobbling around on

Wonder Boot burned off a lot of calories), before taking a cab to the airport.

Luckily, small commuter flights from Paris to London flew out of Paris's Charles de Gaulle almost every other hour. We had two seats on the seven-thirty flight, arriving in London one hour later. I briefly contemplated stopping at the hotel first to pack a couple of items, but considering that was where I'd most likely run into Mr. Pissed-off Voice Mails, I decided to chance it and travel light.

By the time we were flying over the famous London Eye and taxiing onto the runway at Heathrow, the sun had set, the city was a brilliant mosaic of twinkling lights, and, I'll admit, that familiar Farrah excitement was starting to niggle at the back of my brain. Dana and I hailed the first cab we saw and gave the driver the address I'd written down.

Which turned out to be a squat brick building in a seemingly upper-middle-class-looking neighborhood. Small trees lined the street, televisions flickered behind windows, and a guy in a checked cardigan sweater that looked like it came from a garage sale was walking a little terrier on a leash up the street.

"Doesn't exactly look like a jewel thief's place," Dana observed.

"Well, you don't exactly look like Kate Jackson."

"Hey, I thought I was Cheryl Ladd!"

"Come on," I said, grabbing her by the sleeve as the cabdriver gave us a funny look in his rearview mirror.

I asked the driver to wait. He nodded, then pulled out a copy of the *London Times* as Dana and I hopped out.

The front doors to the building were locked, four call

buttons on the wall indicating the flats inside. I hit the one marked JEFFRIES. Unfortunately nothing happened. I waited a beat, then tried again. No answer. Just for good measure I whipped out my cell and keyed in the phone number again. After four rings the machine kicked in.

"Great. Now what?" Dana asked.

I glanced down the street as the guy in the cardigan stooped down to pick up a terrier dropping in a plastic baggie.

"Let's go talk to the neighbors."

We crossed the small expanse of lawn in front of the building, and the dog walker straightened as we approached, awkwardly fumbling with his baggie. "Evening," he mumbled.

"Hi. I was wondering if I could ask you about your neighbor?" I said, indicating the brick building next door.

"Oh, uh, I'm sorry, I don't really know them," he stammered, tying a little twister around the top of his baggie.

"What a cute little doggy," Dana said, crouching down to pet the terrier. It hopped up, putting its front paws on Dana's knee to lick her face.

"Oh, my, Lady, don't do that. Naughty dog, Lady." He tugged on her leash, his face flushed with embarrassment.

"Oh, it's okay. I love dogs," Dana said, straightening.

Cardigan looked from Lady to the poodle on Dana's shirt. He smiled, his stiff posture relaxing a little. "Yes, I can see that you do."

"About your neighbor," I prompted. "Ryan Jeffries?"

"Uh, right. Um, Ryan. He's a model, I think."

"So, you do know him?" Dana asked, stooping down to pet Lady again.

"Uh, well, just to say 'hi' to, I suppose," he said.

"We've been trying to get hold of Ryan. Do you know where he might be?" I asked.

"No. Not really. I haven't seen him much lately. I think he was out of town."

"Any idea where he went?" I asked, mentally crossing my fingers.

"Paris."

Bingo!

"I think," he added. "Not sure. But I know he got back this morning. Saw him hauling luggage up to his place."

"Do you know where he might be now?" Dana asked.

He shook his head. "Sorry, wish I could be more help."

"Thanks anyway," Dana said, giving Lady one last scratch behind the ears.

"Hey, don't I know you?" he asked.

Dana giggled. "Well, I have been in a couple of commercials lately. Do you use Dove soap?"

"No." Cardigan shook his head. "Not you, her." He pointed at me.

"Who, me?"

He narrowed his eyes, nodding. "Yeah, your face looks really familiar."

"Nope," I said a little too quickly. "I guess I've just got one of those faces. Well, thanks, nice meeting you." I dragged Dana back to the cab before Cardigan realized that, according to the latest tabloids, he was face-to-face with the Couture Killer.

"Okay," said Dana as we slid into the backseat again, "so, what now? Do we just wait here until Ryan shows up?"

I glanced up at the brick building. I had to admit that

just sitting around waiting made me feel antsy. With the amount of messages piling up on my voice mail, I had a feeling I was working on borrowed time. Sooner or later Ramirez was going to catch up to me. He was a detective, and a good one. It wouldn't take him long to follow my trail—littered with bread crumbs as it was. And once he did I had a bad feeling there might be handcuffs involved (and not in a good way). No way was that man letting me out of his sight again. So, playing sitting duck wasn't the most appealing of choices.

Instead I leaned forward, addressing our cabdriver, who was perusing the sports section.

"Excuse me," I said.

He looked up, and I read his name tag. Matthew.

"Matthew, do you happen to know if there are any nightclubs in the area?"

Both Angelica and Donata had indicated that Gisella was a party girl. I crossed my fingers that the kind of guy she dated would be a regular on the club circuit as well.

"Sure, there're a couple," he said, his working-class accent thick. "You got the Midnight Bar down that way, and Club Easy a couple blocks south of here. But, uh"—he gestured to Wonder Boot—"they're both dance clubs. I can't say as you'll have much fun there, love."

"Don't worry; I won't be dancing. You mind trying the Midnight Bar first?"

Matthew nodded, folding up the *Times*. "Suit yerself."

Ten minutes later we were parked in front of a large yellowing building with a painted black-and-white sign that read, MIDNIGHT, sitting crookedly above the door. A pair of motorcycles were haphazardly parked along the front, and one window was covered with plywood. All in all it didn't strike me as the type of place a jet-setting male model would spend his evenings.

"Maybe we should try the other one," I suggested.

Matthew shrugged, then put the car into gear.

Club Easy was a larger place, freshly painted in a trendy beige with black trim, sporting a brightly lit exterior and a line to get in that spanned around the building. A steady techno rhythm pulsed from inside as a tall, red-haired bouncer stood sentry at the door, wielding a clipboard in one beefy hand.

Now, this was more like it.

I angled Wonder Boot out of the car and turned to Matthew. "You mind waiting for us?"

He glanced at the meter. "How long you gonna be?"

"Um, I'm not entirely sure." How long did it take to coax a confession out of someone? "But keep the meter running," I said, almost hearing my meager bank account cringe. Then again, if I didn't clear this up soon, I'd be lucky to get a job designing school uniforms.

Matthew just shrugged again, unfolding his paper. "Suit yerself."

I slipped my crutches under my armpits and caught up to Dana as she approached the bouncer outside.

"Hi there," she said, giving the red-haired guy a flirty little one-finger wave.

Big Red gave her a quick up-and-down. But, considering she was showing 50 percent less skin than half the girls in line, he shot back a predictable, "Back of the line."

"Actually, we just wanted to ask you a couple of questions," I piped up.

He crossed his arms over his chest and stared down at me. (And I do mean down—he was at least a foot and a half taller than I was.)

"What kind of questions?"

"We were wondering if you know a guy by the name of Ryan Jeffries. He lives in the area."

He narrowed his eyes. "What about him?"

"So, you do know him?"

He looked from Dana to me as if trying to decide how much to tell us. Luckily Dana jumped in before he could make up his mind. "We met him on a shoot in L.A. and he gave us his number. But he's not answering now, and we so wanted to party with him tonight before we have to go home."

Big Red looked from Dana to me. "You're models?"

"Uh-huh." Dana nodded, flipping her hair over one shoulder in a practiced hot-blonde move.

"Hmph." Big Red glanced at my gimpy leg, obviously not totally convinced.

"We're gonna be so bummed if we miss Ryan, you know? Is he here?" Dana asked, standing on tiptoe to peer over his shoulder.

"No. Ry's working tonight."

"Working?" I asked. "As in modeling?"

He grinned again, showing off a crooked smile that proved he had broken up one too many bar fights. "You could say that."

"Do you know where?" Dana asked, twirling her hair around her index finger.

"Club X. Not really sure it's the kind of place for a couple of nice gals like you, though."

"Oh, we'll take our chances. Would you mind writing down the address for us?" I asked, pulling a gum wrapper and a pen from my purse.

He did. Then beneath it he scrawled a phone number. He handed it to Dana with a wink.

"Just in case you're not into the X scene," he said.

Dana giggled. I grabbed her by the arm and steered her back to the cab before Miss My-boyfriend's-kissing-Natalie-Portman could get too friendly with the natives.

Once in the cab I handed the gum wrapper to Matthew, who had moved on to the local news section.

"Do you know the place?" I asked.

Matthew shook his head. "Sorry, love, can't say as I do. But it's not far, though."

We rode in silence through the London streets littered with clubgoers and all-night pubs, the air starting to thicken with fog as we veered away from downtown and into an older part of the city. Finally Matthew pulled the car up to a dark, two-story building at the end of an abandoned block. Above the door was a lone neon X.

"You girls sure you want to go in there?" Matthew asked.

No. But we'd come this far. "Yep."

Matthew shrugged, picking up his *Times*. "Suit yerself."

Dana and I piled out of the car and up the walkway, pausing only briefly beneath the neon X before slipping inside the club.

The interior was only slightly less dark than the outside. A few strategically placed bulbs gave off an eerie reddish glow, bathing the room in an almost otherworldly light—a room that was packed. Men and women doing the Goth-chic thing filled the room, going back and forth between a tall iron staircase and a long wooden bar spanning the length of the room. Dark, bass-driven music played from hidden speakers, and the decor of choice seemed to be red velvet covering the back wall, as well as a smattering of low sofas and chairs along the room's perimeter.

A woman in black leather pants, a black leather jacket, and with a black leather riding crop attached to her belt walked past, giving us a once-over.

"Gee, suddenly I feel underdressed," Dana mumbled to me.

"Come on, let's find Ryan."

We threaded our way through the club patrons toward the bar, where I relied on Dana's double Ds to attract the bartender's attention. Eventually they worked their magic as he leaned our way.

"What can I get you?" he asked. He had black hair held back in a ponytail, a thick Cockney accent, and about twelve visible piercings on his face, reminding me of an oversize porcupine. I cringed, watching the one in his lip bob up and down as he spoke.

"We're actually looking for Ryan Jeffries. We were told he worked here."

The bartender smiled, revealing piercing number thirteen in his tongue. "Sure. He's upstairs. But he's already doing a scene with someone. You're gonna have to take a number, love."

"Thanks," I said, moving out of the way as the lady with the crop inched her way past me.

"What's that mean, a scene?" I whispered to Dana as we threaded our way up the iron staircase to the second floor.

She shrugged. "I dunno. Maybe they're doing a play."

Though as we reached the second-story landing, I realized that Shakespeare it was not.

A crowd of people was gathered around a low platform, huddled two and three deep, all eyes on a woman in the center of the stage. She had jet-black hair and wore a black leather corset and shiny black leather pants. Her eyes were heavily lined in black, bright red lips her only accent of color. She held what looked like a leather paddle in one hand, in the other a leash. At the end of the leash was a man with pale blond hair, shirtless, crouched on all fours on the floor, wearing a pair of black leather chaps and a studded collar around his neck.

I blinked, suddenly unsure whether I wanted to watch or quickly look away.

"Ohmigod, Dana," I said, grabbing her arm. "I think this is one of *those* kinds of clubs."

Dana's eyes were riveted to the paddle in Leather Lady's hands. "Like a sex kind of club?"

"Like an S and M kind of club. I think she's gonna spank him."

No sooner had I gotten the words out than the paddle made a smacking sound and the crowd went wild, throwing up a cheer as though Lady Leather had just scored a touchdown.

I covered my eyes.

Okay, I'll admit I'm no sheltered virgin. But whips and chains were just a little out of my comfort zone. (And, yes, by "little" I mean light-years.)

Dana, on the other hand, had a very large comfort zone.

"Oh, this I gotta see," she said, moving forward.

"Wait, Dana," I protested. But it was too late. She was already fighting her way to the front of the crowd. I had two choices: stay here alone or follow her to the front row. I looked to my right. A guy in black leather biker shorts and little else gave me the eye.

"Wait for me!"

I wriggled my way forward, hitting only three people in the shins with my crutches, until I finally caught up with her. A long railing had been erected around the perimeter of the stage, and I found Dana with her elbows leaning against it, her eyes kind of glazing over as she watched Lady Leather work her magic on Slave Boy.

"He's kind of cute, huh?" she asked, pointing to Slave Boy.

I wouldn't know. I still had my hand covering my eyes. I gingerly peeked between my ring and pinkie fingers. Of course, wouldn't you know that would be the moment that Lady Leather chose to do away with Slave Boy's leather pants? I felt myself blush all the way down to my blonde roots as I caught an unwanted glimpse of full-frontal Slave Boy.

I grabbed Dana's arm. "Ohmigod," I said.

Dana licked her lips. "I know. God, I miss Ricky."

"No." I shook my head. Not that Slave Boy didn't have an impressive . . . uh, package. But what had me grabbing Dana's arm in a vise grip was the fact that I recognized that package. It was the same one from Gisella's camera.

Slave Boy was Ryan Jeffries.

I left Dana upstairs to watch the rest of Ryan's scene while I walked back to the bar like a fish swimming upstream.

I'm pretty sure 90 percent of Club X's patrons would be going home with purple marks on their shins. I mumbled another "Sorry," as I whacked a girl in three-inch stilettos, fishnets, and a black bodice, and deposited myself on a red velvet sofa to wait for Dana. Fifteen minutes later she finally made an appearance, her eyes shining with an almost high look, one arm linked through Ryan's. I was thankful he'd put the chaps back on, but I still felt myself flush as he and Dana sat down beside me.

"Maddie, you missed a great show," Dana said.

"I'll bet," I mumbled, avoiding eye contact with Ryan.

"Ryan, this is Maddie, the girl I was telling you about."

"Hi," he said. Then he cocked his head to the side. "Say, have we met before?"

I shook my head. Nope, I was fairly certain this guy I would have remembered.

He was tall, at least six feet, with pale blond hair and bright blue eyes. Now that he was fairly vertical it was obvious he had a lean, muscular model's physique. I could easily envision him strutting down a runway in Calvin Kleins. I put his age in his late twenties to early thirties, probably a little old for the runway circuit now—which might explain his latest place of employment.

"You sure?" he asked. "You look very familiar."

I shook my head. "Nope."

Then recognition dawned in his blue eyes. "Wait, you're that designer who stabbed Gisella!"

"I didn't stab her. I swear. It's just a tabloid rumor."

He narrowed his eyes at me, not totally convinced.

"I would never hurt anyone!" I looked up at his collar. "Uh, I mean, not that hurting someone is a bad thing. If they want to be hurt. Which, clearly, you do. I mean, did. I mean, if you like that sort of thing. But I don't. I mean, I didn't. And definitely not Gisella and definitely not with a stiletto heel."

Ryan just looked at me.

I cleared my throat. "Um, do you mind if I ask you a few questions about Gisella?"

I could tell he still had his reservations about me, but he nodded.

"Rumor has it you two were dating?"

"We were."

"How long?"

"About three months."

"And you went to Paris with her for Fashion Week?"

Again, he nodded. "Yes. I thought it would be a good opportunity to make some new contacts. Since I hit thirty things have dried up a little for me. I flew in with her last Friday and stayed until . . ." He trailed off, looking down at his hands.

"I'm sorry," I said. "I know this must be hard on you." When he didn't say anything I plowed ahead. "Can I ask when was the last time you saw Gisella?"

He bit his lip, his eyes focusing on a point just beyond my head. "Four nights ago? At her agent's party."

I frowned. Angelica said she'd heard a male voice the night after that. "Are you sure? You didn't see her the following night?" I prompted.

He shook his head, a sad, faraway look in his eyes. "No. The party was the last time I saw her. She broke it off with me."

I raised an eyebrow. "Oh? Did she say why?"

He gave a humorless little laugh. "She'd met someone new. Someone higher up in the food chain. She brought him to the party. Can you believe that? First she invites me to Fashion Week, and then she shoves this guy in my face. What kind of woman does that?"

Ryan's volume climbed as he talked, his earlier grief quickly being replaced with anger. I wondered just how angry he'd been at the party. Angry enough to kill Gisella the following night?

"Gisella was wearing a necklace at the party," Dana piped up. "Did you see it?"

I leaned in, squinting through the dim light to gauge his reaction.

"Yes," he said without hesitation.

If he'd known Gisella had taken the necklace, he didn't let on.

"She said it was from Lord Ackerman's private collection," he said.

"It was stolen," I said.

His only reaction was to raise an eyebrow. "Really? Who took it?"

I hesitated to share our model-turned–jewel thief theory with him. But on the other hand, if he'd been working with her it wouldn't be news to him. And if he was an innocent bystander in all this, what did we have to lose?

"We think Gisella did. We think she may have even been stealing jewelry from other designers' shows as well."

He shook his head, his eyes on that faraway point again. "Wow. I had no idea. I'm not surprised, though. Like I said, she wasn't the most scrupulous person I've ever met."

"We think she may have had a partner. Someone who sold the stolen items for her," Dana said. "Any idea who that could be?"

He shrugged. "Sorry, I don't know. She didn't have any real close friends. Her agent and me were the only people she really spent much time with."

"What about the new guy?" I asked. "Is it possible he was helping her?"

Again he shrugged.

"You said you met him?"

He nodded. "Yeah. At the party."

"Did you happen to catch his name?"

He gave a wry grin that held little humor. "Oh yeah. She made sure everyone at the party knew who she was there with. That wanker was a real feather in her cap, if you know what I mean."

"Who was it?" I asked.

He snorted again. "Lord Ackerman."

Chapter Ten

Felix? I think my heart stopped beating, the dark room swirling before my vision. Felix and Gisella?!

It had to be a mistake. She had to have been lying. Felix wouldn't go for a girl like that. Felix's type was . . . well it wasn't her.

I thought back. We'd been in her room together; we'd been searching for evidence of a boyfriend. And he hadn't told me he was it! I tried to remember our conversation, but all my brain could focus on was the fact that Felix has been sleeping with a supermodel.

For some odd reason that stomach flu hit me full force again.

"Excuse me," I said, bolting up from the sofa. I made for the front doors as quickly as I could. Air. I needed air. I'm pretty sure I knocked into at least three people, spilling one woman's drink all over her corset in my mad rush to get outside.

Once there I doubled over, leaning on my crutches as I took in big lungfuls of night air that smelled like car exhaust and rotting vegetables.

In a moment Dana was at my side.

"Hey, you okay?" she asked, putting a hand on my back.

"Yeah. Sure. Fine."

"You're a terrible liar."

Unlike some people.

Okay, so I guess I hadn't ever asked Felix point-blank if he'd been sleeping with the victim, but that was a hell of an omission. What else had he failed to mention?

Then one terrible thought occurred to me. He'd been the one to find the diamond necklace in Gisella's room. Had he known where it was all along? Had he been in on it with her? He had said it was insured. Collect once from the insurance company, a second time when he sold it on the black market? Would Felix stoop that low?

Problem was, I didn't really know Felix's stooping limit. Granted, his paper was single-handedly to blame for ruining more than one celebrity marriage with their rumor mill, but that was a far cry from sticking a shoe in someone's neck.

My shoe.

My stomach lurched again and I leaned over, fully expecting a repeat appearance by my ham-and-cheese.

"Do you really think this could have been Felix?" Dana asked, voicing my thoughts.

I shook my head. "I don't know." I paused. "Maybe." Another pause. "No, definitely not." I bit my lip. "Probably not?"

He'd been in Paris the night of her murder, in the same hotel. The victim was *his* girlfriend, presumably stealing *his* jewels.

"I've got to talk to Felix." I pulled my cell out of my purse and dialed his number, my hands shaking harder than the Northridge quake. Unfortunately the call went straight to voice mail. *Shit.* I flipped it shut and threw it in my purse, taking my anxiety out on my Motorola.

"Hey," I said, addressing Matthew, who was fully engrossed in an article in the world news section.

He waited a beat before looking up. When he did he blinked at me as if seeing me for the first time. He looked back to his paper, then to me again.

"It's you!"

I looked down at the *Times* in his lap. Sure enough, there was my mug smiling back at me. Okay, so I wasn't totally smiling. It was a candid shot taken outside the Plaza Athénée as I'd tried to muscle my way through the paparazzi. From the look on my face it was probably when one of the cameramen had knocked into Wonder Boot. I looked either constipated, pissed off, or in pain.

Or, as Matthew had apparently interpreted it, dangerous.

"It's not me."

He looked from the paper to me and back again. "It sure looks like you."

I rolled my eyes. "Okay, yes, the picture is me. But I'm not the killer. I didn't do it. I'm innocent. Which is why I'm here trying to clear my name."

Matthew looked wary. "You sure?"

"Yes, of course I'm sure! Do I look like I could hurt someone?"

Matthew looked me up and down. Then he glanced behind me at the S and M club he'd just taken me to.

"I didn't do it," I said again.

Finally he shrugged. "All right, if you say so. But if I

hear of any dead bodies showin' up at that there club tomorrow, I'm turnin' you in to the police, missy." He wagged a knobby finger at me.

"Fair enough. Listen, do you happen to know where a Lord Ackerman lives?"

He hunched his bushy eyebrows down. "Can't say's I do. He have a place around here?"

My turn to shrug. The problem was, I had no idea where Felix stayed when he was in England. I knew he had an impressive home up in the Hollywood Hills, but as it was becoming clearly apparent, beyond the basics I didn't know much about Felix's life at all.

"Any idea where we could find an address for him?"

He shook his head. "Google?"

Luckily I just happened to know a pair of Googling fiends.

I whipped out my cell, dialing Mom's number. She picked up on the third ring, and I could hear loud music in the background.

"Hello?" she shouted.

I held the phone away from my ear.

"Mom, it's Maddie."

"Hey, hon. Say, where are you? Ramirez has been tearing this place apart looking for you."

I cringed. I was so gonna be on his shit list when I got back. But if it got me off the front page, I'd say it was worth it.

"Dana and I are following a lead. Listen, I was wondering if you could do something for me?"

I heard a sound like a war whoop in the background. "What?" Mom yelled.

I resisted the urge to cover my ear. "Where are you?"

"Mrs. Rosenblatt and I dragged Pierre out to a champagne bar. Mrs. Rosenblatt's on her second bottle and dancing the cancan."

I had a sudden unwelcome vision of Mrs. R's muumuu hiked up to her knees, her thunder thighs kicking heavenward. I shuddered.

"Listen, could you do something for me when you get back to the hotel?" I yelled into the phone.

"Sure. Shoot, Mads."

"I need Felix's address." I filled her in on all I'd learned at the club. (Okay, maybe not *all* I'd learned. I left out the parts about the leashes and paddles.)

"Okay," she said when I finished. "We'll hit the business center as soon as we get back."

I thanked her (though I wasn't entirely sure she heard me over Mrs. Rosenblatt's hollering) and hung up.

"Now what?" Dana asked.

It was late, I was tired, and my stomach still felt wobbly when I thought about Felix and the massive fast one he'd pulled on me. "Let's get a room somewhere."

We piled back in the cab and asked Matthew to take us to a hotel nearby, preferably one that wouldn't make my Visa wince further.

I leaned my head back on the vinyl seat, watching the dark London streets whiz past the window at a rate that sent nausea washing through me again. The more I thought about it, the more foolish I felt for ever trusting a guy like Felix. I'd been the one pleading with Ramirez to get him out of jail. What if it turned out he belonged there? I knew Felix had a moral compass that pointed

just this side of north, but had he really offed his girlfriend? Even worse, would he have framed me for it?

I had to admit at that part my stomach clenched the
worst. Not that I'd thought I meant anything to Felix.
I didn't. And he meant nothing to me. We weren't even
friends. More like acquaintances who sometimes bumped
into each other.

Lips first.

I closed my eyes, willing myself not to think about it.

Matthew pulled us up in front of the Queen's Cozy
Inn and let us out. He gave me one backward glance in
his rearview mirror, eyes still wary, before collecting his
ginormous fare and pulling away from the curb. I had a
bad feeling that if Dana and I didn't find the real killer
soon, that was the kind of look I was doomed to receive
for life.

After I handed over my credit card to the frizzy-haired
girl on duty behind the desk, Dana and I were shown to
a room on the second floor. The bed was standard-issue,
the duvet a pastel floral print. A scarred dresser sat at one
end, a tiny bathroom at the other. A television set with
rabbit ears was on the dresser, and above that hung a
framed lithograph of Queen Elizabeth. The Ritz it was
not. But I didn't care. All I wanted was sleep. Hopefully
in the morning things would make more sense.

The room was dark. A single lamp gave off a dim red glow,
bathing the room in a light eerily reminiscent of blood.
I held my breath, searching the darkness for him. I wasn't
sure whom I was looking for, but I knew I had to find him.
People were everywhere, bumping up against me, pushing

in from all angles. Then I heard the crowd cheering, yelling, hollering. I shoved my way through them, straining on tiptoe to see around them. He had to be here somewhere. I fought my way through the growing crowd to the front. There in the center of the room, standing under a bright red spotlight, was Mrs. Rosenblatt, wearing a leather corset and wielding a long leather riding crop.

"Hey, Mads, wanna play?" she asked, flicking her wrist, the crop doing a menacing snap in the air. The crowd cheered again.

I turned, ready to run from the room.

Then I saw him.

I froze, unable to look away. Felix. He was watching me from the other side of the room. Staring me down.

Suddenly Mrs. Rosenblatt and the rest of the crowd disappeared. It was just Felix and me, eyes locked on each other. I tried to speak, but it was as though I'd eaten too much peanut butter, my mouth sticky, refusing to open.

Felix closed the distance between us, his eyes intent on mine, a little half smile playing on his lips as if he knew a secret that I didn't. He was coming closer, almost floating across the room in slow motion. I tried to speak, tried to move, but my feet were glued to the spot, my limbs too heavy to lift.

Suddenly he was so close he was almost on top of me. "Maddie," he whispered.

He reached out and grabbed my arm with one hand, the other lifting above his head, wielding a black stiletto heel.

Then I really did scream.

I sat up straight in bed, sweat pouring down my back, my breath coming out in German shepherd pants. My eyes whipped around the room, searching for any remnants of the red light, the crowd, the black high heel. Nothing, just a TV, a scarred dresser, and a photo of the queen. And Dana snoring beside me.

I slowly lay back, adrenaline coursing through my limbs, and closed my eyes. It was just a dream.

One that, in light of yesterday's revelations, seemed all too real. That was it. I *had* to talk to Felix.

I rolled over and looked at the clock: seven fifteen. With a groan I slid out of bed and hopped into a lukewarm shower. I turned my panties inside out and redressed in yesterday's clothes, digging in my purse for mascara and lip gloss. Since the hair dryer in the bathroom didn't work, I twisted my wet hair into a French braid and figured I was halfway passable.

I emerged from the bathroom to find Dana yawing, flipping through channels on the television set.

"You were on channel two," she informed me.

"Swell." I plopped down on the bed.

"And Jean Luc called. He said he needs me for a fitting at one. Sorry, Maddie, this Angel has to get back."

I nodded. "I understand." Not everyone's career was in the toilet. "I'll drop you at the airport. Oh, and by the way," I added as she made for the bathroom, "there's no hot water."

I flipped off the TV as Dana shut the bathroom door and I heard water start to run. The last thing I wanted to encounter this early in the morning was another candid shot of myself.

Instead I grabbed my cell and tried Felix's number again. As before, it went straight to voice mail.

Instead I bit the bullet and dialed Ramirez's cell.

I prayed hard to the saint of forgiving boyfriends as I listened to it ring once, then twice. On the third ring he picked up.

"That was a dirty trick," he said, his voice hard.

"Sorry?" It came out more of a question.

"Where the hell are you, Maddie?"

"Um . . ." I looked around the room. The queen stared back at me. "I'm safe."

"That's not what I asked."

"Listen, I just wanted to call to tell you that I'm okay, not to worry, and I'll be back soon."

"Where. Are. You."

"I'm following a lead."

There was silence. Then he muttered a curse in Spanish. "Maddie, detectives follow leads. The police follow leads. Fashion designers draw fluffy little shoes. What the hell are you doing?"

"I have to clear my name, Jack. Do you know I was in the *London Times* yesterday?"

"London?"

Oops. I slapped a hand over my mouth. "Or so I heard," I added feebly.

"Maddie, listen, you've got to have a little faith in the system. Moreau will get to the bottom of this. But you running around following your so-called leads is just going to make things worse. This disappearing act doesn't exactly make you look innocent."

As much as I loved him, it was the "so-called" that put me over the edge.

"I'll be back tonight," I said. Then I hung up, cutting Ramirez off midcurse.

Ramirez might have faith in Moreau, but the way

he'd interrogated me, I certainly didn't. And if I didn't do it, someone else had. Someone who, as of right now, was not only ruining my life, but also getting away with murder.

I just hoped that someone wasn't Felix.

After Dana got out of the shower we both headed down to the Duck's Head Pub on the corner, where we ordered something called bangers and mash for breakfast. Which, when it arrived, turned out to be sausages and mashed potatoes. Personally I thought it was pretty tasty. Dana, on the other hand, scrunched up her nose and asked the waitress if they had any grapefruit halves. The waitress gave her a funny look, then appeared with a mealy apple, saying it was the only fruit on the premises. Dana ate the apple while I made yummy sounds all the way through my sausages.

By the time Dana had hit core, my cell chirped to life in my purse. I pulled it out to see Mom's number on the LCD screen.

"Hello?" I asked around a bite of mashed potatoes and thick onion gravy. I'm telling you, these Europeans know how to eat.

"We got it." Mom relayed an address she and Mrs. R had found off a peerage directory Web site. It was in Hertfordshire, which, once Mom pulled up a Yahoo! map, she informed me was just north of London.

I thanked her and promised I'd call her later. She said to take my time. According to Mom, after the cancan display last night, Pierre had warmed to Mrs. R, and they were all going on a river cruise up the Seine. I wondered if Pierre had "warmed" or been coerced under influence of champagne. Either way, I told her I hoped she had fun and hung up.

Dana and I quickly finished eating, then paid our bill and asked the waitress the best way to get to Hertford-shire. She suggested renting a car and taking the M1 straight up. She gave us directions and pointed us toward a car rental place down the block.

Half an hour later we were squeezed into one of the smallest cars in existence, Dana's knees practically touch-ing her chin as I tried to figure out the gearshift. The thing handled like a tin can on wheels, and every time we went around a corner I yelled, "Lean," to Dana for fear we'd tip over.

By the sheer grace of God I managed to drive her to the airport without hitting anything, even though I for-got and pulled onto the wrong side of the street twice.

After getting stuck for only fifteen minutes in the roundabout outside the terminal, I finally found my way to the motorway and headed out of the city, toward Hertfordshire.

The drive was actually surprisingly pleasant. Rolling green hills spanned either side of the roadway, groves of trees dotting the landscape and a low, thin fog covering it all like something out of a postcard or an Enya song. Overall it was an effect that, by the time I was passing a large wooden sign that indicated my turnoff, had helped diminish the nerves of possibly driving toward a mur-derer's home.

I drove through a small, quaint village complete with stone chimneys and thatched roofs out of a Thomas Kin-caid painting, and up a winding road that led to the ad-dress Mom had given me. I made a couple of wrong turns onto overgrown roads that had clearly seen better days, before finally finding the right one. I wound around a grove of trees until a large structure loomed in the distance. My jaw dropped open. It was a castle.

Felix lived in a freaking castle!?

When had my life become a twisted fairy tale?

Granted, it was small by castle standards, a brick structure with green moss growing along the sides. And I could clearly see that modern additions had been made— double-paned windows, paved driveway and car park, electric lights by the front door. But it still held two large brick turrets that I could easily see Rapunzel throwing a lock of hair from.

I parked my midget car in the massive drive near a row of green hedges and approached a huge wooden door that screamed for an alligator-filled moat.

A modern doorbell sat beside the door and I rang it, hearing the sound echo inside. I waited a beat before the door was pulled open and I found myself face-to-face with dear "old" Auntie.

It took her a moment before recognition registered.

"Maddie. What a surprise," she said, looking behind me as if wondering where I'd come from. She was dressed today in a pale peach miniskirt that maximized her tan, which, if the weather was any indication, was obviously fake. She'd paired the barely there skirt with a short-sleeved white blouse, the sleeves cut on a bias that showed off the muscular curve of her upper arms. I silently wondered if the castle had a gym too.

"Hi, Charlene. I was wondering if Felix is in?"

A small frown settled between her blonde brows. "Yes. But I thought you were in Paris?"

"I was. I . . ." I paused, not really sure how to voice the jumble of thoughts that had been circulating through my head all day. "I need to talk to Felix."

She arched a slim eyebrow but, ever the polite Brit, stepped back to allow me entry. "Please come in."

I did, my crutches squeaking against the polished hardwood floor as she shut the door behind me. Inside, the modern conversion of the castle was even more apparent than it was outside. In fact, the foyer looked as if it could have belonged to any home in Beverly Hills—light, airy rugs, sweeping staircase to the right, dark wood side table, and a crystal chandelier hanging above us.

"Felix is in the study," Charlene said, leading the way down a wide hall. "He's been on the phone with his lawyers all day. He was arrested in Paris, you know." She paused, stopping to look at me. "Of course you know. You were there."

I felt a guilty flush creep up my neck.

"Anyway," she continued, "I flew home with him, though I'm due back in Paris tomorrow. I never miss the Hermès show. Felix is trying to get this matter cleared up to travel with me."

She stopped outside an open door to a large, dark room. "If you'd like to wait here I'll fetch him for you," she said, flicking on a light for me.

"Sure. Thanks, Charlene."

She nodded, that frown settling between her brows again as she turned. It was clear she wasn't fond of me. But I was thankful she was too polite to let on. Instead she swayed those very undoddering hips down the hall, disappearing to the right.

I took a moment to look around the room she'd left

me in. A massive stone fireplace taller than I was stood
at one end. Above it were a pair of weapons—a stick
thingie with a spiked metal ball at the end and some
kind of sword. Very medieval-looking. I shuddered.
The same hardwood floors continued here, broken up
with area rugs in deep burgundies and forest greens.
Large, masculine furnishings filled the room: two sofas
in dark leather, a pair of club chairs with ornate feet, a
handful of end tables, and an antique writing desk in
the corner. I gingerly perched on the edge of one sofa,
feeling as though I'd entered a museum where some do-
cent might pop out at any second and tell me to stay behind the ropes.

"Maddie."

My head whipped around so fast I feared whiplash.

"Felix," I squeaked out.

He was wearing his trademark rumpled white button-
down and khaki pants with a worn pair of sneakers. He
leaned casually against the door frame, his hands in his
pockets. "What are you doing here?" he asked.

I licked my lips, my throat suddenly dry at the sight
of him.

"I, uh, need to talk to you. Your phone was off."

He frowned. "The battery died. What's going on? Are
you all right?" He came into the room and sat down beside me. I immediately jumped up as if he'd shocked me.
I licked my lips again as I wandered over near the fireplace. "Me? Yeah, uh, I'm fine."

Again the frown. "What's going on?"

I cleared my throat, not really sure what to say now
that I was here. Being careful what I said around Felix
was nothing new—let the wrong thing slip out and you

were libel to be front-page news next to Bigfoot. But being careful he didn't stab me with my own pumps? That I was still trying to wrap my head around.

"Um, well, see, here's the thing. I, uh . . ." I took a deep breath. "Why didn't you tell me you were dating Gisella?" I blurted out.

"Ah." He rose from the sofa, taking a step toward me. Instinctively I took one back.

He frowned again, this one deep enough to create little lines between his eyebrows. "We went out a couple of times. Nothing serious. I didn't think it relevant."

"Relevant? Felix, she's dead."

His face became blank. "Yes. I know."

"Why didn't you tell me you'd been in her hotel room before? That you were at the party? Why did you keep this from me?"

"I didn't. When I got the room key I told you I'd been seeing her."

"You told me you *tricked* the front desk into thinking you were seeing her."

"I never said 'tricked.'"

"You could have told me you were with her at the party."

"We had a few drinks, and I walked her to her hotel room. That was it."

"And that was the last time you saw her?"

He paused, then shook his head. "No. I saw her the night she died."

"The night she died?" I thought back to what Angelica had said about hearing a man in the next room. "Ohmigod, you're Mystery Man?"

Felix cocked his head to the side. "Who?"

"You . . . you were in her room the night she died. You were fighting. You slept with her, then started fighting."

Felix looked down at the floor, the toe of his sneaker toying with an invisible spot on the rug. He said in a low voice, "Yes, we fought. She wanted me to accompany her to a party the next night. I said I didn't think we should see each other anymore. She got angry."

"Wait, you were dumping a supermodel?" I asked with a snort. "Why do I find that hard to believe?"

He looked up. "Some men are looking for more than a pair of long legs, Maddie."

I wasn't certain, but I could have sworn his eyes flickered to my own short pair, currently half encased in a foam Smurf boot.

"So why sleep with her first if you knew you were going to dump her? That's low, even for you."

He shook his head. "I didn't sleep with her."

"Angelica heard you. She was in the room right next door."

Again that frown settled between his brows. "I didn't sleep with her, Maddie."

I let it go, focusing on the more important part. "So, you fought, and then what?"

"Then I left her."

"Alive?"

Felix took a step closer.

I backed up again and bit my lip. When had his dimples and rumpled khakis suddenly become so menacing?

He cocked his head to the side, an odd look coming over his features. "No, don't tell me."

"Tell you what?" I asked, my hands starting to sweat at my sides.

"Don't tell me that you of all people think . . . ?"

I threw my hands up in the air. "Well, what am I supposed to think? The necklace belongs to you; you were dating the dead woman. Hell, the story about the stiletto in the jugular was printed in your paper. That's a lot of coincidence, don't you think?"

"Ironic—you talking about coincidence."

I squared my shoulders. "Tell me the truth. Did you kill her, Felix?"

He clenched his jaw, his eyes going dark as he took a step forward. "If I were a cold-blooded killer," he said, his voice suddenly growing a hard edge, "do you really think I'd confess it to you?"

I gulped, my heart rate increasing tenfold.

He shook his head, a slight movement, his eyes saturated with some unreadable emotion. "I can't believe you'd doubt me. Not after all we've been through together." His voice went low, almost a whisper. "After you kissed me."

So he hadn't forgotten.

"That was an accident," I said, wiping my sweaty hands on my dress.

Felix raised an eyebrow at me. "An accident?"

I nodded, taking another step backward.

Felix took two forward. "Is that what you think?"

I nodded again. "Look, you don't think I meant to kiss you? I mean, I'm with Ramirez."

"Actually"—he took two more steps forward—"it looks like you're here. With me."

I gulped, my back coming up against the massive stone fireplace.

"Kinda," I squeaked out.

Felix took one more step forward until he was standing directly in front of me, his body inches from mine. I could feel the heat coming off his skin, smell the scent of coffee on his breath.

"W-what are you doing?" I asked, silently checking his person for anything that looked like a weapon. Specifically a stiletto heel.

None that I could see. His rumpled white shirt lay carelessly over a frame that felt a lot more solid than I'd ever imagined.

"Being deliberate," he said, his voice deep and barely louder than a whisper.

I held my breath.

"D-deliberate?"

But he didn't answer. Instead he leaned in, his body pressing into mine. Despite the fear tickling my spine, my body instantly responded. My heart sped up, heat pooling in my stomach as my lungs suddenly couldn't get enough air. I felt his belly rising and falling against mine in sync with his warm breath on my cheek.

He paused there, his blue eyes never leaving me.

Then he slowly closed the gap between us, his lips moving closer until they hovered a breath away. I tasted coffee and toothpaste, felt his lips brush mine.

I closed my eyes in anticipation of what came next.

His tongue flicked out and tasted my lips so lightly I wasn't even totally sure it happened before his mouth covered mine in a soft, slow movement. Nibbling, tasting, nipping. Before I knew what happened I was returning it, doing a little tasting and nibbling of my own. I must have liked what I sampled, because all on its own my body let out a sigh, sinking into his. His hand slid down my side, resting possessively at my waist as he leaned in, pressing his hips closer.

For a half second the rest of the world disappeared as I went warm in all the right places. The twisted thoughts running circles through my mind the past twenty-four hours melted away. All I cared about right now were his lips, surprisingly soft, capturing mine, his hands, warm and oddly tender, holding me. The fact that despite his annoying habit of pasting my head on Pamela Anderson's body, I just might be able to forgive a guy that was this good a kisser.

A damned good kisser.

Then somewhere through the fog of hormones shrouding me, a tiny voice in the back of my head piped up. *What the hell are you doing, girl?* This was a potential murderer. A creep. A tabloid reporter. *Felix!*

I twisted away, breaking the kiss and sucking in large gulps of air.

"What was that?" I asked Felix.

Only it wasn't Felix's voice that answered.

"My question exactly."

I looked past Felix.

And froze.

Filling the doorway, a death look on his granite features, stood Ramirez.

Chapter Eleven

My life flashed before my eyes as I looked from Felix, his lips still wet and swollen-looking, to Ramirez, his eyes flashing fire, his fists clenching and unclenching at his sides.

"I . . . We . . ." I stammered, taking one giant step away from Felix.

Ramirez gave a low growl, and I suddenly feared another murder might take place soon. *Very* soon.

"It's not what it looks like," I blurted out. "I didn't even kiss him back!" *Much.*

Ramirez looked from me to Felix, his unreadable Cop Face slipping into place.

"Jack?" I said feebly.

But it was too late. I could see all emotion draining from his eyes, being replaced with that dead, even look I'd come to know and dread. Then, before I could stop him, he turned around and stalked out the door.

"Shit." I hobbled after him, my crutches slipping on the overpolished floor. I fumbled with them, then ditched them altogether as I turned the corner, throwing them clattering to the floor in the hallway. "Wait," I called desperately, half hopping, half running after him. "Please, Jack, wait," I begged. I was rushing so quickly I plunged right into him when he stopped abruptly and turned around.

"Uhn."

He immediately pushed me away, as if suddenly my touch repulsed him. Tears instantly stung my eyes.

"Please, Jack," I pleaded, sure I was two seconds away from a total girly cryfest meltdown if he didn't at least look at me.

"What." He didn't phrase it as a question. And he didn't meet my eyes.

"Look, I am so, so sorry. You weren't supposed to walk in on that."

"Obviously."

"No, wait, I didn't mean it like that. I meant that I didn't expect you. You weren't supposed to be here. What are you doing here?"

"I was worried about you, Maddie. I made your mother tell me where you were. I thought you were in trouble." He spit the words out, his voice rough and devoid of all emotion. He looked past my head down the hallway. "Apparently you were getting along just fine."

"No, I'm not. I mean, I am, but it's not what it looks like."

"Oh, so you weren't kissing him?"

"Well, yes, but he kissed me this time!"

Ramirez raised one eyebrow, that vein in his neck pulsing like a Latin conga dancer. "*This* time?"

Oh. Shit.

I bit my lip. "Uh, yeah. I mean, last time was totally an accident. He turned his head."

Ramirez held up his hands. "You know what? I don't even want to hear it. It doesn't matter."

A lead weight dropped into my belly. "It doesn't?"

"No." And from the flat, dead tone in his voice I had a sinking feeling it really didn't. I had a feeling, as he turned and walked purposefully down the hall, his foot-steps echoing, that nothing I did was going to matter to Ramirez anymore. That I could beg, plead, promise six ways till Sunday that I hadn't meant to kiss Felix; that no matter how much I promised I had no idea how what had started out as interrogation had ended with his lips locked on mine, Ramirez wasn't going to forgive me. This was it. The end.

And all because of Felix.

I didn't go back in the room. I couldn't face Felix again. Instead I scooped my crutches up and prayed he didn't come after me as I quickly hobbled to the front door and out to my minicar, shoving Wonder Boot in through a thin veil of tears.

He didn't.

And as I put the car in gear and pulled away from Fe-lix's castle, I prayed I never saw him again. Ramirez was right: Felix brought nothing but trouble into my life. Kidnapping, gunshots, arrest—it was all Felix's fault. Hell, he had probably offed Gisella just to screw up my chance at being a designer.

And now he'd screwed up my chances with Ramirez too.

The tears fell in big, fat drops down my cheeks as I sped way too fast through the village and back to the M1. As if to match my mood, the fog thickened into menacing rain clouds, a downpour to match my own sobs hitting the tinny roof of the little car, drowning out my hiccuping and keeping me company all the way back to London.

By the time I returned the rental and hobbled back to the Queen's Cozy I was drenched, shivering, and didn't have a tear left in me. I staggered through the door, stripping off my wet clothes, and took a long, almost warm shower, after which I wrapped myself in a towel and collapsed onto the bed.

I stared at the picture of the queen.

"Your cousin's an asshole," I told her. She didn't respond. I took a deep breath, then grabbed my cell phone and dialed Ramirez's number.

It rang three times before going to voice mail. I swallowed a sharp lump in my throat at the sound of his voice prompting callers to leave a message.

"Hey. It's me," I said. "Look, I just wanted to let you know that I'm staying at the Queen's Cozy Inn in London. If I leave here I'll let you know where I'm going. No more sneaking around. No more secrets. Okay? And . . . I'm sorry, Jack," I whispered into the silence on the other end. "So very sorry."

I hung up. Because honestly there wasn't anything else to say. I'd apologized as much as I could. It was up to him now to either forgive me or . . . Well, I didn't even want to think about the *or*. The *or* made tears I didn't know I had left well up behind my eyes again.

Instead I flopped back down on the bed and stared at the water-stained ceiling.

My love life was seriously in the toilet, my career was virtually over, and I was one DNA test away from being locked up in a Paris prison. I was pretty sure my life could not get any worse.

At the moment there was nothing I could do about my love life, and unless a miracle occurred and Moreau gave back my shoes, the career thing was pretty dismal as well. But I could at least try to keep my butt out of jail.

I rolled over and grabbed a pad of hotel stationery and a pen from my purse.

As much as I absolutely loathed Felix right now, I had to admit that I still wasn't convinced he'd killed Gisella. Not really. Lying, yes. Cheating, yes. Printing vulgar pictures by the truckload, of course. But stabbing her with a stiletto seemed a stretch.

So if it wasn't me and it wasn't Felix, who did that leave?

I clicked my pen and wrote *Suspects* at the top of the page. Only I wasn't sure what to write next. Assuming Gisella was actually stealing jewelry from the shows, obviously her accomplice was my first choice for her killer. Maybe he or she had wanted a larger portion of the proceeds. Maybe they thought Gisella was getting sloppy and they'd be found out. Maybe they just plain didn't like her.

I wrote *Accomplice* down under *Suspects*. The only problem was, I had no idea who the accomplice was. So, I put a big question mark next to that one.

Okay, so who did I know that might have had a grudge against Gisella? Her agent? Suppose Donata was the accomplice. To be any kind of agent she had to have lots of contacts all over Europe. And she had booked

Gisella in the Jean Luc show in the first place. I was beginning to like this theory.

Of course, there was always the angry, jealous boyfriend theory, too. I wrote Ryan's name down next to Donata's. Unrequited love, jealousy—both classic reasons for wanting someone dead. And didn't they always say on *Law & Order* that it was usually the boyfriend?

And, while we were talking jealousy, how about Angelica? I added her name to the list. We only had her word for it that she hadn't gone in to see Gisella after Felix left. It would have been easy for Angelica to slip out of her room and lure Gisella to the tent unnoticed.

I paused, my pen hovering in midair. Why the tent? I wondered. What had Gisella been doing there so early? Was she meeting someone?

Then a terrible thought occurred to me. When I'd walked into the tent she hadn't been alone. Jean Luc had been there, too. I'd assumed at the time that Jean Luc had come in just before I had. But what if he'd been there all along? What if he'd been the one to stab Gisella? Why, I couldn't imagine, but he had both ample opportunity and means. I wondered just how well Jean Luc had known Gisella, and what kind of history lay between the two. He had mentioned how difficult she was to work with. Had he just meant this show, or were there others?

Reluctantly I wrote his name down, too. Then I stared at my list.

One thing was certain: It was time to go back to Paris.

The sun was setting by the time my plane landed again at Charles de Gaulle. I took a cab to the hotel and let myself into my room. A small part of me had hoped a pissed-off cop might be waiting for me there, but that was dashed quickly enough as I entered the dark, empty room. Ramirez's bags were gone. No note. No sign he'd even been there except for the lingering scent of his aftershave in the bathroom. I inhaled deeply, telling myself I was not going to cry again. Instead I pulled out my cell and, true to my word, left Ramirez another message telling him where I was. Then I slipped off my dress and changed into a pair of black capris and a black long-sleeved DKNY tee. I slipped on a silver ballet flat and added an extra layer of eyeliner to compensate for the slightly red, puffy look of my eyes. I took a blow-dryer to my hair, but even that didn't help the French braid–plus-rainwater look I had going on, so instead I pulled it back in a messy ponytail before grabbing my crutches and heading out to Le Carrousel du Louvre.

The first person I saw when I arrived back on the site was Dana. She was sitting with a group of the other models outside the tent, sipping Perrier through a straw.

"Mads!" She jumped up and dragged me to the side, just out of earshot. "What happened?" she asked, her voice low. "Did Felix do it? Did you confront him?"

I felt that lump form in my throat again, but quickly pushed it back down and filled Dana in. She was such a good friend that when I was finished I thought I saw tears in her eyes.

"Oh, Mads, I'm so sorry." She leaned in and gave me a long hug. "Don't worry. I'm sure Ramirez will come around. That man is nuts about you."

I wasn't so sure. But somehow it was comforting to pretend. "Yeah?"

Dana nodded. "Of course. Just give him a little time."

"Right. Thanks. I'm fine. Really." I sniffed back tears—*so* not convincing. "Is Jean Luc around?"

"He's in the workroom," she said. "He got in that case of plain black pumps. He's trying to convince himself they'll work for the show."

I cringed. I'd forgotten all about those. "How bad are they?"

"Bad. I tried to tell him you could work magic on any shoe, but . . . well . . . I'm pretty sure Jean Luc's about to slit his wrists."

"I'll go see what I can do."

I left her sipping her bubbly water and ducked inside. Jean Luc was, as Dana said, about one Xanax away from suicidal. He was pacing the room, a pump in each hand, shouting in French to poor Ann, who was furiously dialing up numbers on her BlackBerry. He stopped when he saw me, throwing his hands in the air.

"Maddie, thank God you're here. These are all we could get on short notice." He held up a pair of black pumps with pointy toes. "Hideous, aren't they?"

I bit my lip. "Um, well, I guess they're not *that* bad."

"Please tell me you can do something with them, darling. If not I may be forced to swan dive from the top of a very tall bridge."

"I can try," I hedged.

"We'll get you anything you need. Just please make these knockoffs into something that doesn't scream 'off the rack' when my girls wear them down the runway. I'll be the laughingstock of Fashion Week!"

I took one pump from him, turning it over in my

hands. Already ideas had started to brew about how to embellish it for Angelica's outfit in the finale. Granted, they were a far cry from what I'd originally planned, but they beat having the models go barefoot.

"Jean Luc, I was actually wondering if I could speak to you for a moment."

He put up one finger. *"Un moment."* He turned to Ann and barked out a quick stream of orders in French. Ann nodded, and I could mentally see her ticking items off a checklist before she scurried off to fulfill Jean Luc's every demand.

Once she was gone he turned to me again. "Not only do we have to find shoes, but now Becca is scared to go on, worried someone will commit random violence on her, too. Models," he said, shaking his head.

I hesitated, wondering if I should share just how unrandom I suspected Gisella's death was. "You know, it's possible that Gisella wasn't just an innocent victim. We think she may have had something to do with the necklace going missing," I said slowly, watching Jean Luc's reaction.

He nodded. *"Oui.* She was much too careless."

"I meant she may have had something to do with it that goes beyond carelessness."

"Oh?" He raised an eyebrow. "But I thought the police found the necklace in one of her coat pockets?"

"Yes," I conceded, "but I'm not sure it was put there by mistake."

Jean Luc blanched, pulling out a fresh roll of antacids. "Please don't tell me I hired a thief."

"How well did you know Gisella?"

Jean Luc shrugged. "How well does anyone know anybody these days? We worked together. I certainly didn't socialize with the girl."

"Had you worked with her before?"

"Once. Gisella has been on the circuit for quite a while now. I had always heard nasty things about her temperament, but once Donata took her on last year she started hitting some of the bigger campaigns and making a name for herself. Honestly, I would have been a fool not to jump when I had the chance to book her. She was in Cannes when I was doing a photo shoot, so Donata asked if I'd like to have her for the day."

"Out of curiosity, anything go missing from the site that time?"

His forehead wrinkled like a shar-pei's as he tried to think. "Not that I remember. But then again it was a swimsuit shoot. Not a lot of accessories involved."

I nodded. "You said she didn't start booking real jobs until she started with Donata. What do you know about her?"

"Donata? She's very well respected. I think she used to be a model herself, but I don't know the details. Of course, that was aeons ago," he said, rolling his eyes. "But she's done well as an agent. She has a good stock of girls. I've used a few. I believe Angelica's with her, as well."

"Really?" Small world. And something Angelica had failed to mention when she'd said Gisella was burning up her cell minutes hounding her agent for a cover. If Donata was sending Gisella out to jobs instead of Angelica, I saw another mark in the motive column for Angelica to want Gisella out of the way.

"Do you have any idea what Gisella was doing out at the tent that morning?" I asked.

Jean Luc shook his head slowly. "Gisella was never early. Not a morning person, as they say. I have no idea."

"So, you didn't call her in?"

"Who, me? No, I know better than to wake her before noon. Besides, Ann usually sets the models' schedules. She takes care of those kinds of details."

I made a mental note to ask Ann about Gisella's schedule that morning.

"When did you leave the night before?"

"Late. It was past midnight."

Considering that Jean Luc was in essence my employer, I worded my next question carefully. "And when, exactly, did you arrive on site the next morning?"

Jena Luc's eyebrows headed toward his hairline. "Why, just before you did, of course."

I nodded. "Of course."

"And before you ask, yes, I was alone." He gave a wry smile. "I suppose I don't have an alibi either."

"Join the club."

"But Ann can tell you that I was with her until almost two that night. We were going over the lineup and couldn't agree on where to put Bella's third outfit. It seemed to clash with everything but was just too stunning on her to leave out."

"I guess you didn't sleep much that night."

"Of course not," Jean Luc responded, popping an antacid into his mouth. "It's Fashion Week."

Of course.

"Speaking of which . . ." He trailed off, pointing to the pump still in my hand. "We have fifteen of those. If anyone can work this miracle, I know it's you, Maddie."

God, I hoped so. But before I could respond, a seamstress pinning an empire-waisted baby-doll dress near the door caught Jean Luc's attention, and he was off with a, "No, no, no, dahling, it's a *loose* drape."

I stared down at the pump in my hands. Well, at least someone had faith in me.

Chapter Twelve

I spent the rest of the evening doing what I could to turn plain black pumps into designer-worthy creations. Little embellishments here and there helped, but the more I looked at them, the more they looked like plain black pumps that someone had tried to embellish. It was depressing that these were what would go down the runway with my name attached to them.

By the time I finally finished the last one I was beat. Dana and I shared a cab back to the Plaza, where I hobbled up to my room and promptly collapsed, fully clothed, onto the bed, spilling half a dozen pillows onto the floor in the process.

Only, tired as I was, as I closed my eyes I couldn't sleep. Part of me kept listening for my phone to ring, silently willing Ramirez to call. Wondering what I'd say when he did. That is, *if* he ever did.

I had almost convinced myself to pick up the phone and dial his number, pleading for the zillionth time for forgiveness, when the door to my room flew open.

"Maddie, I'm so glad you're back," Mom cried, plopping down on the bed beside me. "We need your advice."

I groaned into my pillow as I felt Mrs. Rosenblatt sit on the other side of the bed, her weight causing me to roll toward her. "I'm kind of tired, Mom. It's been a long day."

"I got me a hot date with Pierre tonight," Mrs. R said, completely ignoring me, "and I can't decide what to wear."

I peeked my head up. Then I let out an involuntary, "Eek!" as I took in Mrs. Rosenblatt's outfit.

She was dressed in a muumuu, of course, this time in shocking green with pink hibiscus flowers printed haphazardly across the front. Her Lucille Ball red hair was piled on top of her head in a frizzy lump that looked like bluebirds should be nesting in it, and a pair of pink-and-green plastic palm-tree earrings hung from her ears. She'd followed Mom's more-is-always-better philosophy of eye-shadow application, drawing a thick green line from her eyelashes all the way up to her eyebrows, and, if I wasn't mistaken, a fake little mole made of black eyeliner pencil sat on her upper lip. All in all she made an excellent drag queen.

"I like the green dress," Mom continued, pointing to Mrs. R's current outfit, "but she's afraid it's a little too subtle."

I raised an eyebrow. Compared to what? A neon sign? "Where's he taking you?" I asked instead, propping myself up on my elbows.

"Some fancy-schmancy place on the Champs-Élysées. He says they got the best authentic French cuisine in Paris. Though I told him there's no way I'm eating a snail. I got them suckers in my garden back home. They are *not* food."

I had to agree with that one.

"So can you help?" Mom asked.

I looked down at Mrs. R's outfit again, suddenly wishing I had a pair of sunglasses handy. "How much time have you got?"

"I'm meeting him at nine."

I looked at the digital clock by my bedside: eight forty.

"Then we'd better get moving."

I followed Mom and Mrs. Rosenblatt through the adjoining door back to their room, filling them both in on my latest discoveries about Felix as I instructed Mrs. R to go wash off the makeup (over my mother's protests).

"Oh, we have news, too!" Mom said, sitting up straight on the bed as I rummaged in the closet for something a little less "subtle" to wear. Unfortunately this was Mrs. Rosenblatt we were talking about, and it was slim pickings.

"You'll never guess what Pierre told us last night. Apparently after they found Felix and the necklace in Gisella's room, the police searched the place from top to bottom. They found three other pieces of jewelry stuffed into pockets."

"Seriously?"

"Seriously."

The theory of Gisella the jewel thief was becoming more plausible. "You had said that four designers besides Jean Luc reported missing pieces. Did they find the other missing piece?"

Mom shrugged. "Not as far as Pierre knew."

Mrs. R piped up from the bathroom. "I'll bet she passed it along to her fence already. It's probably circulating the black market right now."

While Mrs. Rosenblatt tended toward overly dramatic language, I couldn't help thinking she might be right. This time.

"If so, that means her partner has to be someone in Paris. Gisella wouldn't have had time to fly them somewhere else without Jean Luc noticing she was gone," I said, flipping through muumuu after muumuu.

"Which brings us back to her accomplice being someone she knew here," Mom said, even as I started mentally going down my suspect list. I had to admit her agent still seemed the most likely candidate.

"How about this one?" I held up a red-and-orange-printed muumuu that could almost pass for tropical chic as Mrs. Rosenblatt came out of the bathroom, her cheeks a freshly scrubbed pink.

She made a face. "You sure that's better than the green one?"

I nodded. "I've never been so sure of anything in my life."

I paired the dress with a red leather belt that gave Mrs. R's Pillsbury Doughboy figure some semblance of a waist, and a red cardigan borrowed from Mom's side of the closet. Granted, Mrs. R had about a hundred pounds and several inches on Mom, so the sweater didn't exactly close in front, but it was stretchy enough that she could fit her arms into it, and it broke up the floral some. After I'd traded in Mrs. R's palm trees for a pair of tasteful ruby drops from my own wardrobe and applied a thin swipe of dusty beige shadow over her eyes (just to the browbone), she looked pretty darn good, even if I did say so myself. Except for the Birkenstocks on her feet. There wasn't much I could do about those. Luckily, as long as she didn't lift up her skirt and bust out with the cancan, the muumuu was almost long enough to cover them up.

"Well, what do we think?" she asked, twirling in front of the full-length closet mirror.

Mom clapped her hands, giving her sign of approval. "It's lovely. Maddie, you are a lifesaver."

Mrs. Rosenblatt smiled. "If this doesn't get me laid tonight, I don't know what will."

I cringed. Big-time TMI.

I left Mom and Mrs. R putting the finishing touches on her hair—she was so on her own there—and dragged my tired self back to my room, where I stripped off my clothes, threw on my ducky jammies, and crawled into bed. Visions of jewel thieves, murderers, and, unfortunately, postmenopausal women in muumuus getting lucky all sloshed together in my brain as I fell into a restless sleep.

Somewhere around midnight I awoke from a dream of Ramirez's granite features invading my sleep. At two A.M. it was Felix's lips that jostled me awake. Three thirty had pink-and-green palm tress dancing through my subconscious. And by the time I dreamed of myself on my knees, pleading with Ramirez not to walk away from me again, I woke up to find it was five fifteen, and I didn't have the energy to dream anymore.

Instead I reluctantly dragged myself out of bed and into a long, hot shower. I did a blow-dry-and-hair-spray thing, adding an extra layer of mascara afterward in hopes of disguising the sleepless night bagging under my eyes. I swiped some Raspberry Perfection along my lips and threw on a pair of jeans, a stretchy black knit top, and a low black wedge-heeled sandal. A wedge didn't really count as a heel, right? It was more of a platform.

I ordered a pot of coffee and a brioche from room service and made myself wait until eight thirty before hopping into a cab and making my way the few blocks to the Hôtel de Crillon, where I promptly took the elevator to the fourth floor and knocked on Donata's door. I paused, listening for any sign of movement from the other side. None. I waited a beat, then knocked again. Still nothing.

I looked down the hall and spied a maid's cart three doors down. I hobbled over to the open door of the room, where a young, dark-haired woman in a pink starched uniform stretched to its limit over her ample derrière was making the bed. I cleared my throat and knocked on the door frame to get her attention.

"Excuse me," I called.

She looked up and said something in French.

"I'm sorry, I don't speak French," I said, doing an apologetic, palms-up thing.

The woman nodded, then smiled and responded in heavily accented English, "I say there are extra soaps on the cart. Take all you like."

"Oh, thanks. But actually I was wondering if I could ask you a question about room 405."

She scrunched up her nose, shaking out a pillowcase. "I suppose."

"Have you cleaned that room yet this morning?" I asked, wondering if maybe Donata was an early riser.

She shook her head. "I did not need to. No one had slept in it last night."

"Why not?"

She shrugged. "I believe the woman checked out."

I mentally banged my head against the wall. "Checked out? Do you know when?"

"Yesterday sometime."

"I don't suppose you happen to know where she went?"

She shook her head, grabbing a clean set of sheets from her cart. "No. Sorry."

Rats.

I thanked the maid, ducking back out into the hallway.

Okay, time to try plan B.

I pulled my cell out of my purse and dialed the Plaza's main number as I rode the elevator back down to the lobby. I asked for Angelica's room, and, after a moment, the woman at the switchboard put me through and I heard the number ringing. Four rings into it, Angelica's sleepy voice answered.

"Bonjour?"

"Hi, Angelica, it's Maddie."

There was a pause on the other end, as if the name didn't register this early in the morning. "Maddie?"

"The shoe designer for Jean Luc's show."

"Oh. Right. The killer."

I rolled my eyes. "Listen, I was wondering if you knew where Donata went. She checked out of her hotel room yesterday."

I heard Angelica yawn on the other end. "She flew back to Milan. She said she had some urgent business to take care of and that she'd be back in time for the show. Why?"

"I just wanted to ask her something about Gisella," I hedged. "Speaking of which, why didn't you tell me that you and Gisella shared an agent?"

She was quiet for a moment. "Look, I know it looks like I was jealous of Gisella," she said. "But I wasn't. I mean, yeah, we were always competing, but I didn't mind. It kept me on my toes, you know?" she said, throwing another Americanism out.

"It never became a problem? Donata sending Gisella out to jobs instead of you?" I asked, crossing the lobby and stepping outside.

Again she paused, as if choosing her words carefully. And I wondered if there wasn't more than a translation issue going on there. "It pissed me off a little, yeah. Last month I wanted to do a shoot for Corbett Winston, but Donata wouldn't even set up a go-see. She said it was Gisella's project."

Corbett Winston. The jeweler. I perked up. "Did she say why?"

I could hear Angelica's shrug in her voice. "No. Just that she knew Gisella was perfect for that job. Though I guess it turned out to be a good thing I didn't get it in the end."

"Why is that?"

"Well, right after the shoot someone broke in and stole the diamond necklace Gisella was modeling. Winston didn't want the theft publicized, so the ad campaign never ran. A lot of work for nothing, if you ask me."

Alarm bells were going off in my head left and right. "Was Gisella upset?"

"Actually, she didn't really seem to care. She said she got paid the same either way."

I'll bet. A diamond necklace was a handsome payoff for a few hours' work in front of a camera.

"Thanks, Angelica," I said.

She yawned again. "No problem," she replied, then hung up.

I flipped my phone shut and hailed a cab, directing him back to the Plaza Athénée as I digested this bit of information, a clearer picture of Gisella's role in all this forming. Suppose Gisella had taken the job at Winston just to get the lay of the land, so to speak. Then she'd gone in afterward to steal the necklace. Or perhaps the partner had? Either way, like the designers showing at Fashion Week, Gisella must have known Winston wouldn't want the media attention of publicly announcing the theft. Instead they probably filed a very quiet claim with their insurance company and swept the whole thing under the rug. Meanwhile Gisella and her partner would sell the necklace and pocket the profits.

I had to admit it was looking more and more likely that Donata had something to do with it. That fact that she refused to send Angelica out on the job seemed proof enough. Either Donata was being bribed by Gisella and company to target specific jobs for Gisella, or she was the mastermind behind the whole thing, orchestrating Gisella's movements like a puppeteer.

Suddenly I wondered what kind of "urgent business" had called Donata away.

I flipped my cell back open as the cab dropped me off in front of the Plaza and hit number one on my speed dial. Before I was even through the lobby Dana picked up.

"Hello?"

"Hey, it's me. Listen, what's on your schedule for today?"

"I'm being fitted for a second outfit. But after that I'm pretty much free. Why?"

"How do you feel about Milan?"

While Dana went to her fitting, I prayed my Visa hadn't hit its limit as I booked us two seats on a flight to Milan for that afternoon, then went to the hotel business center to research everything I could about the Corbett Winston theft online. Which wasn't much. As Angelica had said, they hadn't wanted to publicize the theft, so only a few small articles had run in the local papers, buried in the back of the style section. According to the reports the theft had occurred about six weeks ago. A thirty-carat diamond-and-sapphire necklace had been taken from their showroom. Generally the necklace was kept in the back vault, but since it had been out for a photo shoot the day before it was temporarily being housed in the less secure glass case at their main showroom. No mention of Gisella, though the article had said the value of the stolen necklace was an estimated 220,000 euros, roughly the equivalent of 300,000 American dollars. I gave a low whistle. I was so in the wrong business. I wondered if it was too late to learn jewelry design.

I printed out everything I'd learned and quickly went upstairs. I stopped in briefly at Mom and Mrs. R's room, but no one was in. Instead I left the printouts on Mom's bed with a little note: *Gisella strikes again?* Then I went next door to pack an overnight bag (I learned my lesson with the inside-out panties the first night) before picking up Dana.

As I was throwing my hair dryer into the bag (lesson number two—travel with your own appliances to foreign countries) my cell rang, displaying an unfamiliar number. My heart did a little leap, and I prayed it was Ramirez.

"Hello?" I asked, suddenly breathless.

"Maddie, it's Felix."

"Oh." I felt my entire body slump with disappointment.

"Well, don't sound so thrilled."

"Sorry, I was expecting . . . someone else."

"He still hasn't called, huh?"

I narrowed my eyes at the phone. "How do you even know who I was expecting?"

He sighed. "Maddie, I saw the look on his face. And believe me, if I'd been your boyfriend and walked in on that scene, I'm not sure I would have called either."

"Gee, thanks. I feel much better now."

"Where are you?"

"In my room. Packing. I'm going to Milan to see Gisella's agent. As if it's any of your business," I couldn't help adding.

"You're still upset about yesterday."

"What tipped you off?"

Again with the sigh. "Look, that's actually why I called. I wanted to apologize."

I raised an eyebrow at the phone. Felix apologizing? Unheard-of.

"Go on," I prompted.

"I was out of line yesterday. I certainly didn't mean to bust things up between you and . . . him."

Wow. That had actually sounded sincere. "Thanks," I said, so shocked that I didn't even have a snide comeback ready for him.

"But I hope you'll forgive me for saying that you could do a lot better."

And then he had to go and ruin it.

"Excuse me?"

"He's a bit on the caveman side, isn't he, love? I mean the whole protect-the-little-woman thing."

I put one hand on my hip. "He cares. There's nothing wrong with that."

"Yes. So much so that you have to sneak off while he threatens to lock you up. Are you his girlfriend or his ward?"

"He happens to worry about me," I said, my volume rising. Maybe I wouldn't have been so defensive if a tiny part of me didn't almost agree with Felix. "That's what people who love each other do. They protect each other."

"But does he trust you? Isn't that a part of loving someone?"

I opened my mouth to speak but realized I didn't have a response for that. Dammit, why did Felix have to start making sense now?

"Look, my love life has nothing to do with you," I shot back instead.

He was quiet a moment. Then in a low, almost sad voice he said, "No. No, I suppose it doesn't."

"And for your information, Ramirez happens to be *just* my type. I happen to like the caveman thing, okay?"

"If you say so."

"Yes, I say so!" I yelled into the phone.

He was quiet, the only sound the panting of my own worked-up breath.

"Are you done apologizing?" I shouted.

I thought I heard Felix give a little chuckle on the other end. "I think that about sums up my apology, yes."

"Good. I have to go." I hit the off button, not waiting for Felix's response, and threw my phone on the bed.

I hated to admit just how much the call had gotten to me. What I'd said was true—I knew Ramirez cared about me, worried about me. And most of the time, when he wasn't infuriating the heck out of me, I appreciated it. Who didn't want someone to care about them?

But Felix was right. Ramirez didn't trust me. He never had. Ever since we'd met I'd always been the cute, slightly ditzy blonde who needed his protection. As much as I'd tried to convince him otherwise in the time we'd known each other, I had a bad feeling that was how he still saw me. Granted, I did have an uncanny ability to shove my heel-clad foot firmly into my mouth, and I'll admit I did seem to be a magnet for trouble at times. So, I could see why he didn't always have *complete* faith in my abilities.

But a little trust might be nice now and then.

Only, as I stared at my phone sitting silently on the floral duvet, I realized that I didn't trust him either. He'd asked me to trust in the legal system, to trust Moreau, to trust that, with Ramirez here, I wouldn't end up in jail. And what had I done? Gone off to London on a wild-goose chase that had ended in me lip-locked with Felix, of all people.

No wonder he wasn't calling.

As if on cue my cell chirped to life.

I dove for it, hitting the on button without even looking at the readout.

"Jack?" I asked, my heart leaping into my throat.

"He still hasn't called, huh?" Dana's voice answered.

I gulped down my disappointment. "No."

"Sorry, hon. But give him a little time. I'm sure he will."

If only I were as sure.

"Anyway, I just wanted to let you know I'm through with my fitting and on my way to the hotel. Give me ten minutes to pack a bag and I'm ready to go."

I nodded at the phone. "Okay, meet you in the lobby in twenty."

I hung up, flopping back onto the bed. I looked at the silent phone in my hands. I closed my eyes and willed it to ring. *Come on, Jack. Please, please, please* . . .

I opened them. Nothing. Still silent.

I took a deep breath and scrolled through the numbers in my address book until Ramirez's showed on the screen. I stared at the entry so hard that the numbers started swimming in front of my vision.

My finger hovered over the call button.

I hit it, holding my breath as it rang on the other end. Once, twice, then to voice mail. My heart bottomed out. He wasn't calling, and he still wasn't taking my calls.

"Hey, it's me again. I just wanted to let you know I'm going to Milan," I told his voice mail. "And I . . . I'm still sorry."

I hung up, then flipped my phone shut and stared at the dark LCD screen.

Dana was right. He just needed some time. He'd call back. Eventually.

I hoped.

Chapter Thirteen

Those who know me well, know that I am a bit of a celebrity junkie. I never miss watching the Emmys, Oscars, or SAG Awards, and I'd have to say that my all-time favorite awards-show moment was when Roberto Benigni won the Oscar for his film *Life Is Beautiful*. In true expressive Italian fashion, he jumped up and down, kissing everyone in sight, running down the aisles like a little kid at Christmas. You couldn't help but laugh, cry, and feel your heart beat a little faster right along with him.

Milan was a city full of Benignis. As soon as our plane landed Dana and I trudged our way through the airport amidst boisterous Italians hugging, laughing, and gesturing with their arms in an aerobic fashion. And kissing. Kissing seemed to be the national sport of Italy. Everywhere we went were men kissing each other on both cheeks, women kissing everyone on both cheeks, and children being kissed in all directions by everyone. In Italy everyone kissed.

By the time we hailed a cab at the airport, I was seriously contemplating a disinfectant wipe for my cheeks, though I couldn't help the grin that had spread across my face. The Benigni-esque atmosphere was infectious.

"I like it here," Dana said, waving to a friendly group of soccer players waiting at the curb. I was pretty sure at least one of them had slipped her his number.

"Do you know where this address is?" I asked our driver, handing him the printout Mom and Mrs. R had found for the Girardi Agency.

"*Sì, sì,*" he said, nodding his head. "I take you pretty signoras there." He gave Dana a wink in the rearview mirror. Dana giggled.

"Heard from Ricky lately?" I asked, nudging her in the ribs.

Immediately the smile left her face. "Oh yeah. The cheating bastard."

"Uh-oh. Trouble in Croatia?"

"I guess you haven't seen the latest edition of the *Informer*?"

I shook my head. Considering there was a 90 percent chance of seeing my own picture splayed across their pages, I was trying to stay clear. "What did they say this time?"

"There was a picture, Maddie. Of Ricky and Natalie Portman on a beach. She was in a bikini and he was rubbing sunscreen all over her back. Her *bare* back."

"So he's concerned about skin cancer?"

"So he's definitely doing her."

"You don't know that. For all you know they pasted Ricky's and Natalie's faces on Brad's and Angelina's bodies. They do that, you know."

Dana made a disbelieving *hmph* sound.

"Have you asked him about it?"

She nodded. "He's still denying it. He told me they're 'just friends,'" she said, doing air quotes with her fingers.

"So, maybe they are."

"Yeah, right."

"Look, maybe he has a perfectly good explanation for it all. Maybe he didn't *mean* to rub sunscreen on her; maybe he was tricked, coerced. Maybe it was just a moment of weakness. Maybe he's really, really sorry and really, really wishes you'd just call and forgive him."

Dana gave me a look. "Um, we're not still talking about Ricky, are we?" she asked.

I bit my lip. "No."

She patted my arm. "Don't worry. He'll call."

While I appreciated the sentiment, I was beginning to believe that less and less.

The ride from the airport to the Girardi Agency was, fortunately, a short one. Even with the packed city streets we pulled up in front of the tall, modern, glass building in less than twenty minutes. It was in a densely urban part of the city that, unless you looked closely, could have resembled any part of L.A.: tall office buildings, parking garages, small coffee shops tucked on every corner, and men and women wearing everything from business attire to Bohemian peasant skirts and backpacks rushing to and fro on the sidewalks.

Dana and I paid the driver, then got out and entered the lobby of the cool air-conditioned building. After consulting the directory, we hopped in the elevator and rode to the twenty-first floor, where the agency's offices were housed.

The frosted-glass doors simply read, GIRARDI, in black letters. The reception area beyond was a cool, sophisticated example of modern Italian design. Bright bold area rugs covered the floors; low chairs and tables in sleek chrome and colorful upholstery lined the waiting area. On the tables were a range of fashion magazines, most, I would assume, featuring the agency's clientele. The walls were a soft cream color, punctuated with abstract art in a variety of bold geometric shapes, and the kidney-shaped desk in the center featured a range of sleek, streamlined computers and other office machines I'd be afraid to touch for fear of pushing the wrong button.

Behind the desk sat an Asian woman, a headset glued to one ear, her fingers clacking noisily over a keyboard.

"Excuse me, we're here to see—" I started, but she didn't let me finish, giving the universal one-finger wait signal as we approached.

"*Sì,*" she said into the headset, her Italian tinged with a Brooklyn accent as she rattled off a string of phrases. Finally one came through that I understood. *"No, dispiace, no commento."* Then she clicked off.

"I'm sorry," she said, addressing us. "The press has been calling nonstop lately. I'm about to pull the phone out of the wall."

Been there. Done that.

"Anyway, how can I help you?" she asked, breaking into a pleasant smile.

"We're here to see Miss Girardi," I informed her.

A little frown settled between her brows. "Oh. Do you have an appointment?"

"Uh, not exactly," I hedged.

"I'm sorry, Miss Girardi isn't in. She went home early today. She said she had some personal business to take care of. Maybe I can help? I'm her assistant, Debbie. What is this regarding?"

I bit my lip. *Regarding the fact that your employer might be part of a ring of jewel thieves*, didn't seem like a kosher message to leave with the friendly assistant. I was still trying to come up with an alternative when Dana piped up beside me.

"I'm seeking representation," she said, flipping her hair over one shoulder.

"Oh?" Debbie asked. "Are you a model?"

Dana nodded. "Yes, I'll be walking in the Le Croix show later this week in Paris."

"Yes, we have a couple of models doing that show." Again her features creased into a frown. "Or we did, anyway."

"I heard about Gisella," I said, leaping in. "I'm so sorry."

"Thanks." She gave a tight smile. "But I honestly didn't really know her. I just started working here a couple of weeks ago. The last girl apparently left quite suddenly."

"Oh?" I asked, raising an eyebrow. "Any idea why?"

She shrugged. "I'm not really sure. One of the interns told me that Donata caught her last assistant in her private office one day and fired her on the spot. Tough break for her, but really lucky for me. I'd just moved from New York, where I was studying fashion design, so the timing was perfect. I've made tons of great contacts already."

The phone rang and she let out an exasperated sigh. "Except for the press. If you'll excuse me a minute?"

I nodded as she hit a button on her computer and began talking into the headset again.

Honestly, my mind was still rolling over the fired-assistant thing. Had the former receptionist stumbled onto something she wasn't supposed to? Was there evidence of a crime in Donata's office? Maybe that was where she'd hidden the jewels. I looked beyond the kidney-shaped desk toward the long expanse of hallway on either side, itching to take a look. Mom and Mrs. Rosenblatt had said that only three of the missing pieces from Fashion Week had been recovered. Maybe that was the "business" Donata had come to Milan to take care of. Maybe she was whisking the fourth away to Milan before Moreau and his crew could get their hands on it.

"No, we're not inclined to comment at this time. I'm sorry," Debbie said into the headset. She rolled her eyes as she hung up. "Sorry, where were we?"

"I was wondering when Miss Girardi would be in," Dana reminded her.

"Right. Well, I'm not sure she's expected back today," Debbie said, checking her watch, "but if you have a contact sheet with you I'd be happy to hand it to her."

Dana bit her lip. "Oh, this was kind of impromptu. We were just in the neighborhood, see? I don't really have anything with me."

"Here," Debbie said, pushing a piece of paper at Dana. "Why don't you leave your contact info and I'll let Miss Girardi know that you stopped by. If you're doing the Le Croix show I'm sure she'd be interested in meeting you."

As Dana took the paper I looked down the hallway again toward Donata's private office. I bit my lip, feeling my chance to snoop—I mean, *investigate*—quickly slipping away. I glanced at Debbie, now fielding another call from a Felix clone. I leaned in close to Dana.

"Cover me, Farrah," I whispered.

Dana immediately got that Angels shine in her eyes and nodded.

"Excuse me," I said as Debbie repeated her no-comment spiel into the phone, "but is there a restroom back there?" I asked, indicating the hallway.

"Oh, sure, first door on your left."

I shot her a big smile. "Thanks."

Dana gave me a sly wink as I hobbled down the hallway. I mentally crossed my fingers that Farrah didn't get too carried away.

Instead of turning left, I did a quick glance over my shoulder before swiftly turning to the right and hobbling as stealthily as I could past the restroom and to a door marked, DONATA GIRARDI. I paused outside, listening for any sign of life beyond, before turning the knob and quickly stepping inside.

I shut the door behind me with a little click, my heart hammering as I calculated that I had, at most, a five-minute window before Debbie would start getting suspicious. My gaze whipped around the room for a place to start.

Like the reception area, Donata's office held a tasteful mix of contemporary furnishings—a long desk in light wood with chrome accents; flat-paneled file cabinets; a sleek sofa in a bold print next to a low glass coffee table; a big white clock on the far wall; and two tall, slim bookshelves filled with binders and photographs.

I dismissed the bookshelves right away, instead heading for the file cabinets. I tried the top one. Locked. Well, what did I expect? If I were hiding stolen diamonds in my office, I'd keep them locked too.

I quickly turned to the desk, opening drawers and scanning the contents for anything that looked like a key. I came across three—one marked with the word *provviste*, the other two smaller and slimmer. I took the small ones to the file cabinet and tried the first one. No luck. It fit in the keyhole but didn't turn. I glanced at the clock. Three minutes had gone by. Starting to get that antsy feeling in the pit of my stomach, I slipped the second key in. Again it fit but didn't turn. *Damn.* Where was Felix's lock-picking kit when I needed it? Just for good measure I tried the *provviste* key, but it wouldn't even go in the hole.

I frantically searched around the room for another place to hide a key. If it was in Donata's purse I was sunk.

My eyes roved the shelves. Framed head shots, books, binders, bits of camera equipment. Finally my eyes landed on a camera case next to a shot of Gisella in a skimpy bathing suit on a no-doubt-exotic beach location. Out of sheer desperation I opened it. Inside was an old Nikon camera, a roll of thirty-five-millimeter film—and a key. I stared at the little sliver thing, wondering if maybe my karma was turning around.

I didn't waste time. With one quick glance at the clock (one minute left) I fit the key into the lock and turned it with a little click. My hands were shaking as I opened the top drawer.

If I'd been expecting to find a cache of jewels in a box marked, STOLEN, I was sorely disappointed. The only things in the drawer were files. I felt my heart sink, though I figured that since I was here I might as well be thorough.

There were several files marked with the names of models, all of which contained pictures, but nothing that seemed out of the ordinary. A few of the files held hand-written notes in Italian that could have been anything from details of their last go-see to Donata's grocery list, for all I could tell. I made a mental note that if I was going to do any more foreign snooping—*investigating*—I was going to have to bring a translator with me.

I glanced up. I'd been there seven minutes. I didn't know how much longer Dana could keep Debbie occupied.

I was just about to give up when I saw a file that appeared to be unmarked. With one more backward glance at the office door, still shut (for now), I pulled the file out and thumbed though.

It contained only pictures. They were all eight-by-ten shots of the same young male model. From the styles he was wearing I'd say they were taken sometime in the seventies. One picture showed the man strutting down a runway; another was of him emerging from the surf in designer swimwear. I paused on one that looked like a candid, a full-face shot that appeared to be minus any airbrush touches. Something about him seemed familiar. I cocked my head to the side, taking in his wide hazel eyes, thick dark hair, thick dark eyebrows.

And then I saw it. I squinted down at the photograph and there, tiny as could be, was a heart-shaped birthmark just at his hairline.

I was looking at Donata.

I felt my breath catch in my throat, time standing still for a full two seconds as I flipped the picture over. Scrawled in neat handwriting on the back was a name: Donatello Gardini. It was too close to be a coincidence.

Checking the clock, I quickly shoved the picture back in the file, relocked it in the file drawer, and shoved the key back in the camera case, my hands shaking. I paused only briefly at the door to make sure no one was lurking on the other side before slipping back out of the office and down the hallway, my mind reeling.——

Everyone had speculated that Donata was a former model, but no one seemed to know the details of her past career. Could that be because Donata was a *male* model? I thought about the amount of obvious plastic surgery she'd gone through. At the time I'd assumed it was because the years had been unkind to her. Now I realized it was a different kind of surgery altogether.

I was sure my breath was still coming out in quick, telltale pants as I entered the lobby, but Debbie didn't seem to notice, deep in conversation with Dana about the merits of New York sushi bars versus L.A. ones.

"Ready?" I asked, hoping my voice didn't betray the erratic thumping of my heart against my rib cage.

Dana nodded. "Yep. Thanks, Debbie."

"No problem," she called after us. "I hope to see you again." She flashed us a big smile before her headset rang, and she fielded another hopeful call from the paparazzi.

I waited until we'd cleared reception and were in the elevator before blurting out my finding to Dana.

"No freakin' way!" she shrieked.

"Way!" I assured her.

"But if she was trying to hide her past, why keep the photos around all these years?" Dana asked.

I thought about the unmarked file. The photos hadn't looked aged at all. In fact, they looked like they'd been freshly printed. "Maybe she didn't. Maybe someone else sent them to her."

"Who would do that?"

"How about this," I said as the elevator doors slid open and we crossed the air-conditioned lobby again. "What if someone found out about her past and sent her those pictures?"

"Like, blackmail?"

I nodded. "Maybe that was how Gisella was getting all the right jobs. Maybe someone was blackmailing Donata."

Dana nodded. "I like it."

I grinned. So did I.

"But there's only one problem," she said.

"What?"

"Proving it to Moreau."

I frowned. "I think it's time we had a little chat with Donata."

As Dana hailed us a cab I pulled out my cell, dialing Ann's number. I had a feeling everyone who was anyone had their addresses stored in her BlackBerry. I hoped that Donata's was among them.

"Yes?" Ann answered in a clipped tone.

"Hi, Ann. It's Maddie."

"Yes?" she repeated. Obviously she had no time for pleasantries. I could hear Jean Luc in the background shouting something and could almost picture the pinched look on poor Ann's face.

"I was wondering if you have Donata Girardi's home address."

There was a pause. "Why?"

Good question. I bit my lip, willing my overtaxed brain to think fast. "I feel terrible about what happened to Gisella. I wanted to send her agent a sympathy card." I cringed. That excuse sounded thinner than Kate Moss even to my own ears.

Luckily Ann had about fifteen million other things on her mind and didn't question me. "Hold on," she said instead, and I could hear her shuffling her phone around. "Okay, here it is." She quickly read off the street to me as I motioned to Dana for a pen. She produced one from her purse, and I wrote the address on my palm.

"Thanks, Ann!"

"Sure. Oh, and don't forget, Jean Luc wants you here tomorrow for the final fitting."

The final fitting. My stomach clenched as I realized the show was less than forty-eight hours away. If I couldn't convince Moreau of my innocence by then, I could kiss my chances of a big Fashion Week debut good-bye.

I tried not to dwell on that, instead pushing it to the back of my mind as I assured Ann I'd be there and hung up.

Considering it was closing in on rush hour in Milan, it took us a few minutes to catch the attention of a cab (which was finally achieved only through the very kind assistance of a man in a pin-striped business suit who gave Dana no less than three kisses on each cheek before seeing us off). Once in, I repeated the address that Ann had given me to the driver, who nodded and said he knew that area of town well.

We slowly inched along the busy streets as I watched the sun sinking lower over the gorgeous old buildings. By the time we finally pulled up to Donata's apartment, the sky was a dusty pink and orange, perfect for a picture postcard of Milan. I paused on the sidewalk a moment taking it in, realizing I'd been to three European countries in as many days and had failed to take one photograph. Granted, I wasn't exactly on a typical tourist vacation, but I made a mental note to buy a disposable camera next time I was in an airport. As sordid as our reason for being here was, the beauty of the city was inescapable.

And Donata's building was no exception. Unlike her office, it was the picture of classic Italian architecture: a tall, narrow structure rimmed in detailed moldings from centuries past, set back from the street by an ornate iron fence. As our cab pulled away from the curb, we climbed the stone steps to an intricately carved wood door and knocked.

Only no one answered. Instead the door swung open all on its own.

Dana and I looked at each other. We'd both watched enough horror movies to know that when a door swung open on its own, it was never a good idea for the blonde to go inside unarmed.

"Hello?" I called instead, my eyes scanning the foyer for any sign of life. Marble floor, antique sideboard, a tall, curving staircase to one side. No sign of Donata.

"Maybe she's upstairs," Dana whispered.

"Maybe she's not here."

"Maybe we should come back another time."

And had Ann not just reminded me of the ticking clock on my career's life span, I might have agreed with her. As it was, I ignored all the warning signs and stepped into the foyer, the sound of my crutches echoing on the marble floor. "Miss Girardi?" I called. "Donata?"

"Maddie," Dana said, grabbing my arm. She pointed toward a doorway to our right. A glass of red wine sat on an end table just near the entrance, as if someone had set it down in a hurry.

"Miss Girardi?" I called again, peeking into the room, Dana one step behind me.

We did a simultaneous gasp as we took in the scene. And for once I was infinitely glad to have my crutches to lean on, because had they not been there, I'm pretty sure I would have crumpled to the ground like a sack of potatoes as I stared at the scene before me.

Lying in the middle of an impeccably decorated room filled with clearly priceless antiques was Donata Girardi: faceup on a Persian rug, eyes staring lifelessly at the ceiling.

A slim, black stiletto heel protruding from her neck.

Chapter Fourteen

The room swayed, my stomach clenched, my lungs suddenly became unable to drag in a full breath.

"Ohmigod," Dana said beside me, her face draining of all color. "Is she . . . ?"

I looked down at the stiletto buried midheel, surrounded by a pool of sticky red stuff. I gulped back the taste of bile in the back of my throat. "Uh-huh."

"Ohmigod, ohmigod." Dana started shaking her hands and jogging in place, as if to rid herself of the dead-person cooties.

"I think I'm going to be sick," I croaked out, and swung around so fast one of my crutches hit the end table by the door, jostling the wineglass to the floor, where it broke, spilling red wine all over the marble tiles.

"Shit." I bent down, automatically picking up the shattered pieces.

"Ohmigod, Maddie, what do we do?" Dana asked, still jogging.

I stood up, closed my eyes, and took a couple of deep breaths. "We call the police."

"Right." Dana stopped hopping up and down. She dug

in her purse and pulled out her cell, her hands shaking so badly she dropped it on the marble tile with a clatter. Scooping it back up, she paused, her fingers hovering over the keys. "How do we call the police?"

Good question.

I scanned the foyer, looking for a landline. None was visible, so I squeaked my crutches down a dark hallway to the right, Dana one step behind me. I peeked in the open doors until I found a room that looked like it doubled as an office. On the mahogany desk sat a cordless. I picked it up and hit the zero, hoping for an operator. Luckily I got one. Unluckily she spoke Italian.

"Desidera?"

"Uh, I need help. I have a dead woman."

"Come?"

"Uh." I looked to Dana. "How do you say *dead* in Italian?"

Dana shrugged.

"Uh, dead-o. *Molto, molto* dead-o. *Sì?*"

There was silence on the other end. Then finally, *"Polizia?"*

"Yes! *Polizia*. Lots of *polizia*. Pronto!"

The woman busted out with another string of Italian, which I hoped meant, *We'll be right there.* Then I hung up.

"Come on," I said to Dana, who was still doing her Casper impression. "Let's wait outside."

She nodded. "Yeah. Good idea."

We walked back down the hall, careful not to touch anything else, lest we disturb the crime scene. We both looked straight forward as if we were wearing blinders as we passed the room where Donata had enjoyed her last glass of wine, and did a collective slump once we made it outside, sitting down on the stone steps in silence.

The sky was a pale blue now, the fist glimmer of stars shining above us. A cool wind had picked up, whipping my hair against my cheeks. I inhaled deeply, dragging slow, deliberate breaths into my lungs. After a few beats Dana's cheeks started to return to their normal color, and I almost had the sickening smell of blood out of my nostrils.

"She was killed with a shoe, Maddie," Dana said quietly.

"I noticed that." A fact that made me want to run and hide, quick, before the *polizia* arrived and pulled out their handcuffs. But I knew that would just make me look even guiltier than Moreau already thought I was. Instead I took Dana's hand and squeezed, waiting silently for the police to arrive.

What felt like an eternity later they did, two blue-and-white cars rounding the corner, their lights blazing. Four officers emerged in starched blue uniforms, all advancing on Dana and me, waving their arms and shouting in Italian.

I just shook my head. "I have no idea what you're saying."

Dana pointed toward the house. "Dead woman. In there."

The officers looked at one another. Then at us. Finally one went in while the other three stayed on the porch. He emerged quickly enough and the wild gesturing started again, this time accompanied by the first officer shouting into his walkie-talkie, then motioning for a second guy, a tall, skinny man with a long beak of a nose, to take charge of Dana and me. He did, shoving us into the back of a squad car, where we remained until the rest of the posse arrived.

By the time the sky had turned pitch-black, the street was crawling with cop cars, crime-scene investigation teams, and the Italian equivalent of a coroner's van. Finally a female officer who looked eerily like James Gandolfini in a wig approached our car and wrenched the door open.

"You are the girls what found the body, *sì*?" she asked in heavily accented English.

I nodded. "Yes."

"I interpret for you. Down at the station."

"But we—" I tried to protest, but she'd already slammed the door shut and gestured to Beak Nose to take us away.

I felt desperation bubble up in my throat as the car pulled away from Donata's house to God knew where. French prison hadn't been any fun. I had a feeling I wasn't going to like Italian prison any better.

While the brick facades and high archways on the out-side of the police station resembled a museum more than the utilitarian government buildings in L.A., the interior looked like an almost exact replica of the squad room on *NYPD Blue*, prompting me to wonder if maybe someone hadn't been watching a few too many reruns from Amer-ican television. A tiny reception area was gated off from the main room, a woman in gray polyester manning the desk. Beyond her were rows of gunmetal gray desks, and behind those sat a row of closed doors.

The first thing the officers did when we got inside was

separate Dana and me. I watched as Beak Nose took her through one door, handing me off to the interpreter, who escorted me to another.

The room we entered was a small six-by-six affair with a plain metal table in the center and four folding chairs. A big, round guy straining his uniform at the gut was waiting for us, seated in one of the chairs. Miss Gandolfini gestured for me to sit opposite him, then placed herself at my side.

I sat, twisting my hands in my lap beneath the table.

The big guy said something in Italian, and the interpreter turned to me.

"You find the victim, *sì*?" she asked me.

I nodded. "Yes." I looked to the big guy. "Yes. I found the victim."

More Italian. I turned to Miss Gandolfini.

"He asks, 'You are friend of the victim?'"

"Well," I shifted in my seat. "Not exactly. I'd met her. In Paris."

Miss Gandolfini raised a pair of bushy black eyebrows, then relayed my answer to the big guy. He grunted, then shot back a reply.

"But she is in Italy," she said.

"Yes, she is now. But she wasn't. She was in Paris with Gisella."

We went through the interpretation dance again, until she came back with, "Gisella? Is this the friend you find the body with?"

I shook my head, feeling a headache brewing behind my eyes. "No. That's Dana. Gisella's a model. Well, I guess Dana's a model now too, but that's only because Gisella is dead."

There went those eyebrows again. But she relayed my answer, resulting in the big guy leaning in close, speaking more excitedly.

"I thought the victim is Donata?" Gandolfini's twin sister said.

"Yes. This one. The other one was Gisella. You see, I'm the Couture Killer."

She stifled a gasp, then interpreted for big guy. He threw his hands up, shouting something in Italian.

"Wait, no! I mean, I didn't really kill anyone. I'm just . . . The press, they . . . I mean, it's all a misunderstanding, you see . . ." I gave up. It was clear neither of them had any idea what I was talking about. To be honest, I wasn't even sure I knew anymore.

The door opened and Beak Nose said something in Italian to the big guy and my so-called interpreter. They shared a look; then both quickly got up from the table. I stood as well, but as the two of them filed out of the room Beak Nose motioned for me to stay, then shut the door again.

I bit my lip, fully aware that I'd been doing that so much today I'd eaten off any trace of Raspberry Perfection that might have been lingering. I wondered what had cut my interview short.

I didn't have to wonder long, as the door popped open again.

And there stood Moreau.

Again he was dressed in a suit that was clearly made for someone two sizes larger, the cuffs hanging over his hands as he walked into the room and sat down opposite me. His scraggly little mustache twitched as he scrutinized me.

"You found another body, Mademoiselle Springer?"

I opened my mouth to speak, but nothing came out. I cleared my throat and tried again. "Yes," I croaked out. "Dana and I did."

"This Dana?" he asked. "She is a model with the show, no?"

I nodded. "Yes."

"And you two were here because . . . ?" He raised an eyebrow at me.

I hesitated, wondering just how much to divulge. He must have noticed because he leaned forward a fraction of an inch in his chair, his mustache twitching ever so slightly.

"We had a hunch Donata might be involved in the jewel thefts. We were going to confront her."

"I see." He leaned his elbows on the table, steepling his fingers. "And what happened? Things got out of hand?"

"Yes." I paused. "Wait, no. I mean, we never confronted her."

"You killed her instead."

"No! I didn't kill anyone. She was . . . like that when we got there."

"I see. Anyone see you arrive?"

"We came in a cab. You can ask the driver."

"His name would be . . . ?" Moreau asked, extracting his trusty notepad from an oversize pocket.

"Arturo. Antonio. Something like that."

Moreau gave me a look, then put the pad back in his pocket. "I see."

"No, no, I don't think you do see. I *didn't* kill Donata. She was dead when we got here. The front door was open, and she was lying on the floor."

"The door was open."

"Yes."

"So, you went inside?"

"Yes."

"Where?"

"Into the foyer. And the room we found her in."

"That is all?"

"Yes." I paused. "Wait, no."

"You keep changing your story."

"No, it's the same story. I just remembered we went into the office, too. To use the phone."

"The cordless?" he clarified.

"Yes."

"And this was the only thing you touched, *oui*?"

"Yes."

He leaned in, his eyes intent on mine. "Then why are your prints all over the wineglass in Mademoiselle Girardi's foyer?"

Shit.

"I forgot. I touched that, too."

"You seem to do a lot of forgetting."

"Look, I knocked it over when we found the body, and I cleaned up the pieces of broken glass."

He raised an eyebrow. "You see a dead woman, yet before you call the police you stop to do a little housekeeping?"

"No. Yes. I . . . I don't know. I wasn't thinking clearly. I was panicked."

"Because you had just killed a woman?"

"Because I'd just *found* a dead woman."

"Hmmmm." He narrowed his eyes at me, pursing his

lips in a way that made his mustache dance. "Where were you this afternoon?"

"At Donata's office. Dana was with me the whole time," I said quickly. "I have an alibi."

"This time," he added skeptically.

I didn't say anything, crossing my arms over my chest.

"What were you doing at Donata's office?" he asked.

"Looking for her. She wasn't there, so I got her home address and we came here. Look, you can ask Donata's assistant, Debbie."

"She is being questioned now."

Wow, he was quick.

"Good," I said defiantly.

"We also have a team going though Donata's office. Care to know what they have found so far?"

I froze. *Uh-oh.* He looked a little too pleased with himself.

Only he didn't wait for me to answer. "Your fingerprints. All over the file cabinets in Mademoiselle Girardi's private office." He gave a little smirk. "I suppose you forgot to mention that, too?"

I bit my lip. *Shit.*

"Look, I didn't take anything. I . . . I was just looking."

"For?"

"Evidence."

"Of?"

"Her involvement in the jewel heists."

"Find any?"

"Well, not exactly. But did you know that Donata used to be a man? She was a male model in the seventies, and someone found out and they sent her some pictures of her as a him, and I think they were blackmailing her into sending Gisella on all the good jobs, where she could get her hands on the jewelry. Or her partner could. Like the Corbett Winston account, because Angelica said that Donata wouldn't even let her go on a go-see, so I'm pretty sure that Donata was involved, and that's why she got killed. Not by me."

Moreau blinked at me. His mustache twitched.

But he didn't get a chance to answer as the door opened again and Beak Nose said something to Moreau in Italian. Moreau answered back, then shot a pointed look at me before disappearing through the door.

I thunked my head down on the table. Could life get any worse?

I wasn't sure how long I sat like that, but by the time the door opened again my forehead made a little suction sound when I lifted it up.

Beak Nose stood in the doorway again. "Okay," he said in broken English. "You can go now."

"I can go?" I asked.

He nodded, holding the door open for me.

I stepped out, wondering what had changed. Two minutes ago Moreau had seemed ready to read me my rights. Now I was free to go.

And then I saw what had changed.

Ramirez.

He looked tired, his eyes bloodshot, his posture tilting slightly forward. A generous dusting of five-o'clock shadow covered his jaw, making his cheeks look hollow, as if he hadn't slept. My heart clenched in my chest, and all I wanted to do was give him a hug.

Beside him stood Moreau, the two of them deep in conversation.

As if he could feel me watching him, Ramirez suddenly straightened his spine, spinning around, his gaze traveling my way. Our eyes locked for a full two seconds.

Then he turned away.

He muttered a brief something to Moreau before walking past the gate and through the dinky reception area.

"Wait!" I called.

Moreau looked up, as did several of the other officers, all eyes turning my way.

But not Ramirez. In an instant he was out the door and gone.

I felt my heart sink, my stomach hollow and empty, a feeling that had nothing to do with the fact that I hadn't eaten, and everything to do with the fact that I wasn't sure how many more times Ramirez would walk away from me before he stopped coming back.

I felt tears well behind my eyes, but bravely sniffed them back, instead hobbling over to where Moreau stood waiting for me.

"You are free to go," he said slowly. Then he added, "For now."

I nodded, still staring at the doorway Ramirez had disappeared through. "And Dana?"

"Your friend is waiting for you downstairs. I have a car ready to take you both back to the airport."

"Thank you."

"I expect you will inform me if you feel the urge to travel out of France again?" he asked, though I could tell that wasn't exactly a question.

I nodded meekly, all the fight having drained out of me the second I'd seen Ramirez.

"Good." Moreau signaled to Beak Nose, who led me down a flight of stairs to where Dana was waiting for me at the bottom.

She gave me a fierce hug. "I hope I did the right thing by calling Ramirez?" she asked.

"Yeah," I said, even as tears welled behind my eyes at the sound of his name.

We both piled into the waiting blue-and-white, riding to the airport in silence. Needless to say there were no kisses on the cheek from Beak Nose as he saw us onto our flight.

I tried to sleep on the brief plane ride back to Paris, but it was nearly impossible. Images of Ramirez, Moreau, Felix, and Donata all mixed together, making my head hurt so badly I begged the flight attendant for an aspirin.

By the time we'd landed and caught a cab back to the Plaza Athénée, I was beat. I crawled into bed fully clothed and collapsed just as the sun was coming up.

I wasn't sure how long I slept, but the sounds of room-service carts woke me several hours later. I rolled over, looking at the clock. It was past noon. I felt like I'd been asleep for days. I stripped off my clothes, hopped in the shower, and attempted to wash the previous day's events off of me while trying to keep Wonder Boot dry. The hot water helped, and I was feeling almost human again by the time I stepped into a clean denim skirt, a white tank, and a cropped black collarless jacket. And as much as I would have liked to don a pair of red heels with the outfit, instead I slipped on a black ballet flat and added an extra swipe of lip gloss as a concession.

I ordered room service in and dialed Dana's number while I waited for my waffles and eggs to appear.

"Hello?" she croaked out.

"Are you up?"

"I am now."

"I ordered waffles."

She groaned.

"And a grapefruit half for you."

"I'll be right over."

Ten minutes later I opened the door and let her in. She was in pink sweats and a rumpled T-shirt that read, AERO-BICS INSTRUCTORS DO IT SWEATY. She flopped onto my bed, staring up at the ceiling.

"Get much sleep?" I asked.

"Some." She yawned. "Not enough."

Ditto.

Luckily, when sleep escapes me, sugar and caffeine are readily available substitutes, both of which I indulged in as room service arrived with a big plate of waffles and two carafes of coffee—decaf for Dana, regular with loads of cream for me.

I slathered on some strawberry preserves, my mouth watering. I took one bite. *Heaven*.

Dana scrunched up her nose and dug into her grape-fruit. "So, any thoughts about Donata's killer this morning?" she asked, covering her breakfast with one hand to avoid grapefruit juice in the eye.

I shook my head. "Nope. And here's what's been both-ering me," I said, shoveling a forkful of waffle into my mouth. "Why kill Donata? I mean, assuming Gisella was working with a partner, it seems like they had the perfect setup. Why ruin that?"

Dana shook her head. "Good question. Okay, let's say the partner offed Gisella for a bigger piece of the profits. Or maybe Gisella was getting sloppy and the partner was worried about someone finding out."

"The last one seems more likely to me," I said. "If he was just greedy, he'd want to keep Gisella around, right? Without her the scam is over. On the other hand, Gisella was risking a lot by hitting four designers in one Fashion Week. Someone was bound to start putting it together sooner or later."

"Okay, the partner's worried about being found out, so he kills Gisella. Lucky for him you're in town, and he can throw suspicion on you with the stiletto thing."

"Lucky him," I mumbled, shoving more waffle into my mouth.

"So . . . why Donata? I mean, it doesn't seem likely she'd go to the police, does it? Not when she had a secret of her own to protect."

I shook my head. "No. It doesn't." I took another bite, chewing thoughtfully. "Dana, who did you tell that we were going to Milan?"

She paused, grapefruit wedge halfway to her lips. "Just Jean Luc. Why?"

"Maybe the killer was afraid Donata would let something slip to us."

"You think?"

I shrugged. "Either way, the killer must have known we'd be in Milan. Otherwise there'd be no reason to do the stiletto thing again. He couldn't very well point the finger at me if I'd been in Paris with an ironclad alibi at the time of the murder. He had to have known I'd be in Milan."

Dana put her spoon down. "Wow. You're totally right. Okay, who knew you were going? Jean Luc. Who else?"

I bit my lip. "No one. I mean, I called Ann for the address to Donata's office. I didn't exactly tell her I was going to Milan, but I guess she could have found out if she tried. And I did ask Angelica about Donata. She could easily have followed me there, I suppose. But the only person I really told was . . ." I trailed off.

"Who?"

"Felix."

Dana paused. "Maddie, there is a chance that he actually did it."

I shook my head. "No. I mean . . ." I thought about it, then shook my head. "No. He couldn't have."

"Maddie, I know you like him—"

"I do *not* like him. I *loathe* him."

She shot me a get-real look, completely ignoring my protests. "But all the clues point to him. And, if he did, that means he must have been the one blackmailing Donata about her past in the first place."

"Which is completely ridiculous. You've seen Felix. He knows nothing about fashion. There's no way he'd know about a seventies male model."

"He works at a newspaper. He has all kinds of access."

I bit my lip. "True," I said slowly. "But what would tip him off? I mean, it isn't the type of thing that you'd go looking for unless you knew it was there."

"What about his aunt? You said she never misses Fashion Week. I'm sure she knows all the designers and models. Maybe he saw some old fashion magazines of hers.

Maybe she said something that had him putting two and
two together."

I felt my brow pucker. "I don't know, Dana. I mean,
it's Felix."

Dana gave me a look. "Right. And how much do you
really know about this guy?"

I stabbed at a bite of waffle. She had a point. He'd
kept a peerage secret and had hidden his relationship
with a murdered model. I suppose it was possible that he
had other skeletons lurking in his closet.

"Maddie, don't let one little kiss cloud your judgment."

My head snapped up. "I am not—"

But she shot me down with another look.

I shut my mouth. "Fine. Finish your grapefruit," I said.
"We'll go visit Auntie Charlene."

Chapter Fifteen

I finished my waffle, then picked up my crutches and headed down to the front desk, Dana in tow. Back at the castle Charlene had mentioned that she was coming into Paris to attend a show today. I crossed my fingers that she'd return to the same hotel.

Pierre, aka Andre, was on duty as I approached. He ducked behind the counter as soon as he saw me.

I looked at Dana, then shrugged. I stood on tippy-toe and peeked my head over the counter.

"Uh, Pie— I mean, Andre?"

"Is she with you?" he whispered, crouching on the ground.

"Who?"

"The loud one. Mademoiselle Rosenblatt?"

I shook my head. "Nope."

He gave an audible sigh of relief, then stood, brushing invisible lint off his jacket. "Thank the gods."

"I take it the date did not go well?"

He shook his head. "That woman, she is . . . how do you say . . . too much to handle. All she want to do is kiss me. I am not machine. I am man, with feelings!"

I tried to hide the grin tugging at my lips. "I see. Uh, listen, I was wondering if you could check whether someone is a guest here. Charlene Dunn."

"*Oui*, I will check. Uh, you have not seen the Mademoiselle Rosenblatt today?" he asked, still warily glancing over my shoulder as if she might appear from behind one of the decorative white marble columns.

"No, I haven't." Which, now that I thought about it, was odd. Surely news of my arrest must have reached Mom. I'd expected her to come bursting into my room with a rib-crushing hug last night, demanding to know what had happened to her "baby." Suddenly I felt a little neglected.

"Ah," Pierre said, his fingers flying over his keyboard. "We have one Mademoiselle Charlene Dunn, checked in last night. You wish to call her room, *oui*?" he asked.

I nodded. "Please."

Pierre pulled a phone out from behind the desk and set it on the counter, dialing the room number. He handed the receiver to me just as it was starting to ring.

On the third one Charlene's voice came through.

"Hello?"

"Hi, Charlene. It's Maddie Springer," I told her.

There was a slight pause on the other end. "Yes? What can I do for you, Maddie?"

"I was wondering if I could come up and talk to you for a moment."

Again with the pause. "Well, I was just on my way out. I'm due at the Hermès show today."

"Please," I said, appealing to that famous British etiquette. "I'll just be a moment. It's about Felix."

"Oh." I heard her breathe deeply into the receiver.

"All right, I suppose I could spare a moment. I'll meet you in the lobby."

"Thank you."

I hung up, handing the phone back to Pierre.

"Thank you, Pierre," I said. Then I looked down at his name tag. "Sorry, I mean, Andre."

He shrugged. "As long as you keep the Rosenblatt away from me, you may call me anything you like."

Dana and I settled into a pair of cream-colored chairs situated around a dark cherry end table in the lobby to wait for Auntie Charlene.

"This is ridiculous," I said. "There is no way Felix killed two women. It just isn't like him."

"Maddie, just because he's a good kisser—"

"I never said he was good!"

Dana shot me a look. "You didn't have to. You blush like a virgin every time I mention it."

Damned if I didn't feel my cheeks go red. I crossed my arms over my chest, trying my best to hang on to some shred of dignity.

"And your point?" I said.

"My point is, let's talk to his auntie."

I didn't respond—mostly because I knew she was right. Not about the kissing thing, but about the possibility that Felix could have had a hand in this. Not that I actually thought he'd kill two women. Even a slug like Felix had his limits. But maybe somehow he was inadvertently mixed up in all of this.

We didn't have to wait long, as a few minutes later Charlene stepped off the elevator dressed in a white leather miniskirt and a gold top that looked as if it were painted on. And a pair of sparkly gold three-inch heels. My hatred of her was renewed.

A tiny frown of concern etched her features, settling between her pale blue eyes. "Sorry to keep you waiting," she said, her lightly accented voice as evenly modulated as ever.

"No problem. Charlene, this is my friend Dana. Dana, Felix's aunt Charlene."

Dana raised an eyebrow at me, then leaned in and whispered, "This is dear 'old' auntie?"

No kidding.

"Hello, lovely to meet you." Charlene extended a hand in Dana's direction.

She shook it as Charlene perched, straight-backed, on the edge of an armchair facing us.

"So, what is it I can do for you today, Maddie?" Charlene asked.

"I wanted to ask you about Felix."

"So you said on the telephone."

"Specifically . . ." I looked to Dana, not sure how to broach the subject in the face of Charlene's very prim and proper demeanor.

Dana rolled her eyes at me. "We were wondering if he's shown any special interest in fashion lately."

Charlene raised one perfectly plucked eyebrow. "I think everyone in Paris has this week, don't you?"

"I mean, maybe less recently than that. In the last few months," I said, thinking back to when Angelica said Gisella had signed on at Donata's agency.

The little frown lines deepened, and I steeled myself

against warning her that she was going to have to Botox those out if she kept it up.

"I'm not really sure I know what you're getting at. As I'm sure you know, Felix doesn't really, uh, dress to trends," she said—a kind way to describe his fashion sense.

"Let me ask you something else," I decided. "Have you ever heard of the model Donatello Gardini?"

"Yes."

I sat up straighter, suddenly on high alert. "You have?"

Charlene nodded slowly. "As you know, I'm a bit of a fashion groupie. I collect old copies of fashion magazines. And from what I've read, he was quite well-known in Europe in the seventies. One of the first male models to catch the public's attention, I believe. I've seen his picture in all the old issues, though it's not a name I've heard much talk about lately."

"You haven't?" I shot Dana an I-told-you-so look.

"No. As you'd expect, he's long gone from the scene by now."

"So no one has, say, been asking you questions about him?" Dana asked.

She shook her head, then gave a small smile. "Just you."

"Not, say, Felix?" Dana pressed.

She cocked her head to the side, blonde hair falling over one shoulder. "No," she said slowly. "Why would he?"

Dana shrugged. "Well . . . I thought perhaps Donatello might be an . . . acquaintance of Felix's."

"Not as far as I know. Donatello has been long gone from the fashion scene. From what I understand, he was hot for a season or two, then faded into relative obscurity."

Or so *Donata* would have liked people to believe.

"So, you don't happen to have any of his magazines or photos, do you?"

"But of course."

Dana nudged me in the ribs and shot me an I-told-you-so look of her own. "You do?"

She shrugged. "As I said, I'm a fashion groupie. I've got back issues of *Vogue* since 1963. Donatello is in quite a few of the early issues."

"Where are these magazines?" I asked.

"Back at the castle. I'm sorry, I really don't understand what this has to do with anything," Charlene said, standing up. "And I don't mean to be rude, but I really must be going or I'll be late for the Hermès show."

"Of course," I said, gathering my crutches and rising. "I don't want to take up any more of your time. Thanks so much."

Once she had crossed the lobby, her backside swaying Marilyn Monroe–esque in her tight skirt, Dana rounded on me. "See! I told you Felix knew about Donatello!"

I shook my head. "Just because his aunt has fashion magazines with the guy's picture in them doesn't mean Felix was blackmailing Donata."

"No, but he *could* have been."

I bit my lip. "Okay, fine. He *could* have been." I paused. "But you heard what Charlene said. If Donatello was really such a big deal way back when, anyone with some time on their hands could have dug up those old pictures. And any one of the people on our suspects list knows more about fashion and the industry than Felix."

Dana let out a long sigh. "Yeah. You're right. Which I guess brings us back to square one." She looked down at her watch. "Listen, I have to get down to the tents for my final fitting. I'll see you there later?"

I nodded. "I told Jean Luc I'd be in at three."

Dana and I split, her catching a cab and me heading for the elevators back up to my room. I stopped at Mom and Mrs. Rosenblatt's first, but no one was in. I was beginning to wonder about those two. I briefly contemplated calling Mom's cell, but I knew that meant explaining the whole arrest thing, and honestly I just didn't have the energy for that at the moment.

Instead I walked across the hall to my own room, threw open the door, and lay on the bed, staring at the ceiling.

I closed my eyes.

Obviously Gisella was the key to all this. Why had she been killed in the first place? She had taken an awful risk stealing so many jewels this week. And Jean Luc had been in a tizzy about the necklace. Sooner or later he would have realized it was stolen. Sooner or later one of the designers would have called the police in. Considering this, it had been especially bold of Gisella to wear Felix's necklace out to a party the night before pocketing it.

The party. Had that been the catalyst? Had the killer seen her wearing it and realized she was getting too reckless?

Who'd been at the party?

Felix, of course, I reluctantly admitted. Angelica. Ryan. Donata, though by her current deceased status, she obviously wasn't the killer.

I went over the conversation that I'd had with Felix about Gisella and his last night with her. I'd been a little preoccupied, with Ramirez walking into the room at the time, but something had bugged me about Felix's story even then. Felix had readily admitted to arguing with Gisella, but he'd sworn he hadn't slept with her. And, oddly enough, I was inclined to believe him. (And no, *not* because he was a good kisser. Not that I was even admitting that he was. He wasn't. At least, not *that* good.) What reason would he have to lie about it now? Unless Angelica was making things up, someone else had been in Gisella's room before Felix.

I got up and grabbed my purse, rummaging around until I found the camera and the list of names I'd pulled from it. I turned the camera on, hoping that maybe the files would have miraculously reappeared. No such luck. I hit a few buttons and pulled up a couple of beautiful pictures Gisella had taken of the Eiffel Tower that made me sigh with envy, but no video files. I mentally thunked my head against the wall. The best evidence we'd had of her accomplice and I'd erased it. Some days I swore I really was blonde.

In lieu of actual video, I pulled out the list of file names I'd written down. Had one of these guys been the Mystery Man in her room that night? What if he was her partner? They'd had sex; he'd left, then told her to meet him at the tents early that morning. Where he'd killed her.

Rocco. Marcel. Charlie. Roberto. Ryan.

I'd already met Ryan. And while he wasn't totally cleared as a suspect, the way Gisella had dumped him for Felix didn't speak to me of a continuing criminal partnership. Angelica had said Rocco was a one-night stand, and Roberto was in New York. Both unlikely candidates. That left Marcel and Charlie.

I took my list and went downstairs to the business

center and booted up a computer. Going on the assumption that Gisella's partner in crime had ties to the fashion industry, I figured I would see what I could dig up on the two names. I had to admit I felt slightly awkward at the unfamiliar terminal. I wished Mom and Mrs. R were around to do this for me, as I tried to punch in Google key words to narrow my search.

An hour later I was cross-eyed from reading tiny print on the screen, and not a whole lot closer to finding Gisella's last lover.

There were more Charlies in fashion than I could count—a handful of young, beautiful models, as well as three designers who were showing at Fashion Week, and countless booking agents. And those were just the ones I found. I set that name aside and tried Marcel instead.

That list was considerably smaller, and once I whittled it down to only those currently in Paris for Fashion Week, I had three Marcels to choose from: a makeup artist (whom I dismissed as soon as I read that he was seen at a party with his boyfriend the night before), a style reporter for the TV entertainment show *Paris Spectacle*, and a male model currently living just outside the city.

I found *Paris Spectacle*'s Web page and, after calling up the site directory, a contact page listing the telephone number of a Marcel Dubois, style reporter.

I slipped my cell out and dialed, waiting while it rang on the other end. Finally, five rings into it, a man picked up.

"*Bonjour, ce Dubois,*" he answered.

"Uh, English?" I asked, crossing my fingers.

"*Oui*, how may I help you?"

I sighed in relief. "Hi, my name is Maddie Springer, and I'm a—"

But I didn't get any further as I heard him suck in a quick breath. "The Couture Killer?"

I gritted my teeth. I was really beginning to hate that nickname.

"Yes. I mean, no, I'm not a killer, but yes, that's what the press is currently calling me." I paused.

"You prefer to be called something else?" he asked.

I rolled my eyes. "I prefer not to be called anything! I didn't do it."

"No, no, of course not," he said. "So, you are denying the current allegations, *oui*?" he asked, and I could hear him scrambling for a pen and paper in the background.

I bit my lip. Obviously Marcel thought I was calling him for an exclusive. But, for the moment, I decided to play along.

"Yes, I am denying them. I had nothing to do with Gisella's death. Or Donata's," I added as an afterthought. "I've been"—I cringed, borrowing a phrase from Mrs. Rosenblatt—"set up."

"I see." I heard the sound of furious scribbling. "By whom?"

"The real killer."

"Ah! The real killer," he repeated as he jotted down my comments. "And did you know the deceased?"

"I'd met her." I paused. "Did *you* know her?"

"Me? Uh . . ." He trailed off, not prepared to be the one questioned. "Yes, of course I knew who she was. Gisella Rossi. Everyone knew her."

"That's not what I meant. Did you know her personally?"

"Uh, I met her once or twice. But I am deeply saddened by her death. Which is why I promise a very tasteful segment. Now, the police say you have no alibi for the night of the murder; is this true?"

I bit my lip. "Yes. I was alone at the time of her death. Uh . . . how about you?"

"Me?" Clearly this was not how most of his interviews went.

"Yes, you."

"Well, I was here. Working."

"And other people saw you there?"

"*Oui.* But as soon as I heard, I was at the tent. I am very thorough in my investigations. I promise I will not leave any details out. Anything you want to share with me, I will report."

"Hmmmm." I was beginning to think I was on the wrong track with this guy. If he'd really been working that night, and had witnesses, there was no way he was Gisella's partner. But just for good measure, I had to ask. "Did you ever sleep with Gisella Rossi?"

"Eh . . . no," he answered, taken aback. "Why?" he asked, a devilish note creeping into his voice. "Did you?"

Oh, brother. "No. And I have no further comment at this time."

"Wait I—" he said.

But I hung up. Clearly he was not Mystery Man. That left one more Marcel: the male model, Marcel Bertrand.

I looked up at the clock: two. I was due back at the tent in an hour anyway; I might as well go talk to Miss Everyone Who's Anyone and see if her BlackBerry could spit out a number for Mr. Bertrand.

I popped by Mom and Mrs. Rosenblatt's room one more time (still empty) before grabbing my shoulder bag and heading down to the lobby.

Though as soon as I got off the elevators I froze.

He was standing at the front desk, speaking with Pierre. His worn-in-the-right-places jeans clung to his frame so tightly that every woman in the lobby gave a second (and sometimes third) glance his way. His black T-shirt was just a little too tight across his biceps, and a growth of stubble across his chin made it look as though he hadn't slept or shaved in days. And his dark hair curled at the nape of his neck, as if he were a week past a decent haircut.

Ramirez.

A black duffel bag sat at his feet, and he slid a card key across the counter to Pierre. Clearly he was checking out.

My heart caught in my throat, and I quickly crossed the lobby to him.

Okay, fine, I *tried* to quickly cross the lobby. But thanks to Wonder Boot I didn't do anything quickly anymore. I saw him thank Pierre, grab the duffel, and turn to go.

"Jack!" I called.

He spun around, his jaw immediately tensing at the sight of me.

I hobbled toward him, double-time. But if there are three things that don't mix, they're a freshly waxed marble floor, a pair of crutches, and a blonde in a hurry. My eyes intent on Ramirez's frame, I moved one crutch a little ahead of the other, then felt it slide out from under me. As if in slow motion crutch one went left, crutch two went right, and I slid down squarely in the middle, my arms flailing as my face planted firmly onto the floor.

I heard Ramirez mutter, "Jesus," under his breath, and then he was suddenly at my side.

"Are you okay?" he asked, lifting me up by my armpits.

"I think so," I replied. Only it came out more like, *I ink ow*, as my lip was already rapidly swelling.

Ramirez looked at me, quickly assessing the damage. He reached one hand out and ran the pad of his thumb lightly along my injured lip.

My breath caught in my throat.

"Jack," I whispered.

His dark eyes met mine.

And he quickly pulled his hand away, clearing his throat. He turned and picked up his duffel bag from the floor.

"I never got to thank you for bailing me out in Italy," I said.

No response.

"Thank you."

Still nothing.

"So, you're leaving?" I asked. Though the answer to that was pretty obvious.

He nodded. "Captain called. They've got a double homicide in Inglewood."

I bit my lip to keep from protesting that there was a double homicide *here*. Because, sadly, between his captain and me, I already knew who'd win out.

"My flight leaves in two hours," he continued, making for the door.

"Wait," I called, gathering up my crutches and hobbling after him. "Please just let me explain."

He shook his head. "You don't need to."

"I *want* to."

He didn't stop. If anything his pace picked up as he stalked purposefully toward the front doors.

"It didn't mean anything," I said, trailing after him. "You have to trust me, this was all just a big mistake."

He stopped just short of the front doors, then turned, his face inches from mine.

"Please don't go like this," I said.

He took a deep breath, shaking his head as he blew it out. "Like what, Maddie?"

I swallowed. "Mad."

He gave me his best Bad Cop stare. "I'm not mad."

"You look mad."

"No." He paused. "I'm disappointed."

I bit my lip. *Wow.* Somehow that was even worse. "In me?" I squeaked out.

He looked at a spot just over my head, as if searching for the right words there. Finally he seemed to find them, giving me a long stare. "In us."

Again, worse. "Look, I don't know how many times I can say it, Jack: I'm sorry. It was a mistake. We all make mistakes."

He shot me a look.

"Okay, fine, some of us make more than others," I conceded. "But come on. Nobody's perfect. You have to trust me when I say that this meant nothing."

"Trust you?" he said, throwing his arms up in the air. "Trust you? Right, the way I trusted you to still be in the room when I finished brushing my teeth?"

I bit my lip. "Okay, that was a dirty trick."

"Damn straight," he ground out through clenched teeth.

"But I've told you everywhere I've been since then. I know leaving you was wrong, but I only did it because

I didn't trust *you* not to hold me back. Trust has to go both ways, you know. It's a fifty/fifty street."

He narrowed his eyes and growled deep in his throat. "Okay, sixty/forty."

He stared at me for a long moment, then shook his head. "Look, I've got to go. I'll miss my flight."

"So that's it?" I asked, feeling tears well up in my throat. "You're just leaving?"

He shot me a look. Almost sad. Almost regretful. Totally final. "Yes, Maddie. That's it."

And then he walked out the door.

Chapter Sixteen

I didn't have the heart to watch Ramirez's cab drive away. Instead I ducked into the café and ordered myself a decadent hot chocolate. Large. With whipped cream. And a chocolate pastry. It was shaping up to be that kind of day.

And the thing that upset me most as I dug into my chocolate indulgence was that even though it was me who had screwed up this time, Ramirez had been far from Mr. Perfect up until now. Hadn't I forgiven him when the captain had called, interrupting our evening at the Venice Pier last month, even when Jack had promised he'd take me on the giant Ferris wheel? I'd been bummed, but I'd understood. I'd forgiven him.

And when we'd planned a weekend getaway to Palm Springs, at the last minute he'd had to cancel because of a murder/suicide by the Hollywood Bowl—all our plans, ruined. Our first vacation together. The nonrefundable deposit on the time-share condo, the brand-new bikini that I'd shopped all day for to find just the right cut that made my legs look long, my tummy look flat, and my barely Bs form into something that resembled cleavage.

But had I complained? Okay, fine, I'd complained a little. I mean, it was a rocking bikini gone to waste. But I'd been understanding. I'd known that when he said he was really, really sorry about canceling, he'd meant it. I hadn't stalked off to sulk (much), and I certainly hadn't gotten on the first flight out of the country to avoid him.

I'd said I was sorry. I'd told him the kiss didn't mean anything. If he couldn't get past it . . . well, maybe he didn't deserve someone as understanding as me anyway. Besides, it wasn't like Ramirez had any claim on me. It wasn't like we were married or anything. I was a single girl. I could kiss whomever I wanted. Not that I *wanted* to kiss Felix, but, well, if I did, I could. And I shouldn't have to grovel at Ramirez's feet for forgiveness.

Deciding that anger was a much more appealing emotion than grief, I continued this train of thought all the way though the lobby and out to a waiting cab. By the time I arrived at Le Carrousel de Louvre I'd worked myself into a pretty nice indignant rage, if I did say so myself. I hobbled out of the cab, making angry little divots in the grass with my crutches as I passed the tents and hobbled across the courtyard and into the workroom.

If Jean Luc had seemed stressed before, he was stressed and on crack now. He paced the length of the workroom, arms waving above his head, French, Italian, and English all jumbled together as he spoke, antacids popping into his mouth one after another.

I slipped into the room, trying to get Ann's attention before Jean Luc descended upon me.

"Pssst," I whispered in Ann's direction. She was standing next to Angelica, instructing the seamstress on just how high the hem was supposed to go on the leg. I noticed with a pang of regret that Angelica was already dressed in her makeshift replacement pumps. I'd done a keyhole design along the front and sprayed the heels gold to match the rim of her skirt. They were passable, but certainly nothing to write home about.

Or to mention in a style column as the next best thing to hit feet since Jimmy Choos.

"Ann," I whispered again, waving my hand to get her attention. She finally looked up and saw me, clomping to the door in her clogs.

"You're early. Great. You can help with the girls in the back. We've got Polaroids of each outfit, if you can help get them on."

I nodded. "Sure. But I was wondering if I could ask you something first."

Her face puckered, as if questions weren't on the schedule today, but she didn't say no.

"I was wondering if you had contact information for a Marcel Bertrand. He's a model in the area."

Her forehead puckered. "We don't do menswear again until spring."

"I know. I just . . ." I paused, racking my little brain for a plausible reason for calling him. Unfortunately, what with the dead bodies, dead career, and dead relationship, my little brain had been through too much lately. "I, uh, think he's kinda cute." I cringed.

Ann cocked her head to the side. "Cute?"

I decided to run with it. "Uh-huh. Do you know if he's already seeing anyone?" I asked. *Like maybe Gisella?*

She shrugged. "Yeah, like I can keep up with their love

lives, too. Hang on." She pulled out the BlackBerry. "What was his last name?"

"Bertrand," I repeated, looking over her shoulder. She scrolled through numbers until she got to the Bs. "No direct number, but his agent is David Callabra." She showed me the screen, and I pulled out a pen and wrote down the agent's cell number on my hand.

"Thanks, Ann," I said, ducking back out the door.

"Hey!"

I froze. "Yeah?"

"What about the fitting?"

Oh yeah. "Uh, I'll be back before three to fit everyone— I swear it," I called over my shoulder.

I slipped outside before she could protest, stepping a few feet away, then pulling out my cell and making the call to Marcel's agent. It rang three times before he picked up, and I could hear the steady pulse of loud techno music in the background.

"*Bonjour,*" he answered.

"Hi, I'm with Le Croix designs," I said, fibbing only a little. "We're looking to book a male model next week for a shoot. I heard you represented Marcel Bertrand?"

"*Oui, uh, un moment.*" I heard him cover the mouthpiece. When he came back on the music had faded some. "Pardon, Le Croix designs, did you say?"

"Yes. Marcel came highly recommended to us by Gisella Rossi."

There was a pause on the other end. "Gisella Rossi?"

"Marcel did know Gisella, didn't he?" I asked, crossing my fingers.

"*Oui*," Callabra said slowly. "But I'm surprised she would recommend him."

"Oh? Why is that?"

"Uh, why don't we talk about this in person? I am at the Gaultier show right now."

"Perfect, I'll meet you there in ten minutes."

Gaultier was showing in a large venue in the Rue Saint-Martin. Unlike New York's Bryant Park, Paris's Fashion Week is spread between a variety of historically rich and architecturally gorgeous sites within a few blocks' radius, with top-tier designers showing throughout the week. When I arrived at the Rue Saint-Martin it was packed. We're talking Nordstrom's semiannual clearance sale packed. My cabdriver circled the block twice before double-parking and letting me out at the curb amidst the angry horns of the other drivers.

I threaded my way through a solid wall of photographers, columnists, and general fashionistas until I heard the telltale pulsating music of the Gaultier show.

I ducked my head in, not actually getting any farther without a ticket. But even from there I could see that the folding chairs two and three rows deep were already long filled. The show was standing room only, and I craned to see the last few models strut their stuff down the runway. I slipped between two guys wielding cameras for a better position and caught a glimpse of a long-legged woman in a streamlined wool jacket and thigh-high boots doing a pose at the end of the runway before strutting away. Despite my reasons for being there, my heart gave a little leap at being among the very first to see the season's hot items.

Especially when the next model stopped and posed in a gorgeous off-the-shoulder, midthigh white dress with butterfly cutouts in the back. I *had* to have one of those.

By the time the last model had made her journey up and down the sleek black runaway and Jean Paul himself came out to the sound of thunderous applause, I was right there clapping along with everyone else, and completely caught up in the infectious excitement of Fashion Week.

So caught up that I jumped when someone tapped me on the shoulder.

"Maddie?"

I spun around to face a short, balding man with a pointed goatee that looked like it had been modeled after Beelzebub himself. He was dressed in all black—slacks, sweater, and pointy-toed shoes that matched his pointy features—a sharp nose, small, calculating eyes. In fact, the only thing not pointy about him was his round little head, balding and gleaming under the still-blaring show lights.

"Yes?" I asked tentatively.

"David Callabra," he said, sticking out his hand. "We spoke on the phone."

I nodded. "Oh, right." I cleared my throat. "Uh, how did you know who I was?"

He gave a wry grin. "Your face has been all over the news, Maddie. Everyone in Paris knows who you are."

At any other time everyone in the fashion world knowing my name might have been a good thing. Today it made my stomach hurt.

"Right." I paused. "I didn't do it, by the way."

He waved me off. "Guilty, innocent, I do not care. As

long as the pay is right, I am willing to chance it, as they say." He grinned, and I had the feeling he was at least half kidding.

"So," he said, leading the way outside, "you said you had a job for Marcel?"

I cleared my throat. "Right. Uh, Gisella had recommended him."

He shook his head. "Like I say, I can hardly believe that."

I froze. *Uh-oh.* Was the jig up? And here I'd thought it was such a good jig.

"From what I heard, Marcel was hardly Gisella's favorite person. They didn't exactly part on the best of terms the last time they worked together."

"Oh," I said, relived he hadn't seen through my cover. "What happened?"

"Her allegations were completely fabricated," he said.

Allegations? This sounded promising. "Go on," I said as we threaded our way through the mass of people milling around the street, comparing notes from the show.

"Well, they were working together in Cannes, and Gisella accused Marcel of stealing something."

"Stealing?" An ironic accusation, coming from Gisella.

"It was a silly misunderstanding. Gisella was wearing a tennis bracelet for the shoot, and afterward it went missing. Gisella accused Marcel of taking it."

"He didn't?"

"No, of course not. But that didn't stop them from searching his things. Of course he came up clean, but it left a taint on his name."

I knew how that felt. "Was the bracelet ever recovered?"

"I assume so. I really do not know. After they searched

his belongings Marcel left the set. The whole thing put a, uh . . . as you say, bad taste in his mouth. Especially considering his relationship with Gisella."

"Relationship? So they *were* dating?"

"*Oui*. Were, past tense. Like I said, they did not have anything to do with each other after that. Though I'm glad to hear that there were no hard feelings on Gisella's part. Ah, when did you say you needed Marcel?"

"What?" I was still digesting this information. Another item of jewelry gone missing in Gisella's presence. The girl had balls, I'd say that. Especially to accuse Marcel. Though it didn't seem likely that were Marcel her partner, she'd have thrown suspicion on him that way.

"When is the shoot?" David repeated.

"Oh. Uh, next week."

Callabra clicked his tongue. "A pity. Marcel's in Spain. He has been doing a calendar shoot there for the past week, and he is not scheduled back until the end of the month."

And unlikely just became impossible. How was it everyone had an alibi but me?

"I do have another young man who might interest you." Callabra reached into his briefcase and pulled out a photo of a twenty-something guy in a tiny Speedo lying on a beach. He had dark hair, dark eyes, and a set of abs that looked chiseled from stone.

I lifted my hand to the corner of my mouth, surreptitiously checking for drool.

"Wow."

"Attractive, *oui*?" he said. "Marc has been on three covers so far, and he was featured as the Daily Fix four times last year with Playgirl. He is very hot right now."

No kidding. With some difficulty I tore my gaze away from the picture. "He's very nice-looking." Understatement alert. "But we really just wanted Marcel."

His face fell as he put the pictures back in his briefcase. "Oh. Sorry. But," he said, pulling a card out of his wallet, "let me know if you change your mind."

As he walked away I slipped the card into my purse and mentally crossed Marcel's name off the list. That left just one identity for Mystery Man.

Charlie.

I fought my way back toward the curb in search of a cab, which, due to the mass of people leaving the Gaultier show, took another twenty minutes before I finally ended up sharing one with a reporter from the *Metropole* who kept sending me sidelong glances until I finally gave him a pointed, "Yes, I'm the Couture Killer, and no, I have no comment."

After that he kept his eyes focused out the window the rest of the ride back to Le Carrousel de Louvre.

Even with all the changes, pinning, and sewing that had gone on with Jean Luc's creations over the past week, there were still a multitude of last-minute adjustments that needed to be made: a seam ripped here, something puckering there, a model who had eaten too big a lunch (which, in their world, I supposed consisted of two Tic Tacs instead of one).

I set up at a table in the back, filling in wherever Ann needed me and trying not to look at the empty shoe rack where my first tastes of fashion fame were supposed to be sitting. Yeah. I know. I didn't try too hard. Every time I caught a glimpse of it out of the corner of my eye,

Moreau moved up that much higher on my shit list. Having him take the stiletto that had killed Gisella into evidence I could understand. But holding all of my creations hostage . . . now, that was just mean. I made a mental note *not* to donate to the policemen's fund next time they came knocking on my door.

The only upside of the day was that as each model made her way to my station for last-minute adjustments, I had an opportunity to quiz her about Gisella and her possible beau-slash-accomplice, the mysterious Mr. Charlie. The first two drew blanks, saying they hadn't even known Gisella when they'd signed on to the Le Croix show. The next one, a girl from Northern California, vaguely remembered Gisella talking about some guy, but had no idea what his name was. And from the description ("a dude into handcuffs") I'd venture to guess she'd been talking about Ryan and not the elusive Charlie.

Half a dozen models later, the most I had garnered was that a) Gisella had flaunted all her previous boyfriends to anyone who would listen, and b) no one really paid much attention to what she said.

All in all a rather unproductive afternoon.

Though one girl I spoke with, a long-legged brunette from South Africa, said that she had ridden the elevator up to the fourteenth floor with a guy in khakis and a rumpled white shirt on the night Gisella was killed. She remembered the time exactly because she'd been late to meet a friend for drinks, and, according to the timetable I'd gotten out of Angelica, it served to confirm Felix's story. It had been too late in the evening for him to have been her Mr. Roll in the Hay. Good to know, but I was hardly a step closer to finding our Mystery Man.

By the time Jean Luc yelled for a dinner break I was beginning to feel desperation kick in that we might never find him.

"Hey," Dana said, approaching my table. "You hungry?"

I nodded, even though, for perhaps the first time in my life, food held no appeal at all.

Dana must have sensed my mood. She cocked her head to the side. "What's wrong?"

I gestured behind me to the empty shoe rack.

She laid a hand on my arm. "Honey, I'm so sorry."

"And I yelled at Ramirez."

She raised an eyebrow.

"And I can't find Charlie."

"Charlie?"

I nodded, then quickly filled her in on my afternoon's activities.

"Well, someone must have known this guy. I mean, especially if he's here at Fashion Week."

"I know." I nodded. "But I can't find anyone who heard Gisella talk about him."

"Maddie," Ann called, walking by my table, her headset already squawking at her about something. "Jean Luc wanted me to reassure you that he's still putting your name in the billing as the shoe designer. Even though . . ." She trailed off, gesturing to the empty rack behind me.

"Thanks," I said. Then I cringed at just what my name would be attached to. "I think."

"Hey, Ann," Dana said, grabbing her arm as she moved to walk away.

"Yes?" Ann gave her a look as if human contact were not in her realm of comfort.

"Do you know a guy named Charlie?"

Ann scrunched up her nose. "Be more specific."

"Do you know anyone here in Paris at Fashion Week named Charlie? Who Gisella might have known?"

Ann paused a moment. Then she shook her head. "I'm sorry, the name isn't ringing any bells."

My shoulders sagged. "Thanks anyway," I called after her as she broke from Dana's grasp.

Dana puckered her forehead. "You know, that in itself is a little odd."

"What?"

"The fact that Ann doesn't know him. Ann knows everyone."

I shrugged. "Let's get some food."

Instead of going all the way back to the hotel, Dana and I walked two blocks south and found a cute little bistro that had an even cuter little waiter. We took a spot on the outside patio, next to a pair of tall heaters, and both ordered large pasta dishes with creamy sauces that would make Jenny Craig drool. Okay, fine, I ordered pasta with a decadent cream sauce. Dana ordered a salad and a small platter of pasta in light virgin olive oil.

As Cutie Waiter brought out our food, he was sure to ask Dana's chest if there was anything more she needed.

"He's kinda cute, huh?" Dana asked, licking her lips as she bit into her salad, her eyes riveted to his retreating tush.

"Uh-huh. Heard anything from Ricky lately?" I asked.

"Who?" Her eyes snapped back to me.

"Your *boyfriend*?"

"Oh." Dana instantly became engrossed in her meal. "Um, yeah, sorta. He called."

"And?"

"He said he would be home in a couple of weeks."

"And?"

She sighed. "And that the Natalie Portman thing was totally made up by the press. Maddie, I feel so bad for not trusting him. But, I mean, do you think I can trust him? Damn, this monogamy thing is so hard."

Tell me about it. "If he says she doesn't mean anything to him, then she doesn't."

"But what if she does?"

I was about to give the fifty/fifty trust speech for the second time today when my cell rang from the depth of my purse. I fished around and looked down at the read-out. Mom.

"Where have you been?" I asked, hitting the on button.

Only there was no response. Just breathing.

"Mom?"

More breathing.

I rolled my eyes and hit the off button. Love my mom as I do, she is not the most technologically advanced person on the planet. When she'd first gotten her cell last year, she'd insisted on shouting every conversation into it. I wouldn't be surprised if a compact in her purse had hit the speed dial.

I waited a beat, then called her number back. It rang four times, then went to a recording.

"Hi, this is Betty. I'm either not available or screening my calls and you didn't make the cut."

I rolled my eyes.

"Please leave a message."

A loud beep sounded in my ear and I did, informing her that her purse had just called me, then hung up.

Wherever she was, I hoped she was having a better day than I was.

A completely futile wish, as I was about to find out.

Chapter Seventeen

After dinner I went back to the workroom, where Jean Luc ran everyone ragged until long after the sun had set. At which point Dana and I took a cab back to the hotel, dragging ourselves through the lobby. It was sparsely populated at this time of night, but I noticed Pierre still on duty.

"Don't they ever let you sleep?" I asked.

He didn't seem to mind working again. He had a big smile, and his eyes held a look that could only be called a twinkle. Even his bald head seemed to shine extra brightly this evening.

"Ah, Mademoiselle Springer. What a lovely evening, *non*?"

Honestly, I'd had better.

"You're in a good mood," I replied.

He gave a deep, contented sigh. "*Oui*. It was a Rosenblatt-free day today." His smile widened.

I felt a frown settling between my brows. "Mrs. Rosenblatt isn't in yet?" I asked.

He shook his head. "I have not seen her." Another big grin.

I admit I was beginning to get worried. It wasn't like Mom just to disappear like that.

My concern must have shown because Pierre asked, "You want me to call their room, *oui*?"

I shook my head. "No, no, I'll call later. Listen, I was wondering if you could tell me whether you have a Charlie registered as a guest here," I said. I knew there were a dozen hotels in a two-block radius he could have been staying at, but I was beginning to get desperate.

Pierre hit a button on his keyboard. "But of course. This Charlie's last name?" he asked, his fingers poised expectantly.

"Well, that's kind of part of the problem. I don't exactly know."

A frown puckered his features. "Oh."

"See, he was a friend of the murdered girl, Gisella."

"Ah. Well, I'm sorry, but our database is arranged according to last name. There's no way to tell if Charlie is registered or not without a last name."

Damn. So much for my last resort. "Thanks anyway for looking."

"Anytime," he said, waving as I walked off.

I rode the elevator up to the seventh floor alone, then knocked on the adjoining door to Mom's room. No answer. I opened it, then peeked inside.

"Hello?" I asked.

No response. I flipped on a light and walked in. It was impossible to tell how long they'd been gone; the beds had been made with military precision by housekeeping. I noticed that both Mom's clunky old orange Samsonite and Mrs. R's pink polka-dotted suitcase were still in the room. They hadn't packed for a long trip. I ducked into the bathroom and saw the multitude of moisturizers, eye-rebuilding creams, and antiwrinkle serums Mom used every night, still sitting on the counter. There was no way she would go anywhere overnight without those.

Maybe we'd just been missing one another?

I sat down on the bed and called her number again. Straight to voice mail this time. I left a message saying I was starting to worry, and could she please call me back.

Sadly, I was starting to sound a little like my mother.

I tried to think back to the last time I'd seen her. It had been . . . yesterday? Before Dana and I had gone to Milan. I glanced around the room again, trying to find any sign that Mom and Mrs. R had been here since then. But, thanks to fastidious housekeepers, if there had been a clue it was gone now.

With an uneasy feeling I switched off the light and left the room, trying to tell myself that Mom was a big girl. She could take care of herself. More than likely she and Mrs. R were just having the time of their lives exploring Paris. Probably they'd found some French karaoke club. Who knows? Maybe Mrs. R had even found some nice French guy who liked muumuus.

I shut the door behind myself, promising that I'd check in again first thing in the morning. I took a long, hot shower and popped two pain pills in my mouth, the effects of the day taking their toll on my leg.

But as I lay in bed, my wet hair wrapped up in a towel, I couldn't sleep. Maybe because I'd slept past noon that day, or maybe because of the anxiety of the next day's show, or the hollow disappointment of not having my own shoes go down the runway.

I rolled over and looked at the phone beside my bed.

I wondered if Ramirez was back home in L.A. yet. Maybe still on a plane somewhere over the Atlantic? Was he thinking about me? Wondering what I was doing? Did he even care what I was doing anymore?

I bit my lip and picked up the phone in the darkness. I dialed the first three digits of his cell number.

Then hung up.

No. I was not calling. I had done all I could. I had apologized, explained. I'd laid it all out there. Now it was his turn. I was not going to be the one to make contact first.

Only . . . what if he never made contact?

I stared at the phone again. What if he was waiting for me to call? What if he wasn't sure I wanted him to call? I had been a little mad this afternoon. Maybe I should call just to let him know that it was okay for him to call?

I lifted the receiver again and this time got all the way through his number and heard it ring twice before hanging it up.

I scrunched my eyes shut, rubbing my balled fists into them. *Damn*. I was such a chicken!

And, worse than that, I realized his cell would show a missed call from me. *Great*. He'd see I'd called and hadn't left a message. What kind of message would that send?

I figured I'd better call back and at least explain the hang-up. You know, so he didn't think I'd dialed, then chickened out and hung up. (Never mind that that was exactly what I'd done.)

I picked up the phone a third time and dialed his number. It rang three times, then went to voice mail.

"Hi. Uh, it's me." I cleared my throat. "Uh, Maddie me. You know, in case you were wondering which me.

'Cause, you know, I'm sure you know a lot of mes." I cringed. "Yeah, anyway, uh, I wanted to let you know that I just called you, but I didn't leave a message, and it wasn't because I chickened out or anything. I, uh, I had a bad connection. Yep, connections really suck here in France. So, yeah, just wanted to clear that up, that I wasn't not calling you. Which I guess is pretty clear by the fact that I am calling you. Right now, even. Which clearly you already know if you're listening to this. Which I hope you are. So, um, bye."

I hung up—and doubled over, cringing all the way down to my toes. *Oh. My. God.* I had sounded like a nutcase! He was going to listen to that and thank his lucky stars he got away from me when he did. That was the worst phone message ever.

I sat down on the bed. I took a few deep breaths. *Okay, Maddie, it's all right. You can fix this, girl.*

I picked up the phone and dialed Ramirez's number.

"Hi. It's me again. Maddie me. Listen, I just wanted to apologize for that obviously bad message I just left you. I'm, uh . . . I just took some pain pills, and I think they're going to my head." I bit my lip. "Yeah, I, uh, can't really think when I take them. Anyway, I really just wanted to apologize again for the whole—"

But I didn't get to finish as a loud beep sounded in my ear and a mechanical voice came on the line. "This mailbox is full," it informed me. "Thank you for calling."

Then it hung up on me.

I stared at the receiver in my hand.

"No!" I shook my head. "No, no, no, no."

I dialed Ramirez's home number. After the third ring his voice mail kicked in.

"Hey, it's me." I paused. "Maddie me. Listen, I just left you a message on your cell, but the in-box filled up before I could finish. And I just wanted to say that I am sorry—amazingly sorry—for everything that happened. And even though I've been very understanding, and you're not being very understanding at all, I'm willing to go seventy/thirty and apologize again. Twice. Three times. As many times as it takes. Okay? So, um, I guess I just wanted to let you know that if you wanted to call me I'd definitely want you to call me, and I'd be here. Picking up. Not letting it go to voice mail." I paused again. "Not that I'm blaming you for me getting your voice mail. I'm just . . . here."

I hung up, then flopped my head back on the pillows. That was it; I seriously needed help.

I was on the runway, spotlights blaring down at me, flash-bulbs going off everywhere I looked. Too bright. So bright I could hardly see where I was going. I squinted my eyes, trying to make out the runway beneath my feet. Only it seemed long—way too long. I kept walking and walking and felt as though I'd never reach the end of it. And the more I walked, the more the white noise of reporters chattering, people clapping, the ever-present cameras going off all blended together into one loud roar.

Until suddenly a voice shouted from the crowd.

"Murderer!"

I turned toward the voice's direction, but I still couldn't see anything. I blinked against the bright glare, shielding my eyes with my hand to make out anything.

"Murderer!" he shouted again. And suddenly the spot-light dimmed, shining instead on the voice.

It was Moreau. He was standing up on a folding chair, his head towering over the crowd. He was wearing a black gown and a white wig, reminding me of an English barrister. He had one long finger pointed squarely at me, his dead-squirrel mustache twitching like mad on his scowling face.

"She did it! I tell you, she killed them all!"

The photographers flashed more pictures, the entire crowd chanting the word, "Murderer."

"But I'm innocent!" I tried to tell them. But my voice was soft, so quiet it was almost a whisper. I tried again to shout, but it came out hardly louder than a sigh.

I turned to run away, but suddenly Moreau was there. I turned again and again; there he was. Everywhere I went Moreau seemed to be there, pointing at me.

I closed my eyes, putting my fingers in my ears to silence the accusations.

And when I finally blinked my lids open again, there he was.

Ramirez.

Stony faced, his hands in his pockets, that panther trailing dangerously down his arm.

"Tell them I didn't do it," I pleaded with him. "Tell them I'm not a killer."

But he just looked at me, then slowly turned and walked away.

My eyes shot open, my breath catching in my throat as I squinted against the sudden onslaught of light. For a moment I had the terrifying feeling I was still dreaming. Until I blinked and realized it was sunlight, not spotlights, coming through the ruffled yellow curtains. I turned and looked at the digital alarm clock numbers: seven fifteen A.M. I shut my eyes and let my head fall back on the pillows.

It was show day.

I took in a deep breath, washing the nightmare out of my system as bittersweet feelings set in.

Even since I'd been a little girl playing mix and match with my Barbie fashion plates, I'd dreamed of being in a real live fashion show. Obviously my just-above–Tom Cruise height killed my dreams of modeling haute couture, but once I became a designer, those dreams had shifted. Showing my own collection had become my holy grail all through college. And knowing how close I'd come to that dream here in Paris, only to be let down again, I felt a lump form in my throat as I stared up at the ceiling.

I'd had a small hope that maybe Moreau would release my shoes in time to show today. But I realized now that it had been in vain. As long as I was still his suspect numero uno, there was no way he was letting those babies go. I took a deep breath, forcing back the serious case of feeling sorry for myself.

No, the Maddie Springer who had fought her way to the top of her class at the Academy of Art College did not feel sorry for herself. The woman who had designed Beverly Hills' most sought after line of shoes since Manolo did not feel sorry for herself. And the new designer whom Jean Luc Le Croix had personally requested outfit all his models did not feel sorry for herself. I'd had enough. No paparazzi, no snooty French police officer, and no damned NERF Wonder Boot was going to stand in my way anymore.

I rolled out of bed and jumped into the shower, dressing in a pair of tight black jeans, rolled at the ankles, and a black tank top with little rhinestone studs along the neckline. Throwing caution to the wind I put on a three-inch strappy red stiletto. Screw Wonder Boot.

Okay, fine. I'll admit the extra height was a little awkward with Wonder Boot, but after I adjusted the crutches a couple inches higher, it was manageable. And it felt good.

I suddenly felt like myself again. I was calm. I was in control.

And I had a plan.

I grabbed my cell and dialed Marcel Dubois's number at the *Paris Spectacle*. After three rings he picked up with a "*Bonjour, ce Debois.*"

"Hi. I called yesterday—Maddie Springer."

"*Oui, oui!*" He sounded as though I'd just told him he'd won the lottery. Which, I guess, journalistically speaking, he kind of had. "Mademoiselle Springer, of course. Lovely to speak with you again."

If only everyone were so happy to get my phone calls.

"Listen, I've decided I want to give you that exclusive after all."

I sincerely hoped Felix would forgive me for this. An exclusive to the competition was tantamount to severing a limb. But on the itty-bitty off chance that maybe Felix was involved in all this, however inadvertently, I could hardly pull this off if he were the one I was giving my information to. So I plowed ahead.

"That is, if you're still interested?"

"In an exclusive?" Dubois's voice went high, and I could hear him shuffling papers in the background. "*Oui*, of course. That would be wonderful, fantastic. Uh, where can we meet? I would love to interview you in person."

I shook my head. "I'm sorry, I don't have time until after the Le Croix show today," I said.

I could almost hear his shoulders sag over the phone.

"But I do have something you can run with now."

"Oh?" And just like that he was back. "*Oui*, go ahead."

I took a deep breath, crossed my fingers, and prayed to the saint of little white lies.

"I have incontrovertible evidence that I did not kill Gisella."

This piqued his interest enough that I actually heard him gasp. "What kind of evidence?" he asked, his voice breathless.

"A camera. It belonged to Gisella Rossi. And it contains proof that not only was she stealing jewelry from her employers but also that she had an accomplice. An accomplice who most likely killed her."

He was silent a moment, digesting this information.

"What kind of proof?"

"Video files. Gisella taped her . . . exploits."

"And you currently have this camera in your possession?"

"I do," I said. Which wasn't a complete lie. I did have the camera. It just didn't contain squat. But the killer didn't know that. And if my bluff worked, he would do whatever it took to make sure that file didn't get out.

"And you will release this evidence to me after the show?"

I nodded at the phone. "Absolutely. On one condition."

"*Oui?*" he said.

I was 99 percent sure he'd do anything to get his hands on a story like this.

"I want you to go on the air now, letting the public know that I have this evidence, it's secure in the safe in my hotel room, and that I'll be talking to you and making the evidence public immediately after the Le Croix show."

I could hear his frown through the phone. "Why?"

Because I had a plan to catch the killer red-handed trying to steal the camera. But I figured that was a little too direct. Instead I told him, "Those are my terms. Take it or leave it."

He paused for a moment. "*Oui*, I will do it."

I grinned, then arranged to meet him in the hotel lobby after the show.

I slipped Gisella's camera out of my purse and opened the closet doors, exposing the little floor safe in the corner. I crouched down and opened it, sliding the camera inside before shutting it and securing the door with a click.

Phase one, complete.

Now all I needed was a way to catch the thief in the act.

I made a quick stop in Mom and Mrs. Rosenblatt's room (still empty—where the hell were those two?) before riding the elevator back down to the lobby. Luckily I caught Andre-slash-Pierre at the front desk.

"Good morning," I said, doing an awkward one-heel, one-boot hobble.

"*Bonjour,* Mademoiselle Springer," he responded. He glanced behind me. "Eh, no Rosenblatt?" he whispered.

I shook my head. "No. No Rosenblatt."

He visibly relaxed. "What can I do for you this fine morning then?"

"I wanted to ask if you have security cameras in the hotel?"

He nodded. "*Oui, oui.* Our guests' safety is of the utmost importance to us. Why do you ask, mademoiselle? You are worried about intruders?"

"Um, sort of. I was wondering . . ." I paused, unsure how much of my plan to share with him. "I was wondering if there is a camera in the hallway outside my room."

Pierre nodded. "All the hallways are monitored."

"I have a feeling . . ." I paused again.

"*Oui?* A feeling?"

"A feeling that someone may try to break into my room today. During the Le Croix show."

His eyebrows shot north. "You have received a threat?"

"Uh, well, no."

"A warning?"

"Not exactly."

He narrowed his eyes. "That Mademoiselle Rosenblatt and her mumbo-jumbo premonitions?"

"Um, no. I just . . . well, had a feeling."

"Hmm." He thought about that. "Okay, then. We should inform the police, *oui?*"

"No!"

Pierre jumped.

"Uh, I mean, no. No police. It's, uh, probably just a prank, right? No point in bringing the authorities in for nothing. I just wanted to make sure that *should* I report a theft later, there would be visual evidence of someone breaking into my room. Should they try to break in."

Pierre sucked in his cheeks, contemplating me. Finally he said, "I will make sure the security team has a camera on your door."

I grinned. "Thank you, Pierre!" I slapped a palm over my mouth. "I mean Andre."

"Hmph," he said again.

I grabbed my crutches and hobbled across the marble floor (slowly this time—one embarrassing face-plant per trip was enough for me) toward the glass front doors, where the doorman hailed me a cab.

I slid onto the seat and gave the driver the address of Le Carrousel du Louvre before pulling out my cell and dialing Dana's number. She picked up on the second ring.

"Hello?"

"Hey, it's me. Where are you?"

"I'm at the tent already. I had a six A.M. fitting. You?"

"I'm on my way there now. I'll see you in a few minutes. And, Dana?"

"Yeah?"

I couldn't help a grin. "We're catching a killer today."

Dana gave a little squeal of excitement in my ear before hanging up.

I settled back down into my seat, crossing my fingers that I wouldn't live to regret this, as a mix of anticipation, fear, and excitement churned in my stomach. No matter what else happened today, one thing was for sure.

The show must go on.

Chapter Eighteen

The ride to Le Carrousel du Louvre took longer than normal, as the streets were packed once we neared the Le Croix tent. I finally had the driver drop me off down the block and hopped along on my crutches to get through the milling crowds. At the entrance I was stopped by two security guards who looked like Popeye clones—both sporting crew cuts and forearms larger than most models' thighs. They went through my shoulder bag and did a cursory pat-down before allowing me entry. Which I honestly found a little ridiculous, considering both Gisella and Donata had been killed by shoes, not handguns or switchblades. Though I'm pretty sure they knew there'd be mutiny if they laid a hand on the guests' footwear.

Once I passed inspection I hobbled through the tent toward the backstage area. The newly constructed runway gleamed under the spotlights, three rows of white folding chairs lining either side. Two of Le Croix's assistants were making their way down the aisles, placing programs on the chairs as Ann looked on, talking into her headset to someone about there being too many red hues in the lighting setup.

I passed her with a cursory wave (which she was too busy to return) as I rounded the runway and went through the curtains separating the staging area.

Whereas the runway was in a state of quiet anticipation, the backstage area was already bordering on manic chaos: hair being teased, makeup applied with quick, practiced strokes by a team of professional artists, and last-minute adjustments being made to sew, pin, and tape the girls into their first outfits.

I spied Dana in a director's chair in front of a mirror, getting bright green eyeshadow swiped along her lids. Huh, what do you know? Maybe Mom and high fashion weren't that far off from each other.

"Hey," I said, coming up behind her.

She opened one eye. "There you are. Jean Luc's looking for you. He said he heard on TV that you were doing an interview after the show?"

Wow, news traveled fast. On the upside that meant Marcel had kept up his side of the bargain. While I'd fibbed to him about my motives for getting the story out, I sincerely hoped that I did have the exclusive of a lifetime to give him once this was all over. I mentally crossed my fingers that Pierre's cameras were rolling as I filled Dana in on my plan.

By the time I got to the end, her eyes was shadowed in a dramatic sweeping green and Jean Luc was shouting for "the shoe girl." I gave Dana's arm a squeeze and told her to break a leg while I went off to fit my makeshift footwear on the models.

The rest of the morning went by in a blur of clothing, shoes, accessories, and a myriad of last-minute crises, each one prompting Jean Luc to pop antacids as if he were growing a garden of ulcers in his gut. By the time I heard the sounds of people filtering into the tent, taking their seats in anticipation of the big show, I was a nervous wreck—not only due to Jean Luc's infectious anxiety, but even more so to what lay ahead afterward. And who might, at that very moment, be breaking into my hotel room to steal decoy evidence.

Which was probably why I jumped about a mile into the air when someone said:

"Maddie."

I turned quickly.

Felix stood behind me. Close behind me. Instinctively I took a step back. I hadn't seen him since the incident at the castle, and my cheeks instantly flooded with heat at the sight of him now.

He was dressed in his usual khakis paired with a white button-down, though—I supposed as a concession to the fashion vibes crackling through the air—he'd slipped a dark brown blazer over the top and traded in his Skechers for a pair of dress shoes. Overall the effect was of a casual sophistication that, I had to admit, he pulled off well.

"You look a little flushed."

My hands immediately went up to my fire-filled cheeks.

"Me? Oh, uh, well, Jean Luc's had us running around all day."

Felix nodded, then handed me a bottle of water. "You look like you could use this."

I took it, making a conscious effort not to skim his hand as I did. "What are you doing here?"

He raised an eyebrow. "Jean Luc invited me. A sort of peace offering for the mess with the necklace."

"A mess you started. Did Jean Luc know you were dating Gisella?" I asked, narrowing my eyes.

Felix looked heavenward. "We're not going to let that one go, are we, love?"

"No, *we're* not."

"Look, I told you, we went out a few times. It was nothing serious."

I unscrewed the top from the bottle. "You never did say why you broke it off."

Felix paused. "No, I didn't."

"Well? Come on. For a guy who makes his living prying into other people's private lives, you're nuts if you think I'm gonna let you clam up now."

He gave me a long, hard look. Then: "There was someone else."

I raised an eyebrow. "You're quite the ladies' man. Another model?"

"No."

"Actress?"

"No."

"Come on, who is she? How long have you been seeing each other?"

Felix's gaze didn't waver, his entire body suddenly rigid, at attention, focused entirely on me. "Perhaps I worded that incorrectly. I wasn't seeing someone else. There was just . . . the hope of someone else."

I cocked my head to the side. "The hope?"

"She . . ." He faltered, then cleared his throat. "I suppose I'm destined to admire her from afar. But as long as I am, it's hardly fair to lead anyone else on."

A bad feeling churned in my stomach, one that warned

I never should have started this conversation. I looked left and right, searching for any way out of it.

But before I could find one, Felix did a short, humorless laugh. "You really don't know, do you?"

I bit my lip. "Felix, I don't think—"

He didn't let me finish, instead taking a step forward, his voice low and laced with emotion. "And here I thought I was being pretty obvious." His eyes finally broke their unnerving contact with my own, lowering, settling on my lips.

I sucked in a breath.

Oh. Hell.

I instinctively licked my lips, my throat suddenly drier than my mother's elbows in January. I tried to take a big breath of much-needed oxygen, but my lungs suddenly felt two sizes too small, especially with Felix standing so close. It felt as if he were everywhere, closing in on me, suffocating me. I opened my mouth to speak, but only a little squeaking sound came out, as though I'd swallowed a mouse. I wet my lips again.

"Stop doing that," Felix whispered.

"What?" I squeaked.

"Moving your tongue along your lips."

"I . . ." I trailed off. I had no response for that.

"A man has only so much self-control, Maddie."

The mouse in my throat piped up again.

Felix's eyes went dark and heavy, his breath coming faster. "Maddie, I—"

"Maddie, dahling, there you are!"

I gave myself a mental shake, Jean Luc's voice breaking the way-too-intimate moment Felix and I were having in the middle of a crowded room.

Disappointment welled in Felix's eyes, though he covered it well, taking a step back and casually running a hand through his ever-disheveled hair.

"Maddie, sweets, love, darling, we have got a problem. We are talking showstopper here, honey."

I cleared my throat, willing my cheeks to stop burning. "Yes?" I asked, addressing Jean Luc.

What little hair the man had was standing on end, a sheen of perspiration covering his forehead, his pupils dilated to an unhealthy size. "It's Angelica. She broke a heel. Damned cheap pumps! You've got to do something—now! She goes on in ten minutes, God help us all." He paused, spotting Felix for the first time. "Oh, hello, Lord Ackerman, I trust you are enjoying the circus, no?" he said, gesturing around himself.

Felix gave Jean Luc a curt nod, his eyes still on me.

"I'm on it," I promised.

"You are a lifesaver. I swear, if I can get through this day without killing myself, I will die a happy man. Now, go, go, go!" He shooed me.

I went, trying not to meet Felix's penetrating gaze. I wasn't sure what he'd been about to say, but I was certain I didn't know how to respond. He had to be joking, right? I mean, this was one of his sick jokes. He was teasing. He was just playing with me. He was . . .

I turned around. He was still standing in the same place, his eyes on me, hands shoved in his pockets, a look in his eyes that was surprisingly vulnerable, making his boyish good looks that much more endearing. I'd never seen Tabloid Boy like this. Teasing, yes. Playful, yes. Even infuriatingly selfish, self-absorbed, preoccupied. But never laid this bare.

I snapped my head back around. This was all too much.

I took a sip from the water bottle in my hands, my mouth going Sahara on me as I threaded my way through the makeup chairs, wardrobe racks, and general chaos to where Angelica was holding a broken heel in one hand and trying to zip up a black baby-doll dress with the other.

"Heel emergency?" I asked.

Angelica nodded. "Sorry. I tripped over a makeup case."

I pulled a tube of superglue from my pocket. "No problem." I applied a thin layer to the heel, sticking it back in place. Were she going on a day trip to the mall, no way would this hold. But for a two-minute strut down a runway, it would do.

"Love the outfit," I said, gesturing to the dress. It featured a high Empire waist and a flowing bell shape, à la vintage Audrey Hepburn. Totally sixties chic.

"Thanks. It would have been better if we'd had a real necklace to go with it," she said, adjusting the piece of costume jewelry around her neck that Jean Luc had found as a last-minute replacement for the real deal, still squirreled away in Moreau's evidence vault, along with two dozen pairs of my very best work.

A thought I shoved to the back of my mind, lest I break out in tears right then and there.

"Damned Gisella. Even dead she's still screwing me over," Angelica mumbled to herself.

"Well, at least she can't steal any more boyfriends away," I reasoned.

Angelica cocked her head at me, her red curls flopping to the side. "What?"

"Like she did with your boyfriend Sam."

She grinned at me, showing off a row of ultrawhite teeth. "I never said Sam was a man. *Samantha* was my girlfriend."

Mental forehead smack.

"Oops. My bad. I guess I just thought . . ." I trailed off. Considering the type of files on Gisella's camera, I'd just assumed that we were talking about a guy here. I never guessed Gisella might be stealing a woman away from Angelica. I guess I assumed Gisella swung only one way—something I supposed I shouldn't have.

But in my defense, "Sam" wasn't exactly the most feminine name. Had she said "Sally," I so would have been right there with her.

Angelica waved me off. "No biggie," she said, doing another of her eastern European Americanisms.

"Angelica, you're on," Jean Luc shouted, grabbing her by the shoulders and propelling her into the wings, where Ann shifted her into line.

So, Sam was a woman. Somehow that new bit of information seemed like it should be significant. But I wasn't quite sure how.

As the swell of music filled the air, cheers erupted from the tent. Ann gave Angelica the silent, *Go*, and Angelica took her first step out onto the runway, instantly barraged by flashbulbs. The steady pulse of music continued as bits and pieces of information that I'd collected over the past week turned over one another in my head, like puzzle pieces that didn't quite fit together.

I watched Jean Luc herd models into line, Ann shouting into her headset, giving each model a, *Go*, on cue. Dana fidgeted in line, looking nervous but gorgeous in her teal silk number. She turned, and I gave her a reassuring thumbs-up as Ann shoved her onto the runway. I couldn't help the little swell of pride as I heard the crowd ooh and ahh over my best friend.

Model after model began returning from the runway, their stoic expressions transforming to panic the second they emerged backstage, quickly stripping off their outfits and shoving their long limbs into the next look. They were each immediately attacked by a waiting team; hair was teased, clothes flew, shoes shoved on tired feet, all to the loud, steady bass beat of the music pumping through the hidden speakers.

I took another sip of water. The chaos of the room, not to mention the last week, was getting to me. I felt my hands starting to sweat, my heart beating a little faster.

And then there was Felix. He was standing off to one side, his back to the runway as he leaned casually against the wall. His hands were still shoved in his pockets, his eyes watchful, taking the scene in, no doubt trying to come up with a sensationalized slant to the whole thing to run in tomorrow's paper. Typical Tabloid Boy.

So why were my cheeks flushing again? I bit my lip, the loud music, the crowded room, Felix's revelation, all suddenly feeling like they were closing in on me. I was getting seriously claustrophobic.

I took a deep breath in and out, trying to get the flush under control as I watched Auntie Charlene appear at Felix's side. He turned and gave her a smile, his adorable Hugh Grant dimples punctuating his cheeks.

I shook my head. *Adorable?* Where had that come from?

Charlene leaned in close, whispering something in

Felix's ear. A frown creased his features, and he glanced my way.

Immediately my eyes hit the ground; I was loath to be caught staring at him. I took another sip of my water, then peeked back up at him through my lashes. Only he was gone. Charlene stood in his place, staring straight at me with her pale blue eyes.

I closed my eyes, the warm flush turning into an all-out sweat. When I opened them again the room started to spin, models dancing before my vision, Jean Luc's anxious form fuzzy and in triplicate. I tried to take deep, steadying breaths.

And still Charlene continued to focus in my direction. Eyes watchful. Pale features placid. Body rigid with tension. Charlene. Charlene . . .

And then the last piece fell into place in my brain with an almost audible click. Charlie. Charlie hadn't been a man; Charlie was a woman.

I felt myself sway on my feet as my crutches slipped out from under me.

"Easy there, Maddie."

I blinked hard, my vision blurred as if I were looking at the world through a sheet of wax paper. I saw Charlene's face hovering just above mine.

"You?" I asked, my voice sounding a million miles away to my own ears. "You and Gisella . . . that night . . . the necklace . . ."

"You look a little flushed, Maddie," she said, her voice echoing in that infuriatingly polite British tone.

I blinked again, trying to control the double visions hitting me harder than a vodka martini on an empty stomach. I looked down at the water bottle still in my hand.

The water.

I let the bottle drop, the contents splashing onto my toes as sweat broke out on my brow. What was in the water?

Felix. Felix had given me the bottle. . . . He and Charlene . . . It couldn't be.

The room began to spin again as I whipped my head back and forth, scanning the backstage area for Felix. What had he done to me?

"Easy, now, Maddie," Charlene said, her blue eyes flat as she stared down at me, her manicured claws digging into my arm to hold me up. "Don't you worry, love."

I watched a slow, wicked smile spread across her features as the room closed in on me.

"I'm going to take *good* care of you."

I opened my mouth to speak, but I was suddenly too weak to move my lips. The best I could do was let out a pathetic, strangled sound in the back of my throat.

Just before everything went black.

Chapter Nineteen

I have had the misfortune in my life to be knocked over the head, shot, whacked unconscious, and, last but not least, nearly strangled. (What can I say? Mrs. Rosenblatt is right: My karma *really* sucks.) But drugged was a new one even for me.

And as I slowly blinked my eyes open one painful movement at a time, it was not an experience, I decided, that I ever wanted to repeat. My mouth felt like I'd been eating cotton balls; my eyelids were almost too heavy to lift. And my head pounded louder than a heavy-metal drummer. I groaned. Bad idea. The sound vibrated through my skull, causing stabs of pain to slice through my brain.

"Maddie?"

I froze at the sound of the familiar voice calling my name. I took a breath and forced my eyes open. They moved as if under water, slowly, blinking a few times before the person who'd spoke came into focus.

"Mom?" I croaked out.

"Oh thank God, Maddie, you're alive."

I did some more blinking, trying to get my bearings as the drummer quickened his pace. I was in a hotel room that looked a lot like mine except for the fact that the color scheme was a dusty rose instead of my sunshine yellow. A pair of matching Vuitton suitcases were lined up by the door, the closets conspicuously empty.

I looked down and saw I was propped up in a bed, my back to a bedpost. Tied to the opposite post, amidst a sea of tiny pillows, sat Mom and Mrs. Rosenblatt, back-to-back, their limbs taped down with a length of gray duct tape, a bedpost between them. Mrs. Rosenblatt had a piece of tape firmly covering her mouth. Mom's was hanging down on one side, exposing a pair of raw-looking lips—that I realized were still moving.

". . . and then she just dumped you there, and I had no idea if you were dead or alive or breathing. I swear, I thought she'd killed you, Maddie. Oh, honey, I'm so glad you're okay!"

I wasn't sure that *okay* accurately described my current condition, but, as I wiggled my fingers and toes, I realized I was alive. Though, as I went on to move arms and legs, I realized I also had been given the duct-tape treatment. A thick band of it cut through my middle, inhibiting any more movement than a slight wiggle. Someone had also wrapped duct tape around my ankles, securing my one good leg to Wonder Boot.

"I'm okay, Mom," I said. Only it came out more like. "Mumph, mum, mmmmm," considering my lips were taped shut, too.

"Mmmm, mmmm," Mrs. Rosenblatt replied, shrugging her shoulders.

"Here, Mads, see if you can inch over here. Maybe I can get the tape loose."

I did, wiggling as far as I could, to no avail. I felt pain

starting to work its way up my spine as tears clouded behind my eyes.

"Okay, okay, don't panic," Mom said, though her freaked expression completely matched mine. "Look, maybe I can get it loose with my toe."

My first thought as I looked down at Mom's bright red pedicure was, *Eww!* But the second was that it actually might work. And a little toe in the face was a lot better than whatever Charlene had planned for us when she got back.

I leaned my head forward, jutting my chin out as far as I could. Mom scooched her butt forward, doing a yoga-worthy stretch in my direction. Still a good six inches away.

Mrs. Rosenblatt moved closer, giving Mom a little more leeway, and she tried again. This time her toe touched my cheek. A couple more rounds of this and she finally had a corner loose. I moved my mouth across my shoulder, catching the tape in my tank top and rubbing back and forth until it finally came loose enough for me to speak.

"Oh, Mom, you're a genius. God bless Faux Dad's pedicures."

"Mmmm, mmm," Mrs. R said, jutting her chin toward me.

She and Mom rotated places, and I did a repeat performance of Mom's acrobatics, slipping off my red heel and running my toe along the side of Mrs. R's cheek until a tiny corner of tape came loose.

"My God, I think that's the longest time I've ever gone without speaking," she said, finally wiggling it off on the strap of her muumuu.

I was almost sure of it.

"Mom, what happened? How did you two get in here?"

"It was Charlene," Mom said, even though I'd suspected as much. "Maddie, she was the one working with Gisella. And I think she killed her."

At the moment I had to agree.

"How did you get here?" I asked. "How long have you been here?"

"Well, after we saw the printouts you left us on that Corbett Winston theft, we thought we'd go check it out. At first no one there wanted to talk to us," Mom said.

"And then your mother got this brilliant idea that we'd pretend we was with the FBI. We told 'em that we was looking into a ring of international jewel thieves."

I rolled my eyes. "And they bought that?"

Mrs. R shrugged.

"Anyway," Mom continued, "finally the manager of Corbett Winston spoke with us, and when we asked about Gisella he said that she'd come in with a companion. A woman Gisella had introduced as her manager."

"Only we hadn't heard of Gisella having any manager," Mrs. R said.

"So, we asked the guy to describe the woman, and he told us about this blonde British woman."

"So, we figured that Felix guy was British; maybe he'd have some idea who she was. We came back to the hotel to talk to him."

"Only Pierre rang his room and he wasn't in," Mom said.

"But his auntie was."

"So we came up to her room and told her what we'd found and that we were hoping Felix could help us figure out who this lady was."

"She ordered tea from room service, and we all sat down to wait it out for Felix," Mrs. Rosenblatt said.

"Only she must have slipped something into it when we weren't looking because the next thing I knew the room was doing a shimmy in front of me, and we woke up like this."

"When was this?" I asked.

Mom shook her head. "Yesterday, the day before. It's all a little fuzzy. She keeps giving us tea."

"I've decided I hate tea," Mrs. R said.

I didn't blame her.

"We tried to call you, Maddie."

"But that was before your mom got her tape off."

"You just kept saying, 'Hello?'"

Mental forehead smack. Well, I guess that tells you not to call me in a crisis.

"How long has she been gone?" I asked, staring at the closed door. The matching luggage next to it made me nervous. Charlene had kept two middle-aged women hostage for over forty-eight hours. She wasn't likely just to let them go home to identify her to the police. Charlene had already killed two women. What were a few more?

"I don't know," Mom said. "Maybe half an hour."

I bit my lip. Then, remembering how Angelica had said the walls of the hotel were thin, I cried out, "Help!" as loudly as the heavy-metal drummer in my head would allow me.

Mom and Mrs. R followed suit, screaming at the top of their lungs.

Fifteen minutes later we were still alone and our voices were hoarse. It was no use. Everyone was either at the shows or had taken our cries for a bad police drama on the television.

I tried a different tactic, leaning down and biting at the length of tape around my arms. Which didn't do much. It was amazingly strong. There was a reason that lazy dads the world over used this stuff to fix anything and everything: It held. I continued gnawing at it as Mom and Mrs. R did the same.

Apparently Mrs. R's teeth were pointier than mine, as I finally heard a rip from her direction and her arms flapped free. She didn't waste any time, quickly ripping first at Mom's bonds, then mine. A few seconds later we were all jumping off the bed, lengths of duct tape stuck to us at comical angles, making for the door.

But, of course, nothing is ever that easy.

Just as we reached it, it swung open.

The three of us froze, our eyes ping-ponging between the figure in the doorway and the three of us. On any other day we might have charged her and probably made it. Unfortunately on this particular day she held a shiny silver gun in her hand.

"Where do you think you're going?"

I opened my mouth to speak, but she shoved the gun in my direction. "Shut up."

Apparently it was a rhetorical question.

Charlene edged into the room, letting the door fall shut behind her. "The maid said she heard the television on in my room. Couldn't have been you loudmouths, could it?" she asked.

This time I kept my mouth shut. Definitely rhetorical.

As she moved into the room, her cool blue minidress perfectly matched her pale blue eyes, giving her an icy edge. Granted, the fact that she'd drugged me, then tied me up might have colored that assessment just a little.

"You two," she said, waving the gun at Mom and Mrs. Rosenblatt. "Into the bathroom."

Mom looked at me. I gave a slight shrug. Since she had the gun and we didn't, I didn't think we were really in a place to argue.

Mom slowly moved to the right, inching into the bathroom, her hands up in a surrender motion. Mrs. R followed, waddling awkwardly through the tiny doorway.

"Maddie?" Mom said tentatively.

"I'll be okay," I said with a false assurance I certainly didn't feel. Especially when Charlene shut the door behind them, barricading it with a chair underneath.

"I guess it's just you and me now," she said, a slow smile spreading across her features.

Oh boy.

"I believe you have something that belongs to me," she said, advancing on me.

"I do?" Instinctively I took a step back.

"The camera. Hand it over."

"You know, technically it doesn't actually belong to you, it belongs to Gisella. Who is dead, but I guess you'd know that because you killed her. But really, I think the camera is the rightful property of her heirs. So, unless you're in her will—"

"Shut up!" She pointed the gun at my nose.

I shut up.

"Felix was right. You do have a big mouth."

Hey! "Felix said that about me?"

She barked out a short laugh. "Not in so many words. The man worships the ground you walk on."

"He does not," I protested.

"Oh, yes, he does. 'Maddie this,' 'Maddie that'— you're all he talks about. It's disgusting."

I paused. "So . . . he's not working with you?"

She scoffed. "Felix? Please. You think he'd be man enough to follow through on something like this?"

Hey! Felix might be many things, but he wasn't a chicken. "But the water. He handed it to me."

She grinned. "I asked him to. Said you looked a little flushed. Heaven forbid his Maddie should be dehydrated."

"*His* Maddie?" My cheeks flooded with heat.

"Oh, don't be flattered. Felix has the brain of a fruit fly."

"Hey!"

She scowled at me.

Oops. I'd said that one out loud.

She narrowed her pale eyes at me. "I have had to deal with that man's bullshit my whole life. I've sat by as he was handed everything that I had to struggle for. Do you know what it's like being the *adopted* child of the trophy wife? After dear old Dad died Felix got everything: the title, the land, the money. And what did I get? Nothing. He never had to work a day in his life. All the while I had to grow up dirt-poor going to visit my titled relations in the castle that should have been mine. Felix doesn't even like England! Running off to L.A. to live in the land of bimbos and write for that silly paper."

She was getting so worked up that an unattractive glob of spittle was forming at the corners of her mouth, reminding me of a rabid dog. I cringed, involuntarily ducking to avoid being the victim of an overannunciated P.

"But all that was going to change," she said, her eyes gleaming, "once I got him to marry me."

"But he's your nephew," I said, getting just a little squicked out.

"Adopted. We're not blood relations, remember. As my dear old dad delighted in pointing out at every turn."

"You really think he'll marry a killer?"

"You really think he'll find out?" she asked.

"All the signs that pointed to Felix being the killer . . . they easily pointed to you as well," I reasoned, stalling for time. I heard Mom and Mrs. R shuffling in the bathroom, a thud falling against the closed door. "It was you who found out about Donatello, wasn't it?"

"You mean Donata?" She smirked. "Yes. The moment I met her I knew there was something familiar about her. Then Angelica told me she'd been a model in the past. Of course I looked through my old magazines, and what do you know? She had. As a he. Fashion may be an open-minded sort of business, but there are limits. And Donata and I both knew that a transsexual agent was pushing them a little too far."

"So you and Gisella hatched a plan."

"I hatched a plan," she corrected me. "Gisella had the brains of a canary. Gisella was all about Gisella. Which worked out fine. She did the strutting, and while all eyes were on her I orchestrated the rest."

"You blackmailed Donata."

She nodded. "That part was easy. Donata was happy to comply with our requests. Especially once Gisella started booking things on her own. Donata made plenty of money off Gisella. She had no reason to complain."

"And Gisella?"

She shrugged. "Gisella was happy as long as she was kept in furs and heels."

I heard Mom and Mrs. R make another run at the door. The chair beneath the knob wiggled a little. If I could just keep Charlene talking . . .

"And you two were lovers?" I asked, trying not to glance at the bathroom door.

She narrowed her eyes at me. "What makes you say that?"

"I saw the camera. The kind of bedroom videos she took."

For a moment Charlene faltered. "She took videos of us in . . ."

I nodded. "You didn't know?"

She shook her head. "So that's your evidence, huh? A torrid lesbian affair?" She snorted. "Hardly as conclusive as the television said."

"But," I said, watching her reaction, "enough to make Felix wonder."

She clenched her jaw, the truth of my words sinking in. "Well, you can't very well hand it over to the press now, can you?"

"Uh, it's in my room. Come with me and we'll go get it," I said, remembering the surveillance cameras in the hallway.

"And give you a chance to run? I don't think so, Maddie. No, I'll just wait until we're through here and retrieve it myself, thank you very much."

Crap.

"Speaking of which . . ." she said, pointing the gun at me and taking a step forward.

"Okay, I bluffed," I blurted out.

Charlene stopped advancing. "What?"

"I bluffed. I don't have any video footage."

"Bullshit! The television said you were turning it over after the show."

"Because that's what I told them. It was all a lie to smoke Charlie out of hiding."

She looked at me, her face going white. Finally she spit out a word: "Shit."

Very unladylike. Dear old dad wouldn't approve.

She straight-armed the gun at me. "You mean you don't even have it! You mean you were lying this whole time?"

"No, there was video footage. I just . . . erased it. By accident."

Suddenly the rage drained from her face, and she threw her head back and laughed.

"You erased it?"

I nodded. "Um, yeah."

"You and Felix really are made for each other. A couple of nitwits."

Mom thudded against the door again, inching the chair forward.

"So, um, what now?" I asked. Not that I really wanted to know. But the longer I kept her talking, the less she was shooting.

Charlene took a step forward, going nose-to-nose with me. I could smell Listerine on her breath.

"Now I hop a flight back to England. I live like a queen

on my proceeds until I can convince my dear nephew to marry me, and then I get my happily-ever-after. The end," she said.

I took a shallow breath. "And what happens to me?"

She narrowed her eyes. "The end."

I gulped. "And Mom and Mrs. Rosenblatt?"

That wicked grin spread across her features again. "Oh, *I'm* not going to do anything to them. You're going to do it all. You are, after all, the Couture Killer."

I felt a knot form in my stomach. "What do you mean?"

Charlene took a step back and unzipped one of the suitcases. She pulled out a pair of black stiletto heels. "One for each of them," she said, gesturing toward the bathroom door.

"There's no way anyone would believe that," I said, even as I doubted the truth of the words. People already believed me to be a killer; this would just be confirmation.

"Oh yes, they will. Especially when they read your suicide note."

"Suicide note?" I asked, my voice going small.

She nodded. "You couldn't handle the guilt. The pressure of Fashion Week was too much for you. You snapped. You killed Gisella, Donata, and then the people closest to you. Then you took your own life."

I felt all the color draining from my cheeks. This chick was seriously whacked.

She took two quick steps forward, grabbing a handful of my hair, and hopped me over to the little writing desk, shoving me into the seat, banging Wonder Boot against the side in the process.

I winced, a sharp pain shooting up my leg, but she didn't notice, instead pushing a pad of paper and pen at me. The cool metal barrel of the gun came up against my temple.

"Write," she instructed.

I gulped, grabbing the pen in my shaky hand.

" 'I, Maddie Springer,' " she dictated.

I stared down at the pages. Okay, fine, I would write. At least it would buy me a little time. I vaguely heard the sounds of Mom and Mrs. R still trying to break down the bathroom door behind me.

In a shaky hand I wrote, *I, Maddie Springer.*

" 'Leave this note as my last confession.' "

I looked up at her.

She shoved the gun at me hard, twisting my head to the side. I felt tears well up behind my eyes.

I wrote what she said, deliberately making slow loops with my letters.

" 'I killed Gisella,' " she said, still dictating. " 'I also killed Donata Girardi. It was too much for me, the pressure of Fashion Week. I'm sorry.' "

I continued writing, willing someone—anyone—to hear us. Where was housekeeping when you needed them?

"Sign it," Charlene demanded.

I did, my signature trailing off at the end as I realized this was it. I was officially out of time.

I took a deep breath as I felt Charlene stiffen behind me. She knew it too.

"Now," she said, her voice oddly flat, "stand up."

I did, on one shaky leg. I could hear Mom and Mrs. R thumping against the bathroom door, but the chair was still in place. I was on my own.

It was now or never.

"Ow, my leg," I moaned, shifting my weight to Wonder Boot.

Obviously Charlene didn't care if I was in pain. Obviously Charlene wanted to shoot me. But it distracted her long enough that she glanced down at my foam-clad foot.

That was all I needed. In one swift movement I kicked my good foot up, my red three-inch stiletto flying up toward her face. Instinctively she staggered back to avoid a heel to the head and I lunged forward, head down, arms out, doing the best imitation of a linebacker a girl who only watches football for the tight pants can.

Charlene gave an unladylike, "Oof," as I connected with her midsection, and she went tumbling backward, the gun in her hand going off and taking out a chunk of the ceiling.

"What's going on out there?" Mrs. Rosenblatt yelled from the bathroom.

"Maddie! Are you okay?" I heard Mom screech.

But I was a little too preoccupied to answer at the moment. I had one hand on Charlene's wrist trying to point the barrel of the gun somewhere other than at my person, balancing on one foot. Charlene grabbed a handful of my hair, ripping backward.

My head went with it, my eyes rolling back in their sockets.

"I think they're fighting," I heard Mrs. Rosenblatt yell.

"Maddie, are you winning, honey?" Mom called.

It was hard to say.

I may have had the element of surprise, but Charlene

had about five inches on me and liked the gym way better than I did. She twisted her wrist, pointing the gun at my ribs. I moved at the last minute and it went off, shattering a lamp by the bedside.

I leaned my head down (no small task with her hand firmly grabbing my hair) and bit her on the wrist.

"Son of a bitch!" she screamed. I guess being in a fight to the death excused one from good manners.

She dropped the gun, which luckily fell to the floor and slid toward the bed.

"You bitch!" she cried, diving for the gun.

My turn to grab a handful of hair. I yanked on her roots for all I was worth, and was rewarded with a high-pitched screech as she twisted on the floor, her long legs sweeping my one good one and taking me down with her.

She sat up, then did a WWE wrestler full-body slam.

I felt the air rush out of my lungs in one big whoosh.

"Maddie? Baby, are you okay?"

"Claw her eyes out, *bubbee*!" I heard Mrs. R yell.

Hey, not a bad idea.

I reached up, my manicured fingers digging for her eyes. Only I missed, drawing a long red scratch down her cheeks instead. But it didn't even faze her. She'd tipped over that edge of crazy where she had only one objective. Her lips curled back from her teeth, her pupils wild and dilated, her gaze locked on mine. She reached up and wrapped her fingers around my throat, squeezing with all her might.

I made a strangled sound in the back of my throat, my hands instantly going to my neck, trying to pry her manicured claws from me.

"You are so going to pay," she said. "Felix's girly little whore."

"Hey, he kissed *me*," I breathed out. Then I kneed her in the pelvis.

She grunted, rolling over and loosening her grip on my throat.

"Right. The second time."

"The first one was an accident."

"Accident, my arse. He told me you spent the night." She elbowed me in the face, and I swear I actually saw stars. Huh, who knew that wasn't just an expression?

"In the guest room. I spent the night in the guest room."

She snorted. "So you say."

"Look, I am not—N-O-T," I spelled out as I slapped her across the face, "involved with Felix. He's so not my type."

"Rich," she said, raking her fingernails across my cheek. "Titled." She grabbed a handful of hair and pulled. "Tight ass. Not your type?"

I tried to shake my head, but her grip on my hair was too strong. Instead I wrapped my one good leg around her middle and pinned her to the ground. "No."

"Oh, really?" She wiggled, twisting out from under me. "Then what is?"

My mind instantly flashed on a dark-stubbled jaw, a sleek panther trailing down one thick bicep, and a pair of dark espresso eyes.

But instead of answering I rolled to the right, twisting Wonder Boot under me and pinning her beneath its bulk. I grabbed both her hands and sat on her chest.

"Ha! Who's girly now, huh?" I asked.

She narrowed her eyes at me, then looked to her right.

We'd rolled along the floor until we were right next to the bed. And the gun.

Oh shit.

In one swift movement she broke my hold, reached out, and had the gun in both hands.

A wicked grin overtook her features, made all the creepier by the fact that our tussle on the floor had her white blonde hair sticking up like an Edgar Winter mohawk.

"Get off me," she seethed between clenched teeth.

I put my hands up in a surrender motion and slowly stood up.

"What's going on out there. Who won?" Mrs. Rosenblatt asked from the bathroom.

"Shut up!" Charlene yelled, punctuating it by shooting at the bathroom door.

I thought I heard Mom shout, "Holy shit," but my mother never swore.

"You," Charlene said, aiming the gun at me. "You have been more trouble than you're worth. Up against the wall."

I complied, my hands still up, retreating until I felt my back hit the wallpaper.

"Just tell me one thing," I said, doing a silent prayer that someone—anyone—had heard the gunshots.

She narrowed her eyes at me. "A dying request?"

"Why kill Gisella? Was it because she was getting sloppy?"

She shook her head. "Gisella was always sloppy. She was so obvious no one would have ever suspected her."

"So then why kill her?"

Her eyes went cold. "Because of Felix. I killed her

because she was dating Felix. Felix was mine! He wasn't supposed to marry her. There was no way I could let that greedy little stick figure ruin everything. Felix belongs to me. That castle belongs to me!" She paused, reining in her volume. "So I had to put an end to our business arrangement."

She took a step forward, the gun pointed at my chest. "Just like I'm putting an end to this farce. Good-bye, Maddie," she said, her voice low, her eyes flat.

Chicken that I am, I closed my eyes. I know—silly. But if my brains were going to be splattered all over this lovely Parisian hotel room, that wasn't the last thing I wanted to see.

I held my breath and felt tears well up.

And my final irrational thought as I stood there was that I was sorry. So amazingly sorry for dragging Mom and Mrs. Rosenblatt into this. Sorry that I'd ever thought the killer could be Felix. And most of all, sorry that I'd hurt Ramirez. A picture of his face as he'd stared at me from the doorway of Felix's room haunted me as the tears fell down my cheeks in wet, hot streams. I would never, ever be able to forgive myself for hurting him. I hoped, though, that maybe someday he might forgive me.

I gave a little hiccup sob as I heard Charlene's gun cock, time seeming to stand still.

I held my breath and turned my head in anticipation.

But the next sound I heard was not the report of gunfire ripping into me, but the sound of a door bursting open.

I peeked one eye open.

"Freeze!" a voice yelled.

I froze, willing myself not to pee my pants.

Until I realized the command was not directed at me—but at Charlene.

Only she wasn't quite as compliant as I was. She turned her gun toward the voice, shooting off two rounds.

"What's going on out there?" Mom cried from the bathroom.

"Duck, Betty," I heard Mrs. R. say.

The owner of the voice returned fire, hitting Charlene once in the shoulder and again in the kneecap. She screamed, dropping her gun and falling to the floor like a sack of potatoes. Then three armed officers wearing bulletproof vests ran into the room, converging on Charlene. One applied pressure to her gunshot wounds while another handcuffed her, and yet a third kept a gun trained on her.

I blinked, the air rushing out of me, the tears flowing freely again, but for a whole different reason as I looked up and saw the fourth guy walk into the room.

Moreau.

I shook my head, my mouth moving but no words coming out. Finally I managed one. "How . . . ?"

Moreau smiled. "You didn't really think I suspected you, did you?"

My shoulders sagged and I crumpled to the ground.

Amid cries from the bathroom of, "What the hell is going on out there?"

Chapter Twenty

I'm not sure how long I was crumpled like that on the floor, but at some point a uniformed officer scooped me up and moved me across the hall to another hotel room full of police scanners, walkie-talkies, and other electronic devices with functions I couldn't begin to guess. He sat me on the edge of the bed, and a man in a white uniform with a red cross on it asked me a bunch of questions in French, to which I just shook my head, more tears falling. Finally he gave up, pulling out a first-aid kit and checking me from head to toe. I had a few scratches and bruises and a sore scalp, but other than that I think he gave me a clean bill of health—though my leg throbbed like crazy under Wonder Boot. I guess fighting off a homicidal maniac was putting a little more pressure on it than Dr. Pontytail would advise.

I don't know long my exam took, but a few minutes later Mom and Mrs. Rosenblatt were ushered across the hall as well. I jumped up, giving them both a hug. For a second we kind of stuck to one another from the duct tape residue, but I didn't care. I'd never been so happy to see anybody in my life.

"I've never been so happy to see you in my life," Mom said, voicing my exact thoughts. "Oh, honey, are you okay?"

She finally pulled back a moment to look at me. I'm pretty sure I had long horror-movie streaks of mascara running down my cheeks, but at least I was minus gunshot wounds.

Which was more than I could say for Charlene. I could still hear her howling across the hallway as more guys in white stabilized her.

The man with the red cross did a repeat of his head-to-toe exam with Mom and Mrs. R. Mrs. R said the guy got a little fresh, but I'm pretty sure that was just wishful thinking on her part. Finally they were pronounced fine—a little dehydrated and hungry from being locked up and given drugged tea for two days, but with a meal and some fluids they'd be okay.

Which prompted another round of sticky hugging and grateful tears all around.

Finally the guy with the first-aid kit left, and Moreau walked into the room.

"Madame Springer, Mademoiselle Rosenblatt," he said, nodding in Mom and Mrs. R's directions. Then his eyes settled on me. "Mademoiselle Springer. We meet again."

I crossed my arms over my chest. "Yes, we do. And I think it's you who has some explaining to do this time. What did you mean back there about not suspecting me?"

The dead squirrel on Moreau's upper lip shifted, and I think it might have been his attempt at a smile. He sat down on an armchair opposite the bed.

"I'm sorry to have kept you in the dark, but I knew that as long as the killer thought you were the prime suspect, she wouldn't flee."

"You used my daughter as bait?" Mom asked, doing a twin crossed-arms thing.

"Uh . . ." Moreau looked from Mom to me, clearly feeling outnumbered. "No. Not exactly. But we felt that as long as the killer thought her job of framing Mademoiselle Springer was working, she would feel safe enough to stay in Paris."

"So, you knew it was Charlene all along?"

He paused. "I'll admit that at first you were the focus of our investigations. It was impossible to overlook the similarities in the current deaths and your past, no?"

I shrugged. "I suppose."

"But," he went on, "as soon as we saw that your DNA did not match the hairs found at the crime scene, you were cleared."

I'd forgotten all about the DNA sample I'd given up. "What about Charlene? What made you suspect her?" I asked.

He spread his hands out wide. "It was a simple matter of finances. She had recently made some large deposits that were unaccounted for. We did some digging into her life and found she had a record of petty thievery as a teenager. We were in the process of obtaining a warrant for a DNA sample from her when we were informed that you might be here with her."

I cocked my head to the side. "Informed?"

"Eh . . ." He paused. "How do you Americans say . . . a tip-off?"

"Who?"

He paused, his mustache twitching. "I'm sorry, I cannot say."

I narrowed my eyes. "Cannot or will not?"

He looked down at the ground, up at the ceiling, everywhere but at my eyes.

I cleared my throat. "Look, I think after letting the press brand me as the Couture Killer to the entire free world, you owe me. Who was it?"

He gave a little sigh, his mustache blowing north. "Detective Ramirez."

I felt my breath catch in my throat. "Ramirez?"

He nodded. "We got a call from the airport this morning. He was going back to the U.S., but apparently he missed his flight. He had to wait until this morning. Then he said he saw a news program and heard about your evidence and the interview scheduled for after the Le Croix show. He called, saying he smelled a . . . how did he put it . . . 'harebrained scheme'?"

For once I wasn't even peeved at the term. All I cared about was that he'd called! Okay, so he hadn't exactly called *me*, but he'd called someone *about* me. That was close, right?

I realized Moreau was still talking.

". . . and he warned me that we should keep an eye on you until he got here. That it was likely you would try to engage the killer. So we put surveillance on you at the show. A good thing too, *oui*?" he asked, gesturing across the hall.

"*Oui, oui!*" Mrs. Rosenblatt piped up.

"Got here?" I repeated, feeling a bubble of hope well

in my chest. "Ramirez is here?" I craned my neck toward the door.

"Uh . . ." He looked away again, not meeting my eyes. "No. He left."

Just like that the hope crashed and burned.

"He left?"

Moreau nodded. "As soon as he knew you were safe."

"Oh," I said, my voice suddenly very, very small.

He was gone. Again. Okay, so he didn't want me to become maimed by some British nutcase. But he also didn't want to see me.

Moreau continued, "Detective Ramirez said he felt it best if we handled the situation from here. But he was with us as we followed Charlene from the tent."

"You know, you could have come in a little sooner," I said, rubbing at my bruised neck.

Moreau shrugged. "We needed to hear her confession first. You did a fine job getting it out of her. You did wonderful!" He clapped his hands in front of him.

"Gee. Swell."

"Say," Mrs. R said, "if you knew Maddie didn't do it, how come you took all her shoes?"

"We had to make it look as though we suspected her."

I narrowed my eyes at him.

Moreau's expression softened. "I'm sorry, Maddie. I know you wanted to show at Fashion Week."

I had. And at the time it had meant the world to me. But just now, knowing Mom and Mrs. R were safe, I couldn't care less where my shoes were.

"So, I get them back now?"

Okay, fine, maybe a teeny-tiny part of me cared a little.

He grinned, that dead squirrel on his upper lip twitching. "Yes. You may have your shoes back."

Two hours and many, many blue-uniformed officers later, Mom, Mrs. R, and I were all escorted back to our rooms. It was past midnight before we finally said good night in the hallway, promising to meet in the morning for breakfast. I closed the door to my room, the sudden silence after the night's chaos almost unreal. I stripped off my jeans and tank in the dark and crawled into bed. I closed my eyes and, willing myself not to dream, fell into a much-needed sleep.

I'm not sure how many hours I slept, but by the time I cracked my eyes open my hotel room was filled with sunshine, and there wasn't a part of my body that wasn't sore. I slowly got out of bed, flexing my limbs, and dragged myself into the bathroom. Bruises covered my upper arms, and a nice shiner ringed my left eye where Charlene's elbow had connected. My leg throbbed almost as badly as the day I'd been hit, and my hair looked like it belonged on a troll doll.

I turned away, figuring mirrors were not my friends at the moment. Instead I took a long, hot shower, probably using half the hotel's hot-water supply, and did the best I could with concealer to hide the majority of my bruises. I slipped into a comfortable pair of white capris, a pink tee with rhinestones that spelled the word PRINCESS on it, and one pink flat.

I called Mom's room, but she and Mrs. R still had the do-not-disturb on their phone. Instead I dialed room service, ordering croissants, brioche, jams, cheese, orange juice, coffee, and one grapefruit half (no need to go over-board).

No sooner had I hung up than a knock sounded at the door. I checked the little peephole and saw Dana standing in the hallway.

I opened the door and barely got out a, "Hi," before she was grabbing me in a bear hug.

"Ohmigod, Maddie! I'm so glad you're okay. I couldn't find you after the show, and then you weren't at the after-party either, and then I came back to the hotel and there were these policemen everywhere, and I tried to go see you, but they wouldn't let me through, and then finally that detective guy said you were okay but that you'd gone to sleep, and I've been totally waiting to come wake you up. And ohmigod, I can't believe it was Charlene!"

"Dana, I can't breathe."

"Oh." She let go of my midsection. "Sorry."

I ushered her into the room, and we sat on the bed as I filled her in on the previous evening's events, ending with the good news that Moreau had promised my shoe collection would be placed back at the Le Croix tent this morning.

"Oh, that reminds me," Dana said, grabbing her purse. "Have you seen this morning's *Informer*?"

I shook my head. I figured that even with the news of Charlene's arrest, it might be a while before tabloids were my friends again.

Dana pulled the folded paper out of her purse. "Okay, good news first, better news second. Check out page seven."

I grabbed the paper from her, open to page seven, and

saw a picture of Ricky and Natalie Portman. They were outside a restaurant, stuck together in a lip-lock.

"Oh, honey, I'm so sorry," I said. Then I paused as I looked up and saw Dana beaming from ear to ear. "Uh, I don't get it. You're happy Ricky is kissing some movie star?"

She giggled. Then she pointed to Ricky's left hand, which was zoning in on Natalie's boobs. "Look," she instructed. "He has a little mole right by his thumb."

"Uh-huh."

"Well, Ricky doesn't have a mole! Don't you see? They totally pasted his head on someone else's body. My boyfriend is not kissing Natalie Portman." She sat back, a smug smile on her face.

I couldn't help but grin back. "Congratulations."

"Thanks," she said, taking the paper. "Okay, now for the better news. Ready?" she asked, flipping to the front page.

"Always ready for good news."

She slid the paper across the bed to me.

The headline read: *Couture Killer Cleared*. But the part that immediately caught my eye was the photographs. Somehow they had gotten pictures of every single one of my shoes that were supposed to have been in the Le Croix show and blown them up on the front page. Okay, so it wasn't quite the same as showing in Paris, but you couldn't buy this kind of publicity. I quickly scanned down to the byline. Sure enough, it read, *Felix Dunn*.

I bit my lip, suddenly all the more sorry I'd ever suspected him of having anything to do with the deaths, let alone his crazy aunt drugging me.

"Wow," I said. "I can't believe he did this for me."

"Believe it, girl," Dana said. Then she added with a smirk, "So, tell me again what a terrible kisser he is."

I snapped my head up.

But I didn't get to answer as a knock sounded at the door. I padded over and looked out the little peephole, only all I could see were flowers.

I opened the door.

"Mademoiselle Springer?" asked a voice. I wasn't sure whose, as the guy's face was completely covered by a huge bouquet of red roses.

"Yes?" I asked tentatively.

The guy lowered the flowers, and a pimply kid with a shock of red hair appeared. "A flower delivery for you."

"Who are they from?"

He shrugged. "There is a card. Please sign here, mademoiselle," he said, shoving a clipboard at me. I awkwardly balanced the roses in one hand while I took his pen in the other and signed his form.

"*Merci*," he said before turning down the hallway.

I looked at the roses. I sniffed them. I couldn't help a little lift at the corners of my mouth.

"Whoa! Who are those from?" Dana asked as I came back into the room.

I shrugged. "I don't know." I sat down on the bed and fished a little white envelope from the plastic fork-shaped thing at the top of the bouquet.

The outside simply said, *Maddie*.

I opened it and felt my heart speed up as I read the card. *We need to talk. Meet me tonight. Nine P.M. The top of the Eiffel Tower.*

I flipped the card over. It wasn't signed. I bit my lip. The Eiffel Tower. The most romantic place in all the world.

But who was I meeting?

"My money's on Felix," Dana said, digging into my grapefruit twenty minutes later as we devoured the last of my room-service breakfast. I'd put the mystery roses in water in the hotel-issue ice bucket on the dresser and couldn't help staring at them every ten seconds.

"Felix?" I scrunched up my nose. "Why?"

"Well," Dana said, a frown settling between her strawberry blonde brows, "first the article. Now flowers. I mean, has Ramirez ever sent you flowers?"

I paused, then shook my head.

"So it has to be Felix."

"But Felix hasn't sent me flowers before either."

"Yeah, but does Ramirez seem like the roses kind of guy?"

I had to admit she had a point.

"What do you think Felix wants to talk about?" I asked, thinking back to our last interrupted conversation at the show.

Dana shrugged. "Maybe how he's madly in love with you."

"He is not!"

Dana sent me a get-real look.

"Okay, so maybe he likes me a little."

"And you like him."

"I do n—"

Dana shot me that look again.

"Okay. Fine. He's a good kisser." I paused, sniffing the roses again. "But so is Ramirez. *Very* good."

"Okay, so maybe Ramirez sent them." She popped a wedge of grapefruit into her mouth.

I absently shoved a piece of croissant into my mouth. "You think?"

Dana nodded. "Sure. He said you needed to talk. I mean, you guys really have unresolved issues."

I nodded. "But then again, so do Felix and I. He was about to tell me something at the show, but he was interrupted."

"Okay, so we're back to Felix again?" Dana asked, the frown increasing.

I shrugged. "Or Ramirez."

"Maddie," she said, setting down her spoon and leaning in close. "Who do you want it to be?"

I bit my lip and stared at her. But I didn't say anything.

Because I had no idea.

The rest of the day moved in slow motion. After Mom and Mrs. R got up we went down to the police station to give Moreau our official statements. Then Jean Luc called, saying my shoes had arrived—most of them minus fingerprint dust—and he was having them sent to the hotel. Marcel called, wanting to know when he'd get his interview, and Ann left a message saying she was booking the next Le Croix photo shoot and could they use my designs? But I couldn't concentrate on any of it. All I could think about was the Eiffel Tower at nine o'clock as I watched the time crawl by.

Finally, at quarter past eight, I threw on a black formfitting dress with a high neck (to cover my bruises), a short hemline (to give my legs the illusion of length—or at least the one good one), and a low scoop in the back (to make the boys drool). I went heavy on the mascara, light on the eyeliner, and puckered up for a swipe of Raspberry Perfection lip gloss, then pulled my hair up into a flattering French twist. I slipped on one black, strappy, two-inch pump, and, while there was nothing I could do to dress Wonder Boot up, I had to admit I looked pretty damn hot.

On instinct I grabbed one of the roses from the bouquet to take with me, holding it to my nose as I made my way down the elevators and across the lobby.

I took a cab to the Eiffel Tower, my stomach doing the dancing-butterflies thing as my palms grew sweatier the closer we got. As we drove through the city, the sky just starting to turn a dusky pink, the setting sun illuminated the old architecture and captured the light off the fountains spurting along the plazas.

And then I saw it.

The cab rounded a bend, and suddenly there it stood in front of me in all its glory: the Eiffel Tower. I sucked in a breath, the beautiful pink-hued sky behind it breathtaking.

By the time the cab pulled up in front, I was lucky I could walk, my stomach was wobbling so badly. I paid my fare with shaky hands and took a ticket, riding the elevator all the way up to the top of the tower. I awkwardly hobbled out on Wonder Boot, taking a spot in the center of the platform, just a little scared to stand too close to the edge this high up.

Though I had to admit the view was amazing, the entire city of Paris spread out before me, the air clear and cool. I inhaled deeply, trying to steady my nerves.

And watched the elevators.

Group after group came up, families with cameras around their necks, students toting backpacks, all speaking a variety of languages. People snapped photos, laughing and pointing down below us. And I stood, twisting my hands together, two words tumbling over and over in my mind. *Ramirez. Felix. Ramirez. Felix.* I had no idea who would come off those elevators next.

And then another elevator car arrived. The doors slid open. Three teenagers and a family of four from Japan filed out.

And him.

I sucked in a breath, not realizing until that moment just how very badly I'd wanted it to be him. I felt tears well behind my eyes and let out a long breath as he approached.

"Maddie," he said.

I took a deep breath. "Jack."

His dark eyes looked down at me, and even though they were rimmed in sleepless circles, they were the most beautiful sight I had ever seen. His stubble-covered jaw flexed, some emotion that I couldn't read flitting across his face. But I didn't care. He was here. And that was all that mattered.

"Oh God, Jack, I'm so sorry. I'm so glad you're here, but I'm so sorry about everything. I don't know how I always seem to make such a mess of everything, but I promise I'm going to be the best girlfriend ever from now on. I just—"

"I can't do this."

I paused midsentence. "What?"

His eyes took on a sad look. "Maddie, I asked you to

meet me here because I needed to talk to you. I'm sorry, but I just can't do this anymore."

My heart froze. "W-what do you mean, you can't . . . ?"

Ramirez shook his head, his dark hair falling across his forehead in a way that made me itch to brush it away with my fingertips. Instead I clasped my hands tightly together around the flower stem, hoping the death grip on the rose would somehow help me get a grip on reality.

"All we do is fight, Maddie. We're butting heads. Me, I'm a straightforward kind of guy. What you see is what you get. And you . . ." He paused, running a hand through his hair. "I don't know if I'll ever figure you out. Hell, you drive me nuts."

I felt tears welling behind my eyes. "I'm sorry. I don't mean to drive you nuts."

"I know," he said, his voice soft, almost if he didn't want to say the words any more than I wanted to hear them. "I know you don't. But I swear, you've taken ten years off my life since I've known you. I don't know how trouble finds you, but it does. I don't want to do this anymore—stay up nights wondering where you are, not knowing if you're safe, if you're in danger, if you're . . ." He trailed off, and I could mentally see the scene at Felix's playing out in his head.

"I'm sorry," I squeaked out again, at a loss for anything else to say.

He took a deep breath, staring out over the roofs of Paris. "I just can't do this anymore. I don't want you to be my girlfriend."

The tears started blurring my vision, and I fought to keep them back. If he was breaking up with me, the last thing I wanted to do was cry and beg for him to stay.

I gave a loud, unladylike sniff. The sweet scents of roses and the cool Paris air seemed oddly incongruous with the hollow, gnawing feeling in my stomach.

"What are you saying, Jack?"

He took another deep breath, his nostrils flaring, his jaw set at a determined angle. Then he turned and looked me squarely in the eye. It wasn't his Bad Cop look. It wasn't his lustful Big Bad Wolf look. Just him and me. It was the most real I had ever seen him. As if suddenly he was letting me in to see the real guy behind everything else.

And then he bent down on one knee.

His hands reached into the pocket of his jacket, and out came a little blue velvet-covered box.

A ring box.

I blinked and dropped the flower.

My heart stopped beating, my breath doing short little gasps, my eyes going big and round. The tears couldn't be held back any longer, wet lines streaming down my face even as I felt my lips curve up into a smile.

"You're shitting me!" I said. I know, not the most romantic thing in the world. But I seriously couldn't believe my eyes. A ring? It was like I'd stepped into the end of a Meg Ryan movie.

Ramirez's gaze didn't waver, his eyes steady on mine, though a small corner of his lips twitched. "Jesus, Maddie, don't cry." He reached one hand up and gently wiped my cheek with the pad of his thumb. "At least wait until you see the ring."

He opened the box, and the most brilliant emerald-cut, sparkling two-carat diamond winked back at me. The tears gushed like Niagara Falls, and I think I actually laughed out loud. Okay, so it wasn't Tiffany, and it wasn't the biggest thing I'd ever seen. But it was the most beautiful.

It was from Jack.

Ramirez's Adam's apple bobbed up and down, his eyes suddenly vulnerable, his breath coming fast and hard. One of his large hands covered mine in a warm embrace.

"Maddie, I don't want you to be my girlfriend. I want you to be my wife," he said, his voice shaky but his dark eyes steady on mine. "Madison Louise Springer, will you marry me?"